I0615874

The Princess and the Guard

by

Abigail J Grace

The Frozen Chronicles

The Princess and the Guard

Contact Information: info@thewildrosepress.com

Cover Art by *Lisa Dawn MacDonald*

The Wild Rose Press, Inc.
PO Box 708
Adams Basin, NY 14410-0708
Visit us at www.thewildrosepress.com

Publishing History
First Edition, 2025
Trade Paperback ISBN 978-1-5092-6277-9
Digital ISBN 978-1-5092-6278-6

The Frozen Chronicles
Published in the United States of America

Dedication

To those seeking Light amidst the darkness

Acknowledgements

First and foremost, I want to thank my Lord and Savior for giving me the genuine love of writing. Whether or not this story blows up into the next big Netflix adaptation, writing and creating stories had brought me so much joy in life and I'm so grateful that He saw fit to bless me with, and through, being an author.

Secondly, I of course have to thank my wonderful family for always encouraging me and bolstering me along when things got sticky. Dad, you taught me what patience and perseverance looks like, and it has certainly paid off. Mom, you always made me feel like something when it came to my writing, never something that "could be."

My critique partner, Rebecca, girl—this story would not have been where it is now without your help and feedback. You truly helped me solidify the story and characters in a way I wouldn't have been able to do without your help. I'm so incredibly grateful the Lord brought us together as writing friends and partners.

All my beta readers have been invaluable with their feedback and hype! Veronica, Kristen, Isabela, Samir, Eden, Bethanie, Soumaya; thank you all so much!

Hannah was a beast when it came to helping me hone the details, both big and small. Those hours spent over Discord were, and are, invaluable to me and I can't thank you enough for all the help you gave me!

The entire team at The Wild Rose Press has been absolutely amazing and I can't wait to see what the future holds. Ally, you rock; Lisa, your graphic designs are impeccable; Rhonda, thank you for answering all eight millions of my questions!

Here's to the next chapter!

Chapter One

Juliette's heart thudded against her ribs so hard it was difficult to breathe. She fought against the urge to sprint, knowing that would only amplify whatever noise she made. The wooden steps beneath her creaked, but she kept moving up, up, up. At the top of the stairs, two short hallways spilled out in front of her, and at the end of one was a small door concealed in the wood.

A closet.

Her refuge.

She darted inside, carefully closing the door after her and then inching as far back as she could. Around her, the scent of wood was strong. There had always been something oddly comforting about that smell. It smelled calm, serene. Peaceful.

It smelled like freedom, something she would never know.

A whole ten seconds ticked by. Juliette's chest ached with every inhale. She tilted her chin to the ceiling. The footsteps grew louder. She thought for a second she'd been discovered.

But they passed, and silence rang.

With a relieved sigh, Juliette pushed the closet door open and stepped back into the hallway. She took off back up the narrow stairs, pushed at a spot in the wall that, on the outside, was a painting. Part of the wall opened, and she peered outside, seeing if anyone was there before crossing to another opening that led her to a narrow, twisting stairwell that went so far in both directions she couldn't see the top or bottom. She bunched her dress in her fists, afraid of tripping or getting it caught.

By the time she reached the top, her heart was racing again, but it was worth it. A small room stretched out before her, big enough to move around in, but too small to have been an actual room. She wasn't sure what this little place had originally been intended for, but it made a fantastic hiding place. There was a tiny circular window with a wide ledge that looked out over the gardens surrounding the palace.

Juliette climbed onto the windowsill, propping her chin on her knees and breathing a sigh of relief.

Below her, the wooden steps creaked.

Juliette's head snapped to the side, her heart leaping to her throat. She stood, mindful to be quiet as she moved behind a panel in the wall that had fallen. Or rotted off.

The groaning wood grew louder and louder, until it cut off with a single, deep creak.

"Where are you? It's just me."

Juliette's shoulders dropped, and she stepped out, relaxing into a grin. Noah was standing in the doorway. Or, rather, standing one step below the doorway since he was too tall to fit in the doorway.

"Is this your newest hiding place?" he asked, casting a glance around.

Juliette almost shrugged. "She keeps finding my other ones."

Noah looked like he might have laughed if Juliette wasn't serious. If she didn't have to hide all the time. If she could have roamed the palace in peace instead of fear.

Juliette leaned back against the window, wishing there wasn't so much space between them. She couldn't put her finger on it, but she'd been feeling different around him lately. A way that made her heart lurch in her chest and chest fill with warmth. A way that made her feel like she was made entirely of wax and would melt completely.

It was not an unpleasant feeling.

Juliette licked her lips, then got to her feet. "She's not due back for another hour and a half. Are you hungry?"

"No, I ate. I could really use a nice, week-long vacation, though."

Juliette pressed her lips together. She hated how hard he worked, but he didn't have a choice. Guards weren't given the luxury of taking time off whenever they wanted.

As if realizing he'd spoken a thought aloud, Noah cleared his throat and called up a smile. "Come on."

Juliette reluctantly followed him back down the stairs. When they neared the bottom, Noah stopped short.

"Guards," he said.

"You're a guard," Juliette reminded him.

"Yes, but I'm one of the good ones. And I'm not one of hers."

Juliette could have kicked herself. "I thought her shuttle wasn't supposed to arrive back until two." She glanced at the digital watch strapped around her wrist, the light almost blinding in the darkness. It was just now twelve thirty.

Noah grimaced. "So did I. Come on, let's take a shortcut around back to your room." He glanced down at his white T-shirt. "I should have grabbed my jacket."

"If she catches us, we'll just tell her I got lost and wandered down to the guards' area and you walked me back," Juliette said with more confidence than she felt.

"Out of uniform?"

Juliette shifted her lips, jogging to keep up with Noah as they cut through the library toward Juliette's room. "Noah, just go back down. I can make it from here."

"It's fine. She'll probably be coming in from the front." Still holding her hand, Noah pulled her through one of the servants' passages, effectively shaving a good three minutes off their trip.

Noah stopped again. Voices filled the air, and he waited until they passed.

Juliette held her breath. "That was close."

"Too close." Noah started forward again, pausing at the door that opened into the main corridor.

"If she's going straight to her room, we may as well walk in the regular hallway so we aren't so cramped," Juliette muttered.

"Yeah, I suppose," Noah replied carefully, inching the door open and checking the corridor.

Juliette followed him, stifling a sigh. She just thought to suggest they see if they could raid the kitchen when the ground lurched beneath her. Juliette let out a yelp of surprise, falling. She fell to the ground, her knees slamming into the thick carpet. She tried to stand up, twice, only to be knocked down again by the force of the trembling.

The quakes that had been plaguing the small

kingdom of Demetria for her whole life were growing closer and closer together. It might have been her imagination, but it felt like their intensity was worsening every time.

"They always come at the worst possible moments," Noah said, getting to his feet and then helping her up.

Juliette shook her dark hair out of her face. "Yeah." She started to say something else, but as she and Noah rounded a corner, she ran right into her sister, Queen Odette.

Chapter Two

Odette shoved Juliette away. Juliette, surprised, lost her balance and stumbled into the wall.

Noah was quick to catch her.

"Don't. Touch. Her," Odette ordered, her voice even.

Noah dipped into a curt bow, his hands locking behind him. "Your Majesty."

Juliette straightened, smoothing her hands down the front of her dress. She could feel warmth flood her cheeks, but she stood straighter.

Odette was alone and dressed in an elegant, deep blue dress that swished around her feet as she moved. Her hair hung down her back in glossy, rich brown curls that bounced with every step. Her face, naturally beautiful, was masked in disapproval, and her grey eyes glittered with irritation.

Her gaze was pinned on Juliette. "I thought I had ordered you to your room for the rest of the week. Are you really that forgetful?"

Juliette clenched her teeth, resisting the urge to glance at Noah. Odette didn't seem bothered by a guard out of uniform, and Juliette didn't want to draw any attention to him. Instead, she focused on stamping down the rise of fear that always flooded her brain when Odette was nearby. "I was," she replied carefully. As much as she hated the idea of giving Odette the impression she was submissive, she knew standing her ground would get her nowhere. There were other ways to be strong, a lesson she had learned by the time she was eight.

Besides, in all likelihood, Odette would make Noah pin her down while she inflicted her punishment. She'd done it before. Not with Noah, thank the skies, but with whichever guard was with her at the time.

"I thought since you were gone for the day, you wouldn't mind if I went for a walk and got in a little exercise."

Odette sneered, the corner of her mouth tilting in disgust. Her eyes darkened, and she inspected her fingernails. "You must enjoy being punished."

Juliette's heart skittered. Dread settled in her stomach. One would have thought she wouldn't be so afraid of Odette's lashings by now, as often as they happened, and in a way she wasn't. She could deal with pain. Bruises healed. Lashes mended. Scars faded.

It was what Odette might do in front of Noah that made her fingers turn to ice.

"Forgive me, Your Majesty. It was my fault," Noah said, his voice even. Calm. Serene. He didn't move in front of Juliette; he didn't give any indication he was trying to protect her.

"Juliette should have more sense than to run around the palace with a guard. A guard out of uniform, no less," Odette hissed, her eyes narrowing to slits, her gaze slithering to Noah.

Noah's face remained expressionless, and thankfully Odette's attention shifted right back to Juliette without lingering on Noah.

"No, it was my fault," Juliette said, taking a step

forward. "I'm sorry. I was feeling antsy and wanted to take a walk. I ended up in the guards' wing. Ryder was off duty, and I ran into him. He wanted to make sure I got back to my room safely."

Odette blinked. Slowly. Like a snake, waiting to devour her prey.

Juliette lightly cleared her throat, risking a subject change. "How was your trip to Russia? I haven't heard anything from you since you left."

Odette waved a hand in Noah's direction. A dismissal. He bowed again, then turned and disappeared down the corridor.

Juliette breathed a sigh of relief for him.

"You must think I'm an idiot," Odette sneered with an eyebrow raise, "to think you just 'bumped' into that guard."

Juliette's mind sorted through all the different things she could say, the roles she could play. The meek, afraid princess cowering in the shadow of the queen. The stupid, airheaded girl who was so naïve she couldn't be blamed for another mistake. The awestruck baby sister gazing up at her wise, all-knowing older sister.

Even though the role she wanted to play was the one who pushed back when Odette hurt her, the one who stood her ground, the one who showed she wasn't afraid. But she'd learned the hard way that Odette had countless people to back her, and standing up to her would accomplish nothing.

Odette was too strong; she had guards to back her. She had resources at her disposal.

Juliette was nothing.

"You should remember, little girl, I have eyes

everywhere, even when I'm not here," Odette continued. "I should have that guard punished for your behavior, to teach you a lesson."

Fear wrapped around Juliette's fingers. It coiled around her spine, planting in her stomach and shooting its icy tendrils down her legs, her arms. It squeezed her lungs, suffocating her.

Juliette worked to keep her face neutral. "All that would do is warn the other guards to stay away from me. He was only helping, doing his job. It was my fault," she repeated, keeping her words slow so as not to give the impression she was being snarky.

Odette jammed a finger in Juliette's direction. "I have need of you. Come with me," she said.

Not for the first time in her life, Juliette was tempted to say no.

But she already knew what would happen if she did that. Odette would whip Juliette and then probably have Noah or one of the maids whipped as well. Odette loved doling out punishments, but even she wasn't stupid enough to punish a guard for protecting a royal. She needed a better excuse, and Juliette rebelling would be perfect.

As they passed through the Great Hall, Juliette's eyes landed on the world map splayed out on the wall above the fireplace. It was almost two hundred years old, from before the third world war had started, and way before the South Pole had been colonized as its own country. Only within the past century did Demetria fully secede from Russia.

They rounded a corner. Juliette tried to imitate the way Odette carried herself—shoulders back, head held high, graceful steps.

"I hope your playtime was worth it."

Juliette clenched her teeth, barely stifling an eye roll. "We weren't *playing*—" She let out a yelp of surprise when Odette pulled her arm down a narrow corridor.

Odette finally paused, shoving Juliette into the wall and then backhanding her across her face. The blow itself was more surprising than the pain, and the force of it caused Juliette to hit the back of her head on the wall.

Juliette stifled a gasp, pressing a hand to her stinging cheek and enduring the pain in silence. Just another bruise that would heal. Pain was temporary.

"I expect you to do as I say, even when I'm not here. When you don't listen, there must be consequences. Do you understand?" Odette demanded, lowering her voice to a harsh whisper. She raised her eyebrows. When Juliette didn't reply, she gripped her chin in a viselike hold, her other fist driving into Juliette's stomach. "Answer me."

Juliette's jaw ached from grinding her teeth, but she managed not to groan. She forced out a "yes," biting the inside of her cheek. Her survival instincts started to kick in—don't let Odette see she was afraid, be quiet, draw as little attention to herself as possible.

Odette scoffed. "I'm sure." She stared at Juliette for several moments before finally straightening. "I don't know how much you are aware of our relationship with Russia, but every world leader has already begun establishing alliances with each other. No one has any interest in Demetria. I'm concerned that our solitude will draw unwanted attention and leave us vulnerable."

Juliette's eyebrows twitched in a frown. She coughed, resisting the urge to hold onto her stomach. "Why wouldn't anyone want to form an alliance with us?"

"Because we're small, we're insignificant." Odette sighed shortly. Her gaze wandered to the side, as if she were thinking aloud. "What they don't realize is that Demetria is home to unique minerals that aren't found in other parts of the world. We're a solid country, our economy is thriving. We have so much to offer. But why trade with someone when you could steal it instead?"

Juliette could only blink. Her eyes wandered to the window. "What do you want me to do?"

"I am still trying to get a peace treaty signed with the president of Russia to settle our differences and establish a solid relationship. I want you to see about tapping into their private conference calls."

Juliette's eyes popped open. "You want me to hack into a secure network?"

"Don't play stupid," Odette snapped. "I don't have the time or the patience for it. I know you can do something that simple. You've done way more complicated work before."

Juliette opened her mouth to reply but thought better of it. She'd done tons of work for Odette over the years—creating a private network for the palace, monitoring feeds across the other Houses that made up Demetria. Odette knew Juliette's capabilities and didn't hesitate to push her.

"I'll try."

"I don't want you to try. I want you to do it." Odette straightened. "Now, about your little lapse in judgment—" She yanked open a small utility door, jerking her chin at one of the guards, who then grabbed Juliette by her shoulder and shoved her inside. "You will go without dinner tonight and sleep here as punishment for your disobedience," she said, as casually as if she were discussing the weather. "I will not tolerate your behavior."

Juliette scraped her arm on a piece of wood. She glared at the guard who grabbed her, but he had already stepped back behind Odette. Juliette twitched to dart right back out, but Odette blocked her escape.

Odette wasn't overly strong, but she was taller and broader than Juliette, which gave her just enough of a physical advantage. When she needed extra help, she had guards.

"And if you even think about trying to defy me, I'll break your ribs again. And this time I won't let you go in the cryo-wrap for a speedy recovery. Do I make myself clear?"

Juliette clenched her teeth. Odette usually stuck to whippings, but last week she'd been especially angry at something—Juliette didn't even know what—and had accidentally broken two of Juliette's ribs. Thankfully Juliette had been allowed to spend the day in one of the cryo-wraps at the palace infirmary which expedited the healing process.

At Odette's eyebrow raise, Juliette forced a nod. It wasn't so much being in a small space that made her wary, but being locked in. The palace was full of nooks and crannies, hidden compartments, and passages. This one was especially small, and Juliette knew from being locked here before that there was no escape route. Chills shot down her arms, and she shivered, wishing there was enough space to stand up or even fully extend her legs. But it wasn't airtight; she wouldn't run out of oxygen. She'd survive. She'd survived a lot worse.

Odette handed her a tablet. "You may as well get started and save some time."

Juliette worked to keep the glare off her face, daydreaming about striking Odette the way she did to Juliette. About leaving a bruise on her face, or welts on her back. Making her cry because she felt stupid and just wanted her sister to love her. She imagined it would be very satisfying.

Odette straightened, swinging the door shut with a bang. Juliette heard a lock click, followed by Odette's heels stomping away until they faded completely.

Only when silence rang, did Juliette feel the smallest bit of relief.

With a sigh, blinking her eyes clear, she settled back into her temporary prison. Most of these utility closets had long since been abandoned, but a few—like this one—still housed some electrical equipment.

Not sure how to go about programming a device for listening purposes, Juliette did a quick Nexus search, then narrowed the results for some more specific solutions. She didn't know what kind of device Odette wanted—a chip installed in a computer or phone, or a separate bug she could plant beneath a lamp—but it looked like there were a few options regardless.

After gathering as much information as possible and creating several different plans of attack, Juliette raked her hand through her hair, scratching the underside of her wrist until it stung. She didn't know when Odette would be back for her, so while she waited, Juliette caught up on the news. She checked the eleven different news feeds from each of the nine Houses that made up Demetria. Nothing new was happening anywhere.

Out of curiosity, she looked at some of the most recent world news, not at all surprised to see that Odette was in fact correct. There were plenty of articles centering around the ongoing world war, the war that Odette had pulled out of in an effort to save Demetria and their pathetic military. It was one of the few things Odette did that Juliette actually thought the best thing to do.

Juliette pressed her lips together. She knew that the civil war between Demetria and Russia had depleted their military, back in her grandparents' day, and the start of the third world war—the longest war to date—had barely given them the chance to pick themselves back up.

Chapter Three

Odette filled her lungs, then let the air out in a steady sigh as she walked down the black carpeted hallway toward her wing of the palace. One of the chandelier's light bulbs was out in the hallway and needed to be replaced, and there was a smudge on the pale marble wall.

Seas, did no one do any work while she was away?

The two guards posted outside her bedchamber pulled the doors open, letting her in. Odette crossed the room and stepped into her closet. She hated this room. Hated how small it was, how dark, how dreary. Way too many of her dresses had to be pressed daily because they were so wrinkled. One might say she needed fewer dresses.

One would be wrong.

Odette reached onto the top shelf for the box containing her crown. Well, one of her crowns. She had at least five tiaras, but this was the crown she was coronated with. This was the crown she wore as queen. It was so different from the one her mother wore, which had been made of white and green diamonds. She was nothing like her mother and had no desire to be.

Odette's was entirely black. Black diamonds, interspersed with small pieces of obsidian, and set in ruthenium.

Smiling to herself, Odette brought the glittering

black crown out into the light, watching the way it sparkled. Dark rainbows filled the room.

It had been two years since she was coronated queen of Demetria. Two years of building this frozen Russian colony into what would one day be an empire of a kingdom, one that stood tall and proud, strong and able to defend itself.

When Odette was crowned, she did what her ancestors should have done and pulled out of the world war altogether.

The rest of the globe was still fighting, and Odette couldn't be certain that another country had plans to attempt a takeover. She wasn't about to give them a leg to stand on. It was time to do what her parents didn't have the strength to do.

Someone knocked on her door, and when Odette opened it, she stepped aside at seeing several maids with boxes waiting in the hallway.

"It's about time," she said, waving them in. "These clothes in here are to be carried, not folded, to my new suite. Bring them right into the closet and hang them up, but take away anything that's wrinkled and have them pressed."

One of the maids dipped her chin, bobbing a quick curtsey. She and one of the others started taking the dresses from the closet.

Odette then directed the third and fourth as to how she wanted the things on her vanity to be transported. It wasn't far to her new room, but she didn't want anything broken on the way.

While the maids were going about their assigned tasks, Odette gathered her crown, her five tiaras, and a few of her more expensive pieces of jewelry. She set them down carefully on the edge of her brown-quilted bed.

Brown was such a dreary color, Odette realized with a sneer.

"Ah, the moving process has begun?"

Odette turned, almost smiling as her lady-in-waiting, Natasha Prya, walked in and cast a glance around. "It has. I really hate to waste so much time on something as trivial as switching rooms, but I want to be closer to the entrance to the sublevels—" Odette stopped, barely managing to catch herself. Cleared her throat. "Don't just stand there. Here, you can help," she added, handing Natasha one of the jewelry boxes.

Natasha took it, walking with Odette out into the corridor. "I have the final guest list for the celebration dinner and ball, and then I have the gown downstairs in the sewing room for you to try on. Madame Miller will be here in a half hour for a final fitting."

Odette stopped. Blinked. "Celebration ball—? Oh, great skies above, I'd forgotten."

"Do you want me to cancel it?"

"No! No, not at all." Odette licked her lips, kicking herself for not paying closer attention to the date. She'd planned this ball almost six months ago, as an anniversary celebration of her two-year reign. It seemed a little foolish now, given that she still hadn't formed a solid alliance with another country, but maybe a ball would give her something to look forward to.

Odette pushed the door of her new bedroom open, setting her things down on the larger vanity.

As soon as a handful of maids had gathered, Odette relayed the instructions as to how she wanted everything set up and arranged.

"Come with me to the sewing room?" Odette asked, turning to Natasha. "I'll need a second opinion, and I have some things to discuss with you." She brushed her hands together, even though they were clean, and then waved Natasha to follow her. "I really should have my hair trimmed at some point," she added, twirling a thick strand around her fingers and studying the ends.

"That will be easy to arrange," Natasha said around a smile. "If you like, let me know when works for you and I will take care of it."

Odette nodded. "I will, thank you." She involuntarily slowed, a frown settling on her face. "You know, Natasha, you have been invaluable to me these past years."

Natasha blinked, seemingly taken aback. "That—Your Majesty, that greatly pleases me."

"It pleases me more. Since my parents have passed and I've taken the role of queen," she added with barely a concealed rush of thrill, "you have been there for all of it, stepping in and doing whatever I needed done without a second thought."

Natasha's lips twitched in a smile.

"I know you've been my lady-in-waiting for a long time now, but what with recent…" Odette hedged for the right word, "developments, I'll need some additional help. I'll need an official, designated second-in-command."

Natasha drew in a lungful of air, slowing.

Odette paused, turning to face her. The light from the window made Natasha's blonde hair look white. "I would like to offer you the position. Frankly, there's no one else quite suited to the job, and there are very few people, if any, who I trust as much as I do you. I will need someone to delegate, someone to take charge of various tasks that I am unable to do myself."

Natasha dipped her head, her pale lashes fluttering. "I am flattered beyond words, Your Majesty."

Odette started walking again. "Think about it, as it is no small offer. But I will need an answer soon."

"I don't need time, Your Majesty. I would be honored to accept."

Odette inclined her head. "Good. I will have the necessary paperwork drawn up, and we will make it official by the end of the day. One of my biggest concerns at the moment is our military. I can't know what Russia, or any country for that matter, could be planning. I can't see an end to the war in sight. Regardless, given that my attempts at establishing an alliance have gone unanswered, it seems only smart to develop our military. We have no way of defending ourselves, and regardless of what alliances we form, it's been far too long that we've remained vulnerable."

Natasha nodded along.

"Our population isn't big enough to support a decent army. We don't have enough manpower, and even if we did, it would be impractical to expect every single citizen to be a soldier. Being a soldier takes training, and that's not something we'll be able to accomplish in a year. That leaves us will few options, but I believe I've come up with the perfect solution."

Natasha delicately arched her eyebrows.

Odette paused outside the sewing room doors, waiting for the guards to open them before stepping inside.

A smile stretched across her lips. She ignored the

mess around her. Bolts of fabric took up every wall. Shoes and buttons were scattered across the floor in a haphazard mess, but it was the dress on the mannequin that captivated Odette's attention.

The material might as well have been alive. The lights in the room were dim, causing the material to sparkle and shimmer. The effect was ethereal.

It was all Odette could do not to tear it off and hug it against herself, however juvenile it would have been. Instead, she stepped behind the dressing wall and disrobed, then donned the new gown. She squared her shoulders, as she stepped back around and stood atop the stool so Madame Miller could adjust the hem and neckline. The dress tinkled when she moved, the result of so many diamonds being clustered together.

Odette drew a careful inhale, trying to ignore the nagging worry that lingered in the back of her mind. A small spark of sorrow washed through her, and she almost wished her parents could have been here to take some of the burden off her shoulders.

Of course, if they were here, she would have never been crowned queen and Demetria would be crumbling. Her parents never had Demetria's best interests at heart. They lacked the willingness to make sacrifices for the good of the country.

Odette didn't. Odette would do whatever it took to protect her country, her people.

Her crown.

Chapter Four

"Juliette?"

Juliette, sitting at her desk with her tablet propped in front of her, turned around. Odette was standing in the doorway, one hand on her hip.

"I'm almost finished," replied Juliette, already turning away.

"Then take a break."

The tone in Odette's voice gave Juliette pause. She wasn't irritated, but there was a tenseness about her that wasn't usually there.

"I need you to come with me. It's time for your doctor's appointment."

Juliette's eyebrows shot up. "My what?"

Odette arched an eyebrow. "Have you gone deaf now, too?"

"No, but I thought maybe you'd started speaking in tongues," Juliette muttered under her breath.

Odette waved a hand in Juliette's direction. "Hurry up, I don't have all day."

"Why am I going to the doctors?"

"Because some people need medicine to function." Odette shot her a smug smile. "You would be one of the 'some people.' "

Juliette knew Odette was goading her, trying to provoke a response. Despite years of hatred that Odette displayed toward her, Juliette still longed for her sister's approval. Odette's words still stung. They pierced her heart, shooting barbed stingers through her ribs, pricking the tender flesh beneath.

"I don't know what that means, but I'm not seeing a doctor for no reason."

"Oh, we're back to the defiance again. Fantastic." Odette arched her neck in a stretch, glancing over her shoulder as two guards walked in.

Juliette shot up, frozen to the spot. The two guards grabbed her arms, unbothered at her attempts to break free. "Let me go! What do you think you're doing?" she demanded.

"Taking you to the doctors, as I said. Since you're determined to disobey orders, I've had to resort to getting help, and Mother isn't here anymore to protect you." Odette smiled as Juliette was led through the door and dragged through the corridors.

Juliette struggled, determined to make the guards' job as difficult as possible. She remembered, not too long ago, when the guards had been ordered to protect Juliette *from* Odette. Their mother had seen the hatred festering, the abuse starting, and stood as a barrier.

It had been two and a half years since Odette and Juliette's mother died. Two and a half years—thirty months, one-hundred-and-thirty weeks, nine-hundred-and-eighty-four days—of living with Odette and her newfound freedom to hit and beat and scream at Juliette whenever she felt like it.

"I don't know if you're aware, but House Canyons has been working on new technological advances," Odette said, unbothered at Juliette's attempts to break free. "From what I can tell, the software should impress even you and make your work easier and more efficient."

House Canyons was one of the Houses that made up Demetria, and since their primary export was technology, it was Juliette's favorite.

"I have taken the liberty of ordering you a series of new data tablets," Odette continued. "Which means you won't have any more excuses since they will let you work more efficiently."

Juliette stopped struggling just for a moment. A new tablet? It had been a while since she'd gotten anything *new*.

Odette abruptly stopped walking, wheeling on Juliette. "Don't get excited," she snapped, jamming a finger in Juliette's face. Juliette wanted to smack her away so badly, but her arms were still being held. She twisted her wrist, but to no avail. "They're for working. And if you can't work effectively, they will be taken away."

Juliette glared at Odette. "You're so kind."

Odette cleared her throat, continuing down the corridor. "Have you made any progress in accessing the other world leaders' conference calls?"

Juliette scoffed. Odette really wanted to talk about this now? "I thought I was just supposed to be looking into Russia."

"If you can get into Russia, then getting into the others shouldn't be a problem. It can't hurt to have more information."

Juliette reluctantly agreed. "Nothing concrete, but I've been working on establishing a stronger signal so it will be consistent and not quite so spotty."

Odette seemed relieved. "Keep at it. I cannot predict when this war will be over, but it would help if we knew what the other world leaders are planning, or who is looking to form an alliance with whom."

Juliette didn't reply. She glanced over at Odette, who looked like she wanted to say something but wasn't sure how to go about it.

"I'm sure even you are well aware of the struggles we're facing at the moment," Odette finally said, slowly, as if she were choosing her words. "It's important we all do our part for the greater good." She rounded the corner to another corridor. The carpet ended, and her heels clicked on the shiny, marble ground.

Juliette dug her nails into the palms of her hands. She'd been told ever since she could remember that it was important for everyone to do their part. Even when her parents were alive, it was Odette who ran most of the kingdom. She was smart, intuitive.

For the longest time, Juliette worked hard to do *her* part, doing whatever Odette asked her to. It seemed like the only value Juliette held was when Odette needed a new computer installed or built, or needed access to something.

"As I've told you countless times before, your part," Odette continued as if she were reading Juliette's mind, "is to follow orders and do it without having a meltdown."

I know, she inwardly drawled. Juliette stifled another sigh. Meltdown. Panic attack. Tantrum.

"The tasks I've been giving you are extremely important, but they aren't enough, not on their own. We must solidify Demetria, both as a country and as a kingdom. There is a war going on. We can't be so foolish as to think we will be overlooked."

Juliette frowned to herself, but she said nothing. Why did it sound like Odette was trying to convince herself, as well as Juliette? The two guards holding her slowed at Odette's command.

"Now, are you going to cooperate on your own free will? Or do I need to drag them in with you?" The corner of her mouth tilted in a cruel smile. "And don't forget you won't be wearing much."

Juliette worked her jaw. "I'll cooperate."

Odette looked at the guards, and they both released her. "Come."

Juliette forced her feet forward. It was much colder inside, and she involuntarily shivered. She followed Odette through several white corridors until they came to a private room. A long counter ran along one wall, with a computer mounted in the corner. A folded gown was resting on top of the exam table.

Juliette hovered by the table. She pointedly ignored the folded gown, not about to undress in front of Odette, who always told her she was too skinny and looked like a walking skeleton.

"It should be fairly simple today, just a basic physical," Odette said, finding sudden fascination with her fingernails.

"And *why* am I here?" Juliette asked again.

"I told you. I can't stand your behavior and want to do something about it."

Juliette narrowed her eyes. She could tell Odette was lying, but she wasn't sure why.

"When the doctor is finished with you, I want you to go back to your room and finish your work," Odette said, leaning against one of the sleek walls.

Juliette drew in a lungful of air. "Yeah, sure. Are

you staying?" she asked dubiously. For once, Odette looked completely out of place in her elegant gown and glittering tiara seated in the middle of a hospital room.

"Yes. Someone has to make sure she actually does something." Odette lifted her head. "And I don't want any trouble out of you," she snapped.

A laugh bubbled in Juliette's throat before she could swallow it back. She should have seen it coming, but Odette kicked her in the backs of her knees, forcing her to the ground.

"You're getting entirely too comfortable being a brat."

The door swung open, and a woman wearing square glasses and whose grey hair was pulled into a bun walked in, carrying a data tablet. She froze in the doorway, glancing from Juliette to Odette.

"Your Majesty, Princess Juliette," she murmured.

Juliette blinked her eyes clear, her knee aching from hitting the ground. She wished she was bigger. Bigger, stronger, taller, braver. She wished her body's response to fear wasn't always tears. She'd stand up to Odette in more ways than fighting the guards who pinned her down.

"We're here today for just a basic physical, correct?"

Odette nodded, sinking gracefully onto the chair. Her skirt poofed out around her. "I need you to run some tests. Make sure she's healthy and up to standard."

Up to standard. As if Juliette were a product being tested.

Juliette wordlessly donned the gown when Dr. Greene instructed her to, ignoring the glare Odette shot her. She was weighed and measured, her heart rate and blood pressure checked, and a bright light shone in her eyes.

"How have you been getting eight hours of sleep?" Dr. Greene asked, lowering her voice just a little. Not that it mattered; Odette was listening intently.

"Probably closer to six, if I'm being honest. Work has kept me up lately," she added with a pointed look at Odette.

Odette made a face.

Dr. Greene turned away, loading a syringe with a large, empty vial.

Chills shot down Juliette's spine. "Is that a shot?" she asked, trying to stifle a groan.

"Not quite. I'm just going to run a quick blood analysis and make sure there's nothing abnormal going on," Dr. Greene said, smiling. She took Juliette's arm and turned it over, wiping the inside of her elbow off with a cold wipe before inserting the needle into her skin.

Juliette winced, even though it really didn't hurt. Dr. Greene removed the needle and pressed a cotton pad to her elbow.

"Keep pressure on it so you don't bruise," she said gently.

Juliette mechanically flattened her other hand around her elbow.

"I should have her results back by the end of the day," Dr. Greene assured Odette. "But I don't see anything that's cause for concern."

Odette visibly relaxed.

On her way out the door, Dr. Greene cast a glance back at Juliette.

Juliette looked away.

"Hopefully she'll be able to confirm that you're fine, and we can move forward," Odette said with a sigh. "If not, we'll have to come up with something to combat it. Whatever *it* may be."

A frown settled on Juliette's face. Move forward with what? She was fairly certain Odette was trying to be provocative, but what if the reason she hated Juliette so much was actually her own fault? What if a simple solution was all it took to get Odette to love her? What if Dr. Greene came up with an easy solution that would fix whatever idiosyncrasies Juliette displayed that irritated Odette so much?

Chapter Five

The clock on the mantel said it was well past midnight. Odette could feel her eyelids growing heavier as the minutes ticked by, but there was still so much to get through. She was really looking forward to going to bed. Her maids had finally finished transferring all her things from the old suite to the new one. It was so much more spacious, with a much larger bed, a massive bathroom, and a two-story closet. The windows were larger, letting in more light, and she'd had the entire floor done in a blood-red carpet.

She couldn't wait to climb into her brand-new bed, with her brand-new mattress atop brand-new, crisp, freshly washed sheets.

During the initial moving process, she'd considered taking her parents' room since it was bigger than the old queen's suite, but that felt…wrong. She hated her parents. If she could, she would have burned just their room, ridding the palace of the last trace of them once and for all. Their weakness had almost been the undoing of Demetria. They should have kept Demetria out of the war in the first place.

Odette stifled a sigh, glancing up at the clock again. There simply were not enough hours in the day.

"Your Majesty, as you're aware, we are experiencing increasing issues due to Demetria's expanding population," the head of her cabinet was saying. "Which is a good thing. We want to be growing but will require some more strategy on our part."

Odette scoffed, dropping her hand down on the table. *Our part*. More like *her* part. She was the one who had been working tirelessly to come up with ways to save Demetria. Her parents had failed on so many levels, but Odette had risen above the challenges they left her. She had started the process of putting Demetria on the map and giving them a chance of long-term survival, and nearly a decade later she was beginning to see the fruits of her labors, despite some minor setbacks.

Odette straightened. "I've been speaking with our chief science officer in Fatir, and I would like to divert some of our attention to recycling."

The head of Odette's cabinet blinked. Lightly cleared his throat. "Recycling, Your Majesty?"

Odette drew a steadying breath. "The minerals we have been mining thus far have been being used and discarded. Demetria, as of right now, can function on its own but barely. We need to be smarter about the resources we use and so easily discard. If we continue with this present rate, we will soon be at the mercy of other countries, and we'll once again be reduced to nothing more than a meaningless colony. Something I have no desire to do." Odette's gaze involuntarily flickered to the old map spread out on the wall opposite her. Specifically Russia, the country responsible for sending a small group of scientists to the uninhabited South Pole over two centuries ago.

The one thing Odette's ancestors—her grandparents, specifically—had done right was legally seceding from Russia, but then they just stopped there.

They didn't establish the military; they didn't set Demetria up for a chance of success as its own country. With the third world war in full swing, Odette was the one to pay the price for their negligence.

It was time to start making changes in that direction. Countries that had been around for centuries had existing relationships, had ways to stand tall amidst these uncertain times. Demetria needed to prove herself.

Odette arched her eyebrows, waiting for a response.

The man nodded, the jacket of his uniform causing the skin beneath his chin to pucker. He didn't look convinced, but it hardly mattered. Odette couldn't even remember his name, so he clearly wasn't important.

"I thought creating an incentive program would give the people some motivation to continue in the direction of being self-sustaining. I know it's a small step, but I'm hoping it will make a difference in the long run," Odette continued thoughtfully, writing things down on her tablet beside her. She didn't need to keep notes, but it helped her focus. Her gaze shifted to Juliette, sitting in the corner of the room, also taking notes.

Dr. Violet better start producing results fast.

"I, for one, think that's an excellent idea," Casimir, the secretary of state, said, bringing Odette's attention back to the problem at hand.

"Good." Odette waved at one of the maids off to the side, taking a glass of water when it was placed in her hand. She delicately sipped at it. "Then Natasha, forward my request to the science officers in Fatir."

Natasha stepped forward. "Yes, Your Majesty."

Odette stood up. Her back ached from sitting for so long, and she needed to be alone to clear her head. "We'll finish this tomorrow, but it's been a long day, and I need to sleep. Natasha, walk with me."

Natasha fell into step behind Odette, walking with her to her room. Once they were alone, Odette reached for her own tablet.

"I received a report from Dr. Greene, about the princess's test results," Odette said. "She's fine, which gives us the all-clear to move forward."

Natasha blinked, her eyebrows shooting up. "Move forward with what, Your Majesty?"

Odette chewed the end of her thumbnail, forgetting she had them polished that morning. "I forgot; I never finished telling you. My recent visit to Russia wasn't as productive as I had hoped. They're hesitant to sign a peace treaty and won't commit to an alliance. I don't know why, but regardless, we need a stronger military. Demetria is vulnerable."

Natasha dipped her head. "Understandable. I take it you have a solution?"

"I do. It came to me on the way home," she replied, turning her tablet and handing it to Natasha.

Natasha took it, silently studying the text. The expression on her face didn't change.

Odette tried to be patient while she waited. "Well?"

"Who's Dr. Violet?"

"One of the scientists here I've been working with."

"I don't think I quite understand. You're going to build a weapon?"

"Not just any weapon, a *human* weapon." Odette could feel her eyes glowing, though she had to repeatedly remind herself not to tell Natasha everything, not until she started testing. Until it was *ready*.

Natasha's eyebrows shot up.

"When I stopped in Armament to oversee the newest training recruits en route back to the palace," Odette continued, "I realized that most of our draftees are sixteen or seventeen when taken, so they don't have much time to build up their physical strength or learn how to fight. That, coupled with the lack of numbers we have, puts us at risk. So, what if they were given a special serum that would alter their brain chemistry and turn them into the perfect war machines in a matter of days?"

Natasha's frown deepened into one of concern. "Are you wanting to invade another country?"

"No!" Odette drew back, rolling her eyes. Natasha could be so slow sometimes. "Of course not. I want to strengthen *our* military. That's what this is about, but we're severely limited. I'm not anticipating any sort of invasion, but if we stand a chance at succeeding and getting other countries to take us seriously, we must be strong. We must be *solid*."

"No, it—it does seem like a brilliant idea, and it makes sense."

Odette deflated, just a bit. She snatched her tablet back, irritated at Natasha's lack of enthusiasm.

"I'm sorry, I don't mean to frustrate you. I suppose I just don't have your vision for it. Isn't it dangerous? How have you taken steps toward testing if it's even possible?"

"I spoke with one of my chief sciences officers from Fatir, Dr. Violet, and explained my idea to her.

She's on her way now and will start development on it right away."

Natasha nodded, slowly at first and then a little faster. "You've certainly been working hard."

"A great deal. I know even with the unique resources we have they won't be enough to last us forever. Sooner or later, we'll have to open larger trade arrangements among other countries. I'm hoping my serum will be ready long before that point. In fact, I think it'll be ready within the next year."

Natasha shifted her lips to the side. She opened her mouth to say something, then closed it again. "What does this have to do with the princess getting a pass from Dr. Greene?"

Odette blinked. Waited for Natasha to connect the dots. "She's going to be my main subject, isn't that obvious? I needed to make sure she didn't have any preexisting conditions I was unaware of."

Natasha took half a step back, coughing into her elbow. "Apologies. You're planning on using Princess Juliette as…as your test subject." It wasn't a question. "Would this experiment be in the form of a medical procedure?" she asked.

Odette thought about her answer. "I'm not sure yet. I will be speaking with Dr. Violet this evening and going over the plan with her."

Natasha barely nodded again, though she still didn't look convinced. "Are you sure it's safe?"

"Of course not, I've barely begun development on it." Odette paused outside her bedchamber doors. "I'll keep you appraised."

Once she was alone, Odette pulled the pins from her hair and shook her curls free. She was too tired to go through her regular night routine and instead undressed herself, tossed her clothes on the bench at the end of her bed, and slipped on her silk nightdress.

Seas, her bed was even more comfortable than she could have hoped. She'd just started to fall asleep when she perked back up, her brain flickering back to life.

With a tired sigh, Odette turned onto her side, stuffing her pillow beneath her head and drifting off to sleep.

Chapter Six

Juliette stepped from the shower, shaking a towel through her damp hair. Her eyes caught the bruise blooming on the inside of her elbow. It had turned into an ugly purple and ached anytime she touched it.

Running a comb through her hair, Juliette pulled a night slip over her head and then braided her hair to keep it from getting tangled. She studied her reflection in the mirror, but a sharp knock startled her. Standing up, Juliette tugged a sweatshirt over her head as she twisted the doorknob. The door was shoved the rest of the way open, and two figures pushed their way in.

"What are you doing?" Juliette asked, involuntarily taking a step back, her heart leaping to her throat. She opened her mouth to order them back out, but one of them locked a damp rag around her face, the other pushing her down to the ground. Something sharp pricked her side, and blackness swallowed her whole.

Juliette blinked her eyes open. Her eyelids were heavy, and blinking was difficult. The lights on the ceiling were blinding, and her eyes filled with tears. When she blinked, they dripped down the sides of her face. She swallowed, a dull ache spreading through her entire body.

"What's happening?" she asked, the words thick in her mouth. She tried to move, but her entire body was weighed down. There were restraints around her wrists and ankles. She could hear people moving around, talking. Something sharp pricked the inside of her arm, and she winced, struggling to break away.

"Leave me alone!" She thought to yell, but she couldn't even feel the words in her throat and was afraid she didn't say anything at all.

"You're fine. Try and hold still. We're almost finished."

Who was that? A woman, it sounded like, but Juliette couldn't place the voice.

"Trust me, Highness, you won't remember any of this. It'll be easier for everyone if you're out of it."

"Any of *what*?" Juliette coughed, her throat parched. Her lips were dry and cracked, and her head felt like it was packed with cotton. Something else pricked her, this time in her neck. The sensation seemed to wake her brain up, at least a little. Her vision started to clear, and she was vaguely aware of three people in the room. One of them was clearly the one in charge, as the other two were clothed from head to toe in scrubs.

The third, a woman, was wearing a white lab coat and had hair cropped short. A perpetual scowl seemed to be frozen on her face. She locked eyes with Juliette.

"You're not going to give us any trouble, are you?"

"What's happening?" Juliette asked again.

"Nothing too bad. Her Majesty found a use for you, and we're starting the preliminary testing tonight. Mostly just monitoring how your body reacts to different solutions."

Juliette couldn't wrap her mind around the words, but she knew whatever was going on couldn't be good. "Solutions?"

"Don't worry about it. We're almost finished, and

then you can leave."

Juliette reluctantly dropped her head back down. Paper crinkled beneath her, and she realized she was still wearing her thin nightdress, but her sweatshirt had been removed. Panic momentarily flared, until she saw it wadded up in a corner on the floor. It had been Noah's at one point. He gave it to her when she was cold, and she never gave it back. She didn't often think of herself as sentimental, but she loved that sweatshirt.

One of the clothed figures felt the pulse in Juliette's neck. The woman in the white lab coat stabbed a hypodermic needle into a small jar with a clear solution in it. She mumbled something to one of the other two with her, before taking Juliette's arm.

Juliette resisted, but the restraint kept her hand in place. Another needle was pressed into the crook of her elbow, and the solution emptied into her bloodstream.

"What…? What are you doing? What's…what's happening?"

Blackness once again crept into the corners of her vision. Emptiness overtook her, but only for a second. Her eyes flew back open, and she scrambled to get up, the blankets of her own bed tangling around her legs. She fell to the carpeted ground of her bedroom, scrambling to get to her feet.

Her eyes scanned the area around her, her heart hammering wildly in her chest. She yanked the hoodie off, snapping the light on and examining her arms. She already had a bruise from the other day, but it was darker. Bigger.

Juliette pressed a hand to her forehead, crossing the room and yanking her door open. The hallway was dark, empty, and quiet. No signs of life. It may as well have been a tomb for how still it was.

Stepping back inside, she slammed her door shut and turned the bolt, then leaned her body weight against it and tilted her head toward the ceiling. Hot tears trickled down her face, anger coming to life inside her and making her squirm.

She hated that everyone so willingly did anything Odette told them, regardless of what it was. She hated that she was smaller, that she had no power, no real way to fight back. She'd endured countless beatings and slaps at the hands of Odette, for no reason. As she'd gotten older, the beatings became closer together. Now, to add to that, a whole new kind of torture appeared to be starting.

She hated Odette. *Hated* her.

Chapter Seven

Noah stifled a yawn, arching his back in a stretch. He used the light from his tablet to read, not wanting to get up and turn the light on. His eyes burned, and he kept yawning, but he was almost finished with the last section of his textbook.

He heard the nearest door to the guards' wing open and shut with a thud.

"You're still up?" Philip, Noah's older brother, asked as he paused in Noah's doorway.

Noah didn't look away from his book. "I was just finishing some school. I have a test tomorrow. My last one, thank the seas."

Philip's eyebrows twitched in a partial frown, unbuttoning his jacket. "Let me guess, fooling around with the princess again?"

Noah lifted his head, and he shot Philip a glare. "Don't say it like that. And no, I haven't seen her all day."

"You're going to get us both in trouble one of these days."

Noah scoffed. Aside from the other day when Odette had gotten home early, he hadn't once been caught with Juliette. He'd been busy lately. School was ending, and when he wasn't in school, he was training. When he wasn't training, he was working.

"Relax." Noah snapped the book shut and tossed it

on his nightstand. "We've been friends forever and have somehow managed to survive."

"Being friends when you're seven and eight is different than being friends at sixteen and seventeen."

Noah didn't think it needed mentioning that Juliette hadn't turned sixteen yet.

"Especially when you're a newly instated guard and she's a princess," Philip added.

"I've been working for almost two years now, that's not exactly new." Noah stood up, feigning a yawn and willing Philip to give up and go to bed.

"It doesn't matter." Philip lowered his voice, taking a step inside and partially closing the door. "There are guards and maids and servants everywhere, and as Juliette gets older, she'll have more and more people around her. More people to see things and more things to talk about."

Noah chortled. He didn't like that the back of his mind whispered Philip was right. Juliette had been working for Odette more and more lately, and given the close call they both encountered a few days ago, maybe he did need to back off a little.

"I, uh…I have some news," Philip continued after a few seconds of silence.

Dread settled in Noah's stomach. "Oh?"

"Yeah. I got new orders. Reassignment orders." Philip shifted. "To Fatir."

Noah blinked. "What?"

"Yeah." Philip sighed shortly. "I'm supposed to report there by the end of the month."

Noah's heart skittered, but he didn't let it show. He cleared his throat. "Any idea if I will be going as well?"

"Not as far as I know."

The knots in Noah's stomach started to dissipate. If it wasn't for Juliette, he would have been begging to be reassigned, but he couldn't leave her here. Not that there was anything he could actually *do* to protect her from Odette, but at least with him here he could do something after the fact.

"Do you have any attachment to Dad's old ship?"

Noah frowned. "What old ship?"

"The one in the lower garage. He left it to us, but it's in pretty bad shape so I was going to sell it for parts."

"Oh. No, that's fine. I don't want it."

Philip said good night and then disappeared down the hall into his own room.

Noah stood up and collapsed into his bed. Training had been bumped up to five in the morning, instead of six. He was having less and less time to himself during the day, which meant less and less time to catch up on sleep. He was beginning to understand why so many of Odette's guards ended up being reassigned elsewhere in the country after only a few years.

With a sigh, he turned over onto his other side, staring out the small window. He could only see the base of the trees in the distance, given that the guards' rooms were partially underground.

His mind roved back to Juliette. He knew Odette abused her, and he was powerless to do anything to stop it. He was a guard, and he could do nothing to protect her.

Morning came way too quickly, and after wolfing down two protein packets, Noah hurried to the training facility. He had another physical assessment test in the afternoon to make sure he was healthy and had been putting on enough muscle. He'd been told that most of the male guards went through a regression when they were between sixteen and eighteen. There were only a handful of females, but they were all on Odette's guard and mostly served as decoys when the situation needed, so there were different requirements for them.

As soon as he walked back into the training center, farther beneath the palace itself, Noah was directed to a check-in desk and then told to wait with a handful of the other guys his age until their trainer came over.

"If I never have to see another needle for the rest of my life, it will be too soon," Mason grumbled, leaning his head back on the wall.

"Same." Noah sighed. He sank to the ground and pulled out one of his free-read books while waiting.

It felt like they waited for hours before a man came over and gave them a rundown of the day. They were going to start with how quickly they could each run a mile without stopping. Noah beat Mason by five whole seconds.

Afterward, they were led through a series of strength training reps so their endurance could be evaluated.

As the assessment continued with no sign of coming to an end, Noah's strength started to wane. He thought he had fairly decent endurance, but being up late almost every night for the past month had wiped him out more than he thought. Or hoped. He couldn't fall behind now, or he'd be put back in concentrated training.

Trying to give himself a mental boost, Noah focused his attention on the pull-up bar over him. He jumped, catching the rung, but he could only manage ten before dropping back to the ground.

Mason did eleven.

"Don't worry too much, Ryder, I'm sure the princess will move you ahead anyway," one of the other guys, Meyer, sneered.

Noah rolled his eyes, though his cheeks warmed both with the embarrassment at only doing ten lousy pull-ups *and* being teased about Juliette.

"It really makes me wonder why she spends so much time with you and what the two of you are always getting up to."

"I bet it's just killing you," Noah responded with a drawl. "She's my friend, and you know it."

"Sure, sure. Your friend who just so happens to be the princess, and who just so happens to always need *you*. None of us are good enough for her?"

Noah looked him up and down. "Apparently not."

Mason laughed, playfully smacking the back of Noah's shoulder.

Meyer scoffed, shaking his head and dusting his hands together. "Stupid girl."

"She's not stupid," Noah muttered. "And you really shouldn't be talking about the princess like that."

"She's stupid enough to spend so much time messing around with a guard and then get hit by the queen when she does."

Noah shot up, the chair he was sitting on screeching out behind him. Mason and Luis, two of his closest friends, moved in, taking half a step in front of him.

Meyer arched his eyebrows in a challenge. "What? Hey, I'm not blaming you. I mean if I got the chance to move up by screwing—"

Noah rammed into Meyer, tackling him to the ground.

A circle immediately formed, though no one moved to jump in and help. Since Noah had the element of surprise, at least for a few seconds, he was able to get a few hits in before Meyer started attacking right back. Meyer twisted, slamming his elbowing into Noah's face. Pain exploded in his jaw. Noah threw his head back. Something crunched, and then there was blood.

"Hey, hey—break it up!"

Noah and Meyer were both yanked to their feet, the fight ending before it really got the chance to take off.

Meyer had his hand covering his face, blood dripping onto his shirt. "You broke my nose!"

"Serves you right!"

"That's enough," the instructor said. "Who started it?"

"Meyer," Noah huffed.

"Noah," Meyer spat back.

"Anyone else care to chime in?" the instructor asked, casting a glance around.

"Meyer started it," Mason murmured.

Noah smirked. Technically, that was true. Meyer was the one taunting. Noah just threw the first punch.

"Meyer, that'll be enough for today. You're dismissed."

Noah yanked the hem of his shirt down, straightening it. He watched with satisfaction as Meyer was led out of the room.

"He's a jerk," said Mason. He handed Noah a towel.

"The worst." Noah pressed a hand to his jaw, carefully feeling his teeth with his tongue and glad nothing had been loosened. “Thanks for saying something.”

“Sure thing.”

Noah studied Mason’s face. Mason didn’t meet his gaze, his eyes skirting around uncomfortably. Before Noah got the chance to ask what he wasn’t saying, their instructor told everyone to take a seat and wait for their names to be called for their physicals.

“Out with it already,” Noah said when they’d been sitting for a few minutes.

“What?” Mason asked.

“You want to say or ask something, so get it over with.”

Mason almost chuckled. He ruefully shrugged. “I guess I’m just curious. Is there anything going on with you and the princess? I know you guys have always been good friends, and well, I thought maybe it had turned into something more?”

Noah was already shaking his head. “No, nothing’s going on,” he said, even though he wished it wasn’t true.

“You sure? I’ve seen the way she looks at you when no one’s paying attention.”

Noah forced a laugh. “I’m sure. Besides,” he said when one of the physicians poked his head out and called Noah’s name, “she’s a princess and I’ll always be a guard. It’s not like there’s a chance of anything going anywhere.”

Chapter Eight

Odette chewed the inside of her cheek, tasting blood. She tried to settle the thoughts swirling in her mind, ignoring the jitters that wouldn't go away.

A maid was behind her, brushing her hair, while another one was finishing the nails on her right hand.

Odette took another sip of coffee, thinking too late she shouldn't be drinking anything caffeinated given her already anxious state. She couldn't get her soldier serum out of her mind. Dr. Violet and her team had been working around the clock to develop the first stages of Odette's serum. None of them had any conclusive results about how Juliette adapted to her first round of tests. It might not be something plausible after all.

"The catering staff has been working since early yesterday morning on the changes you requested, so there won't be any delay, and the celebration dinner has been lengthened from two hours instead of one," Natasha was saying, glancing at her tablet where her notes were.

Odette clicked her nails together, trying to center her attention back to the current matters at hand, almost wishing she didn't have this dinner party to worry about, but it was too late to cancel. She'd have time to talk to the doctor later. One thing at a time. "Good."

Natasha cleared her throat, a telltale indication she

was about to deliver some bad news. “On a not-so-happy note, we’ve had a few insurrections in House Atworth,” she said, folding her hands in her lap.

Odette almost laughed. “Atworth? They’re all farmers, what are they upset about?”

“Based on my reports from the guards there, there were a handful of people who felt that the capital was getting too much food while they were left with too little. In their minds, they’re the ones doing most of the work to feed Demetria, yet they’re getting the least amount.”

Amusement flared in Odette’s chest. “Really? And what’s been done for their insubordination?”

“Nothing yet, Your Majesty.”

Odette shook her head. She studied her freshly painted fingernails, indicating a spot that had been smudged. The maid started to fix it. “People don’t understand the fragility of Demetria right now. They can’t be selfish enough to withhold food for the capital. These uprisings won’t be tolerated.” She abruptly sat up, waving the maids away and reaching for her tablet. Frustration made her hands tremble. “Send more guards and soldiers and ensure our supply euros are *filled*.”

“Yes, Your Majesty.”

“I want a curfew set; anyone out on the streets is to spend the night in a cell. No exceptions. We’ll see how well citizens begin to realize how well they had it before.”

Natasha nodded once, jotting down something on her own tablet.

Odette sighed, satisfied for the moment. She drew a steadying breath, telling herself everything would be fine once Atworth was under control. “Send guards and soldiers to the rest of the Houses as well, as a precaution. I want to stay ahead of any potential disturbances, and if word gets around, we might have trouble in other Houses."

"Your Majesty?"

Odette swiveled her attention back to Natasha.

"I might remind you that we are experiencing shortages on our staff here at the palace. Guards, specifically. We don't have a lot of extra to spare, unless you want to deplete from your personal guard."

Odette shifted her lips. She pulled up her map of Demetria, surveying the various Houses and each of their contributions to the country.

House Canyons was responsible for keeping the county up-to-date on the latest technological advances.

House Galvan conducted electricity and power.

House Hastings oversaw transportation.

House Luxe kept the palace and elites' clothes in luxury items and fine goods.

House Eldoris harvested fresh seafood, straight from the Indian Ocean.

House Fatir mined the substances native to the southern pole.

House Atworth farmed the land.

House Apatite grew trees that were used in construction.

House Armament provided Demetria with weapons and military personnel, and kept soldiers ready. The young men born and raised there were already headed for the infantry once they turned sixteen.

Odette shifted her lips. She'd been hoping to wait to start drafting from other houses until her serum was further developed. Thankfully, she was flexible.

"We'll pull from Fatir," she murmured thoughtfully. Fatir, which mined the area surrounding Demetria and was the main export of the country's minerals, seemed like the next obvious choice. The people there had to be strong, right? "Anyone fitting a certain physical description will be eligible, and I want the training program here at the palace reviewed as well."

"Yes, Your Majesty. Will you create the program yourself, or shall I take care of it?"

"I'll take care of it and then talk to Aaryn," she added. As the head of her guards-in-training, Aaryn should know what would be best and that Odette would want to oversee everything.

Natasha dipped her head again, then disappeared through the door.

Odette arched her back, the muscles in her spine aching. She stared at her reflection for several moments, noticing the faint circles beneath her eyes and the lack of color in her face. She really needed to start taking better care of herself and not spend so much time working.

The problem was no one else here had half a brain. She *had* to do everything, or nothing would get done.

Odette cast a wayward glance out the window as she climbed into bed and snapped her lamp off. The lights in the dome had long since dimmed. Because the southern pole had six months of darkness, followed by six months of sun, artificial lights had been installed throughout the shield to help keep a semblance of normalcy. At least this way there was an illusion of sun.

And if all went according to plan, one day Demetria's relationship with other countries would allow Odette to travel among them. She’d get to feel the sun, the real sun, on her face and see blue skies.

Seas, what a dream.

Chapter Nine

Juliette forced air into her lungs. In and out, in and out. She tried to tune out the buzzing of the fluorescent lights above her. With all the money Odette spent, she would think it wouldn't be hard to get some lights that didn't make noise. She closed her eyes when Dr. Violet—the same woman from her not-actually-a-nightmare nightmare—turned around with her third syringe, the backs of her eyes stinging.

The guard holding Juliette's arm turned it over. Juliette clenched her muscle, trying to make it as hard as she could for Dr. Violet.

"I don't know why you do that, all you're doing is hurting yourself," Dr. Violet said.

Juliette knew that, but it was the only thing she could do to fight back. The guards who held her down were strong. There would be no point in trying to physically fight. At least this way she wasted more of Dr. Violet's time.

She swallowed against the burn in her throat, afraid for one horrible second she was going to the sick, but Dr. Violet pulled the needle out, and the nausea passed.

Juliette took another deep breath, her skin prickling with sweat.

"Should I have them step back, or are you going to throw another fit?" Dr. Violet asked.

Juliette put as much loathing into a glare as she

could, first at Dr. Violet then at one of the guards pinning her arms.

"Didn't think so." Dr. Violet sighed, as if *she* were tired. As if she were the one who was being forced against her will to be poked and prodded. As if she were the one who would be throwing up later because whatever drugs she was being given would make her sick.

"Keep her arms away from her face," Dr. Violet told the guard. Looking at Juliette, she added, "I need to check your eyes, so keep them open."

Juliette thought to crush them shut, but she knew Dr. Violet would either jam her pen into Juliette's ribs, as she did the last time, or call Odette to come and whip her.

Juliette forced her eyes open, trying not to blink as a bright light shone in her eyes and Dr. Violet held an oddly shaped device against the bridge of her nose. It felt like she left it there an antagonizingly long time, but the light finally vanished.

For a few seconds, the room was an odd shade of green. Tears trickled down the side of her face, and her vision started to adjust.

Juliette could feel panic clawing up her throat, and she swallowed it down, letting out a shaky exhale. This was the second time in a single week she'd seen Dr. Violet. It was also the second time in a single week she'd fought off a panic attack.

"Can I have some water?" Her throat felt like it was made of sandpaper.

"You can go. I'm finished with you," Dr. Violet replied instead.

Juliette yanked her arm free of the guard's grasp.

He took a step back, and Juliette's arm tingled as blood started circulating again. She took another deep breath, waiting until the dizziness passed, then pushed herself up. She fumbled with the hospital gown, trying to get it off, but her hands wouldn't stop shaking.

By the time she was dressed again and walking out of the infirmary, her entire body was trembling so much it was hard to walk. It wasn't just the effects of whatever drugs Dr. Violet had given her; it was rage.

Pure, white-hot rage.

Juliette ran back toward her wing of the palace. She didn't want to go to her room, so she paused in what was supposed to have been her library. It was empty, save for the few pieces of furniture.

Whipping her tablet out of her pocket, thinking to look for a ship out of the country, Juliette froze. Fare on a ship cost money. She didn't even know where the nearest station was. There was a private shuttle here in the palace, but there was no way she would be able to commandeer something like that to leave quickly enough.

She'd have to figure out a way to get her hands on some money, something that Odette couldn't trace.

"Jules?"

Juliette looked up. She choked on another lungful of air. Through her blurring vision, she saw Noah had paused in the doorway. He was in uniform, no doubt on his way to start his shift. "I'm fine," she managed to get out. She could feel her legs going out from beneath her, and she pressed a hand against the wall to steady herself.

Noah caught her, gently lowering her to the ground. "What happened? Are you okay?"

Juliette nodded, pulling in another breath of air. It stuck, and she could only manage short bursts. "I'm fine," she said again in between hiccups. The ache in her chest was growing, and she was afraid if she didn't get in a decent breath, she'd pass out. "But I'm not…staying here…another night."

"What? What do you mean?"

Juliette shook her head, grateful that Noah didn't take his hands from her arms. "Odette, Odette's been having me go…to the doctors. This was the, the second time. I have no idea why, but I'm not…staying here…anymore."

"Breath in, Jules. Take a deep breath."

Juliette tried to, but her sternum was trembling so hard it was almost impossible. She needed to get out of the palace. Whatever Odette was doing, whether there was a reason for it, or it was just another twisted way to inflict pain, Juliette had enough.

She'd been Odette's punching bag long enough; she wasn't about to be her pincushion.

"I'm leaving the palace. I'm running away, and don't try and talk me out of it. I should have seen this coming, her getting worse and worse and—"

Noah, his face twisted in concern, cast a glance around. "Okay, okay. We'll get you out of here, but we can't talk about it in the open like this."

Juliette drew another steadying inhale, the cobwebs in her brain starting to burn away. She cleared her throat. "Fine. But I'm serious."

"I believe you." Noah didn't laugh. Didn't smile. Didn't give any indication he was teasing. He was serious.

Juliette exhaled shortly. She scrunched her

shoulders by her ears, then let them drop. She tried to call up a smile, lifting her eyes to Noah, but it vanished as soon as she realized there was a bruise blooming on his jaw. She immediately stood up, gingerly touching her fingers to his purple skin that stood out as a stark contrast against his skin. “What happened?”

“Nothing.” Noah waved a hand in the air. “Got into a mild scuffle.”

“Yeah? Was he prettier than you?”

A smile tilted at his lips. “No one’s prettier than me. Except maybe you.”

Juliette laughed.

Something on Noah’s face shifted, but she wasn’t sure what. Silence hung between them for several seconds, and suddenly the weight of Juliette’s words sank in. She couldn’t run away. How could she?

“I’m sorry,” she murmured.

“What in the seas for?”

Juliette hedged. For not being strong enough to push back, for keeping her feelings for him to herself, for letting her dramatic side get the better of her. “Making you late,” she finally said.

Noah poked her between her eyebrows. “My primary job description is to serve the royal family.”

Another laugh bubbled in her throat. “That’s fair.”

“Which means if you want help getting out of here, I can help.”

Juliette frowned, though her heart did a little hiccup. “How?”

“I don’t know. Not off the top of my head, but we’ll figure something out. We’ll come up with a plan.”

Juliette filled her lungs. Nodded. “Okay.” She cleared her throat, raking the hair away from her face and working the knots free. “When is your shift over?”

“I’m finished. I opted for a night shift instead of working the party.” Noah ducked his head so she’d look at him, concern once against written on his features. “Are you sure you’re okay?”

“I am now. But I meant it. I’m not staying at the palace a day longer than I have to. I don’t care what it takes. Odette can have the country to herself for all I care.”

Noah straightened his jacket. “Understandable. I’ll walk you back to your room so you can get some rest before everything starts.”

Juliette shook her head, walking with him down the corridor. “I’m not going.”

“Why not?”

“Because Odette won’t let me. Which is fine with me because it doesn’t even sound fun,” she added truthfully. “Going to a ball and dinner, with Odette on the loose? Hard pass.”

Noah almost laughed, but he was otherwise silent. Then, when they neared her room, he paused. “You…you really want to leave?”

Juliette hesitated. Barely nodded.

“Have you thought about it before? I’m not trying to talk you out of it, but leaving the palace—running away—it won’t be easy.”

“I know. I…I have thought about it before. I know it will take some planning, and if it takes years to create a plan, then fine. But I need to be working on a way to leave, I need…to be able to see an end in sight, and nothing will change if I stay. Odette’s always hated me, but she’s gotten worse since—” Juliette stopped, her throat tightening. Since her mother died.

Noah worked his jaw. “Okay.” He drew a steadying inhale.

“Okay?”

“Okay.”

Chapter Ten

As soon as he changed out of his uniform, Noah scoured the entire guards' wing in search of Philip. He found him in the main gym, finishing a set at the bench press.

"You haven't sold the ship yet, have you?" Noah asked, jerking a thumb behind him.

Philip sat up, slinging a towel over his shoulder. "No. Why, do you want it?"

"Yes. I'll buy it off you, if you want. Or, you know, your half."

"What are you going to do with it?"

"I think it would be fun to fix up." Noah shrugged. "Mason got really into ships a few years ago and is always going on about how fun they are to work on. My curiosity has been piqued. Besides, I'm almost finished with my pilot's license, so it would be nice to have my own ship."

"Oh." Philip stood up and started to put the weights away. "Then yeah, have at it. It'll be one less thing I have to worry about transporting."

Noah inwardly pumped a fist. "Great, thanks. I'm going to go tinker around with it for a bit."

"Just don't mess anything up until you know what you're doing."

"I'll try my hardest," Noah replied with mock sincerity. Philip shot him a glare, and Noah took off before Philip changed his mind.

Jogging out to the hangar where the guards were allowed to keep their personal ships, Noah started straight toward Philip's. Or, rather, his and Philip's. It was small, meant for short trips, but a new ship was out of the question. Ships cost money and registration.

A palace guard, or the royal princess, purchasing a two-man ship would *not* go unnoticed.

No, this would be perfect. It needed some repairs before it would be airworthy, but if he and Juliette could get it to work, it would be perfect. He wasn't sure if Juliette had a final destination in mind, or if she had in fact thought through a rough idea of a plan.

Pulling at the door, Noah hauled himself into the cockpit and sat down in the captain's chair. He'd only ever flown the newer models, but from what he understood, these older ships were much easier to fly. He really hoped that was the case and he wouldn't have to learn a whole new system.

As he familiarized himself with the inner workings, he propped his tablet up and turned on the local news for a distraction.

"...worried about the increasing number of quakes in the coming winter months."

Noah absentmindedly listened while he thoroughly inspected the control panel. Most of the instruments he recognized and understood how they worked, but there were a few knobs and handles he wasn't sure about, so he did some Nexus searches.

"Queen Odette had declined to make any comment, but we have it on good authority from a palace source that there is ongoing research into the continued development of the dome."

Noah glanced over, his eyebrows sinking lower on his forehead. He watched on the screen as the camera switched from the woman making her report, to a shot of the sky through the electrified field that separated the entire country of Demetria from the harsh elements.

"You're not going to try and fly this thing, are you?"

Noah turned as Mason jumped into the cockpit. "Eventually. Why?"

"It just needs a lot of work."

Noah stifled a sigh. "Yeah?"

"Yeah. It'll be fun, though. At least, I think so."

Noah licked his lips. "Where would you suggest I start? I've never done a project like this and would like to avoid blowing myself up."

Mason laughed. "I have some basic books I can give you to look over if you want. You got some big trip planned?"

Noah tensed. "No. No, of course not. I just want something to do. I work, eat, and sleep. I need something to look forward to break up the days."

"Makes sense, I can respect that. I'll get you those books later tonight."

Noah waited until Mason had left before moving through the rest of the ship.

Aside from the cockpit, which was in the worst condition, there were only minor repairs needed in the interior. Besides the small kitchen, there was a single bedroom and washroom, a living area with a built-in TV and sofa, a tiny cargo bay in the rear that would maybe hold two suitcases, and plenty of storage space for enough food to get them at least to another country.

The sink in the washroom needed attention, but

when Noah inspected the toilet and shower, they both appeared to be in working order.

The couch in the living room housed extra storage space, and there were cabinets lining almost the entire wall opposite the TV. It would be tight, living like this for a while, but it would work.

Noah thought to see about getting a bigger sofa that he could sleep on, but since it was built into the ship it would take more work to replace, and he needed to focus on the more critical things. Oh well. He didn't mind. Maybe he would sleep on the floor in the bedroom.

Although, he realized with a glance around, the floor could use a thorough cleaning.

Noah stifled a grimace. He would talk to Juliette as soon as he could so they could touch base about who would do what. The engine being in working condition was the most important, and if Juliette could install a new computer, then the rest would be easy to take care of.

Chapter Eleven

Juliette couldn't stop her hands from trembling, and she didn't even know why. She wasn't nervous about anything. Quite the contrary, she'd never felt more confident in her life. There was an end to this life of pain in sight. Nothing she did mattered. Nothing Odette did mattered.

She was leaving the palace. She'd already decided. She didn't know how or when, but it was happening.

She rolled her shoulders, and a dull ache spread from the inner corner of her elbow. She glanced down, gently dragging her fingers over the purple bruise.

Her tablet buzzed with a message from Noah. He had finished for the night and wanted to talk to her about something.

Juliette's stomach clenched, anticipation giving her another bout of the jitters. She checked where Odette was, relieved to see that she had gone to her room for the night and would be out of the way.

Within minutes, there was a knock at her door. Juliette immediately opened it, stepping back so Noah could come in.

"I'm sorry to bother you so late," he started.

Juliette shook her head. "I was still awake."

Noah licked his lips. "Listen, about what you said earlier today."

Juliette's heart stilled. She shouldn't have said

anything without having a better plan, without giving him something to work with.

"I have a ship."

Juliette blinked. Her lips wrapped around a word, but nothing came out. She cleared her throat. "What? Really? How?"

"Yes." Noah nervously smiled. "It was mine and Phil's, but he doesn't want it and said I could have it. It's old and will need quite a bit of work, but I thought over the next few days we could look at it and see if we can get it in working condition." He cupped the back of his neck. "It might not work. We might have to figure something else out, but—"

" 'We'? You're...you're coming with me?" she asked, suddenly aware she'd never asked him.

The smallest hint of a smile brought sunlight to Noah's face. "Absolutely."

Juliette's shoulders dropped, and she sank down onto the end of her bed. She didn't realize how much that meant to her. She was spared being forced to choose between Noah and freedom, even though she knew he would have never made her choose. If he couldn't have gone, he would have made sure she got away.

"So we have a starting place, then," Juliette murmured. "It's one step closer than we were this morning."

"Right."

Juliette picked at a loose hangnail. It took a second for her brain to process what he was saying, and when it did, her heart squeezed. They were going to leave the palace. They were going to *leave the palace*...together.

Juliette cleared her throat, her sternum trembling.

"The ship's in bad shape, but I'm pretty sure we'll be able to fix it. I've started looking into that model and the engine parts. You know Mason, right?"

"I have three guards Noah: you, Mason, and Luis. Yes, I know who Mason is."

Noah almost laughed. "He's really good with ships, and he said I could borrow some of his books on engines and mechanics. I thought I'd start reading up on those."

"What kind of ship is it?"

"0618, Ice Rover."

Juliette pulled up the different years of the ship, giving it to Noah so he could find his. As soon as she knew what ship it was and what kind of electrical housing it was made of, she would be able to start studying the mechanics of it. Engines weren't really her area of expertise, but she wanted to at least understand how it worked so she could learn how to block tracking signals. Plus, if the ship's computer needed any kind of repair, she wanted to have a plan ready to go.

"It's here in the palace garage," Noah added, almost hesitantly. "Maybe tomorrow we could take a more thorough look at it together? I took a quick peek inside. The engine and computer system need a lot of work."

Juliette tried not to feel deflated. It was a ship. They had a starting point. She'd survived Odette her entire life, she would survive another night. "That's okay. Maybe we can tackle the big things first and then worry about the rest later? I mean, I personally would forgo a clean couch if it meant getting away."

Noah laughed through a grimace. "That's fair."

Juliette couldn't keep the grin from her face. Her

hands flew to her mouth, scarcely able to wrap her mind around the reality of what was happening. She didn't think to move, but her body acted before her mind had the chance to catch up, stepping up to Noah and wrapping her arms around him.

He didn't even hesitate to hug her right back.

Juliette could feel her heart in her neck. It was pounding, and she wondered if Noah could feel it as well.

After not nearly a long enough time, he let her go, taking half a step back.

"Anyway, I'll let you get back to whatever it was you were doing, but I wanted to tell you." Noah pressed his lips together.

"Thank you." Juliette walked with him to the door. She wanted to say more but couldn't think of what.

Noah paused. He lightly squeezed her forearm, then turned and disappeared down the corridor.

Alone, Juliette sagged against her closed door. She could feel her pulse in her temple, and she tried to wrap her mind around leaving. Around taking off and flying through the gates, feeling the sun, seeing the sky. She'd dreamed about it for her entire life, she couldn't believe she'd put up with Odette's abuse for so long.

Filling her lungs to capacity, Juliette closed her eyes and smiled at the ceiling.

Chapter Twelve

Odette walked up the stairs toward the observation booth, her dress rippling around her. Her spirits were much lighter than they were yesterday. It had been almost a week since Dr. Violet had begun development of her serum. A week of giving them to Juliette in small doses and monitoring her results.

So far, so good.

Odette felt like finally, *finally*, she was moving in the right direction, making notable progress as queen. With each step she took, she ticked off an item. Her soldier serum was well underway, showing signs of success, her country's infrastructure was growing stronger by the day, she was on the very of establishing trading routes with the rest of the world.

The list went on, but she ran out of stairs.

"This way, Your Majesty."

Odette walked to the edge of the balcony, wrapping her hands around the banister and scanning the crowd of guards-in-training below. There were so many of them. It sent a wave of relief through her mind, seeing just how many there were. With all the insurrection reports, she'd been uncharacteristically anxious about her safety.

"As you can see, Your Majesty, the new training methods we've implemented per your order are already making changes in the upkeep of our current guards, as well as improving the stamina of the new trainees," Aaryn, the head of the training program there at the palace, said proudly. "It's only been two weeks, and already our averages are soaring. The striplings are already running as fast at the medians, and the medians are almost able to lift the same amount of weight as the seniors."

Odette had to remember which group was which. She was pretty sure the striplings were the ten- to thirteen-year-olds, the medians were the fourteen- to sixteen-year-olds, and the seniors were the seventeen- to eighteen-year-olds. She'd never spent much time learning the training ranks in the guard, and only now was she wishing she had.

"Of course, we still have a long way to go. Many of them are reaching fatigue faster than we're used to."

Odette shifted her lips. "Is that normal?"

"Oh very. Any time one's physical limits are pushed, you reach your breaking point much sooner than you otherwise would have."

Breaking point. The words made Odette's chest swell. She wanted—no, *needed*—to break them. These boys were mere children today, but they would be the ones holding her country together.

All at her call. Her order.

"But then their overall strength limits are increasing," Aaryn continued. "In the long run, it's excellent."

"And these are being applied to my military training camps throughout the country as well, yes?" she asked, turning partially around. Having at least a strong foundation would hopefully help bolster the intended effects of her soldier serum.

"Yes, of course, Your Majesty. From what I understand, perhaps even more strictly."

Odette dipped her head, not sure yet whether to be impressed. Or, rather, not sure yet whether she wanted to *show* she was impressed.

"Do any additional changes come to mind?" Aaryn asked, glancing out at the guards training below them. "The curriculum is still new, so it will be quite simple to add or eliminate whatever you wish."

Odette thought about it, her eyes continuously scanning the room, so big she couldn't look at everything at once. Most of the trainees were quiet, save for grunting and panting. It was the trainers whose voices filled the massive hall, echoing off the stone walls. "Nothing that I can think of, at the moment."

A smile tugged at Odette's mouth. She liked watching them. Liked seeing what kind of men they were turning into.

"Nice job, Noah," one of the trainers called, his voice rising above the roar of hundreds of others.

Odette snapped her gaze toward the voice, just as one of the older boys jogged over and smacked his trainer's hand in a high-five.

Odette missed what he did to earn praise, but the name stuck out to her. Noah.

Noah turned, sagging against the wall. Recognition hit her, and the smile dropped from her face. He was the guard from the hallway, the one Juliette had tried to protect.

"That boy down there, who is he? Is his family here?" Odette asked, tilting her head and trying to see what Juliette saw in him. He certainly wasn't unattractive, just not the type of man Odette would have focused in on. Not when there were so many others to choose from.

Aaryn stepped forward, and Odette pointed to Noah again.

"Ah, that's Noah Ryder, Your Majesty. His parents passed away during a quake when he was two, and his brother, Philip Ryder, is also a guard. Noah turned seventeen about two months ago, and he's always been one of our top trainees. He graduated early and has been working as a junior guard for about two years."

Odette hummed to herself. "Is he still a junior guard?"

"No, Your Majesty. He was promoted last month and has been on Princess Juliette's personal guard since then. Given that he's only seventeen, he will take an assessment test when he finished school, and then continue with this level of training until he turns twenty-two."

Odette knew that, but she didn't comment on it. Him being on Juliette's guard explained her infatuation with him. She only had a handful of them to choose from, whereas Odette had the entire palace.

"I want him watched," Odette said. "He's been spending a lot of his time with the princess, and if he slackens off, I want him punished for it. He shouldn't be spending so much time with her in casual conversation, and vice versa."

"Yes, of course. I can speak with him if you wish."

"No. I'd like to see what comes of it on its own."

Odette kept her eyes trained on Noah, glad that the trainers were adhering to the new training methods she'd implemented. Watching the way the boys' strength visibly waned toward the end of the session was satisfying. *Breaking point*. She involuntarily sought out Noah again, watching with satisfaction as he leaned back against one of the walls again after another round and sank to the ground. Even from this far away she could see how fast he was breathing.

Someone tossed him a water bottle, and he downed almost the entire thing in a single gulp. He recapped it and then hurled it at one of the boys in his group.

Odette bristled, thinking she was about to witness a fight, but the other boy broke out into a laugh, and he threw it right back.

"Do they think this is *playtime*?" she hissed under her breath, her cheeks flaring. She wished there was something handy she could throw down at them to get their attention.

Noah leaned his head back on the wall, heaving a tired sigh.

Odette was just about to bring his lack of attention to Aaryn's attention when Noah's eyes flickered up, catching Odette watching him.

Odette smirked, the corner of her mouth tilting in a smug grin. *I'm watching you, boy. If you step one toe out of line, I will take great pleasure in inflicting as much punishment as I need.*

Instead of standing up to bow or even dipping his head, as was expected, he shot her a half-hearted, two-fingered salute that hardly looked genuine. If anything, it looked like he was mocking her.

The smile dropped from Odette's face, only to appear on Noah's.

Chapter Thirteen

Juliette chewed the end of her stylus, her brows furrowed in concentration. She tucked one of her legs beneath her, leaning back against the wall. Beyond the door, where everyone was training, she could hear the faint grunts and groans, voices carrying, and skin hitting the canvas punching bags. She wanted to peek inside and see what it looked like, but the door was closed, and she didn't want to draw any attention to herself.

She'd been working on breaking into the Canadian governments' secured network all morning. Numbers and letters and passwords blurred together, making her eyes burn. She was just over halfway finished, and it was already two in the afternoon. Odette threatened to punish her if she didn't finish it by five. Juliette thought it would have been fairly simple, but now she was starting to grow anxious.

She thought maybe going for a walk, or coming to see Noah, would help clear her mind and give herself a much-needed break, but she was just as on edge now as when she was in her room.

A rush of anger flooded her brain, a guttural cry tearing its way up her throat. Juliette hurled her tablet across the hallway as hard as she could, just as the door flung open and Noah walked out. Sweat trickled down her temple, her hands trembling.

Noah almost laughed. He was panting, his sweat-soaked shirt clinging to his stomach and shoulders. He looked exhausted. "What'd your tablet do to you?"

Juliette stood up, the fury melting in an instant. "Nothing, I just got…frustrated," she said with a head shake.

Noah stooped for the abandoned tablet and handed it back to her, checking to see if it was cracked. "Another program?"

"Of a sort," she mumbled, feeling the heat on her face. She waited for Noah to say something or ask her why she was upset. Thankfully he didn't comment on it.

"I'm done for the day; I was going to go make something to eat, care to join me?" he asked, casting a glance around.

"Yes please." Juliette eagerly fell into step with him.

"What are you working on today?"

Juliette hedged. She didn't want to tell him, not because she was afraid he'd talk about it to other people, but because it was embarrassing. She was snooping, breaking into a private network for the purpose of letting Odette listen in.

"Just another generic program," Juliette finally replied. She twirled a piece of hair around her finger, glancing around to make sure they were alone. "I've been looking into the model of Philip's ship, and those specific engines have tracking equipment built into them," she said, lowering her voice.

Noah slowed.

"That doesn't mean it can't be disabled, but it's not as simple as the newer models where it's a separate housing unit that can be removed and replaced without touching anything else. As soon as I go back to my room, I'm going to look into downloading some blueprints and see if I can learn more about what it takes."

Noah nodded. "I was going to do some work on it tonight as well. If I move it far enough back in the garage, it's outside the security camera's line of sight. Don't suppose I could talk you into coming down there with me?" he asked, almost hesitantly.

Juliette tried to stifle a smile, her cheeks warming. "I'm not sure what's going on, but if I can, I'd love to. It would be helpful to look at it in person so I know what kind of computer to be building."

Noah jerked his chin toward the cabinets as they neared the kitchen. "Hungry?"

She shook her head. "No, I should really work on what Odette gave me before she gets upset and throws another fit."

"You can do your work here if you want, but you really should eat something. I'll make you a snack. What'll you take? We've got some *ponchiks*. Oh, and *sosiska v teste*."

"*Ponchik* please," Juliette said with a smile. She watched him moving at the counter, his hair knotted behind him.

Noah pulled a paper bag out of the cabinet and set it on the table in front of her. Juliette pulled out the fluffiest *ponchik* she could see, immediately taking a bite. She wasn't supposed to have sweets—Odette said they made her hyper and obnoxious—but she didn't care. The deep-fried, sweet bread was worth the risk.

She set her tablet up on the table at the same time

Noah dropped into the chair opposite her, reaching behind him for a few of his textbooks. A frown settled between her brows. He was still in school, in addition to working and training?

Juliette forced herself to finish her task, setting to work with newfound determination. She wasn't the only one who needed to get away from Odette, and if she was going to spend the later part of the night with Noah going over his ship, she needed to keep Odette off her back. Glancing at the clock in the corner of her tablet, seeing she had less than a half hour, Juliette nervously gnawed at her lip.

Twenty minutes left.

Fifteen.

Five.

"I have to go get upstairs," Juliette said, standing up and shoving another *ponchik* into her mouth. She brushed her hands together, then grabbed her tablet.

Noah looked up. "Let me know if you can come down later, otherwise we can nex't about it."

"Perfect."

Noah nodded, and Juliette turned from the kitchen, weaving her way through the guards' section and back into the main area of the palace. She broke into a jog, running the rest of the way to Odette's study.

The two guards standing outside the doors simultaneously opened the doors for her.

"Thanks," Juliette panted, stepping inside, suddenly winded. She really should do more cardio if running for five minutes made her this exhausted.

Odette, sitting with her legs crossed at her desk, snapped her head around. She glanced down at her watch—an actual watch, not like the digital one Juliette had.

"I have your program finished," Juliette said, her heart thudding against her chest. "It's pretty straightforward, and I was able to establish a connection that *hopefully* won't waver. If it does—" Juliette slowed, pausing to catch her breath. Seas, why was it still hard to catch her breath? She coughed. "If it does, I can try something else."

Odette stood up. "I asked for it to be finished by five."

Juliette arched an eyebrow, glancing down at her own watch. She tried to slow her breathing, but her heart was still thumping wildly in her chest. The edges of her vision started to fill with black pinpricks, and she tried to blink them away.

Odette started toward Juliette, reaching for her tablet. "You said it's secure?"

Juliette thought to nod, but her body refused to listen. She had to repeat Odette's question in her mind a second time before it processed. "Yes. For now. Like I said, it should hold, but if—"

A backhanded slap from Odette sent the world spinning, and Juliette stumbled to the ground.

"When I ask for something by five, I expect it to be finished, on my tablet, on my computer, by five. I don't want you running in here panting and out of breath at *exactly* five, understand? Do you have any idea how critical my time is?!"

Odette was shrieking, her words echoed, her face blurring.

Juliette crushed her eyes shut, blinking them open and trying to refocus her attention. She tried to call up some fire. She should have been furious—she'd spent all day working on this for Odette, got it finished, and Odette slaps her for it?

"What's wrong with you?" Odette asked, her face shifting.

"I don't know," Juliette managed to get out. Her arms were shaking, so much that she couldn't even push herself up off the floor.

"Can someone get her?" Odette stepped over her, and one of the nearby guards stooped to help Juliette up.

Juliette's arm felt like it was being yanked out of her socket. Daggers pierced the back of her brain, and a scream was ripped from her. Her legs buckled, and she fell again, but the guard caught her.

"Bring her to the doctor."

Juliette could barely register Odette's words. She couldn't see; she could barely hear. Her throat had closed, but her lungs felt like they were on fire. Blackness bled in from the corners of her vision until the whole world was swallowed in darkness.

Chapter Fourteen

Juliette woke to a bright light shining into her face. She blinked, stifling a groan. Her entire body ached. It felt like she'd been run over with a truck. A groan made its way up her throat. Something crinkled beneath her, and she realized she was on a paper-covered table.

She was back at the infirmary.

Juliette started to get up, but something was wrapped around her wrists and ankles, keeping her rooted to the spot. Her heart thundered in her neck, her eyes widening.

"Dr. Violet?" Juliette struggled to lift her head, but her brain felt like a ten-pound boulder. She kicked at the restraints, but it did nothing.

"Try not to move, Princess. We're running some tests right now," Dr. Violet's voice said, from over a speaker.

Juliette looked around. At least she could still move her head. "Where are you?"

"Behind the glass."

Juliette dropped her head back down, crushing her eyes shut. "Could you at least turn the lights down?"

Dr. Violet didn't answer.

"What happened? Why am I here?" Juliette asked.

The door opened, and Dr. Violet walked in, a tablet in her hands. "You had a seizure."

A trickle of cold fear made its way down to

Juliette's stomach. She licked her lips, her heart skittering in her chest. "A *what*?"

Dr. Violet jerked her shoulders in a shrug. "Thankfully we were able to get you back here and stop it before too much damage had been done."

"Damage? To what?"

Dr. Violet undid the straps around Juliette's wrists, letting some circulation back into her hands. Juliette's muscles ached, and her head felt like it was packed with cotton, but she didn't see any needles in sight.

She'd never had a seizure before, and even with her limited knowledge of them, she knew they were serious. People didn't just have random seizures. They were brought on by *something*.

Dr. Violet was silent, and no matter what else Juliette asked, she didn't answer. She let Juliette go, telling her to get some sleep and drink plenty of water.

Juliette returned to her room, glancing at the clock on the mantel. It was midnight. Noah was probably in bed by now, and as much as she needed to sleep, Juliette could feel the electricity swirling around in her brain.

A seizure? Damage?

Shifting her lips, Juliette changed into a pair of sweatpants and then stole out into the corridor. Her wing of the palace didn't have any guards—not since Odette had been queen and said there was no reason for Juliette to have so much protection—so she felt confident moving without being spotted.

She wandered almost the entire length of her area of the palace, stopping short when she found herself nearing the entrance to the guards' section. She should have sent Noah a nex't to see if he was even still awake, but she was afraid of waking him up if he was asleep. Besides, even if he was in bed, she could poke around the ship herself.

The palace's garage was always so shockingly big. Juliette knew Odette had her own personal shuttle, so she didn't understand why there were so many different ships and cars parked here. Having studied the garage layout and discovering there were only two cameras, she managed to walk through the entire place without being seen.

Noah's ship wasn't here, she realized. He must have moved it somewhere else, but where?

Juliette was just about to turn away, thinking she'd have to wait until tomorrow to ask Noah where it was, when she remembered there was a basement-level garage for the staff at the palace to keep their cars and ships. It took her a few minutes to orient herself, but when she found the door that opened into a set of concrete stairs, she jogged down them with renewed vigor.

The staff's garage was much smaller than the one on ground level, but it made it easy to find Noah's ship. It was parked in the back corner, and Juliette only saw the one security camera. She hung back on the stairs, pulling out her tablet and accessing the security feeds. She disabled the camera, hoping it was late enough to go unnoticed. Safe from prying eyes, she marched into the main part of the garage.

Knotting her hair on the top of her head, Juliette studied the outside of the ship. It didn't look too bad. Nothing a paint job wouldn't fix, but she didn't think repainting it should be the priority.

She tugged on the cockpit's door, relieved that it

was unlocked, and then hauled herself inside. It was a much tighter fit than she was expecting, but when she moved into the main area of the ship, it was a bit more spacious.

Juliette took a quick tour, jotting down the things that needed attention. The whole interior needed to be cleaned, the bathroom sink was sagging and looked about ready to fall, one of the chairs in the cockpit was completely broken, and the main control panel was a disaster. That was the part that was the most important.

The cockpit door swung open, and Noah pulled himself up. His eyes landed on Juliette, and he jumped, stumbling back out and falling to the ground.

Juliette swallowed a laugh, scrambling forward. “I’m sorry, I didn’t mean to startle you!”

Noah waved a hand in the air, getting back up and almost laughing. “It’s all good, I just wasn’t expecting you. What do you think?” he climbed back inside, then closed the door after him.

“I think it’ll work. It’s small, but thankfully there’s just two of us.”

Noah dropped a stack of books onto the main control panel. “Behold, our guidebooks.”

Juliette picked one up when he handed it to her, flipping through the worn, wrinkled pages. Even briefly scanning the text, she could tell it would take some serious studying to understand how to go about repairing an engine.

“It seems similar to the model engine I built last year for an exam, so I’m hoping there will be some crossover,” Noah mused with a shrug. He pulled his sweatshirt over his head, then jumped back down to the ground, crossing the garage to the opposite wall and grabbing a large metal box overflowing with tools.

While Noah lay sprawled beneath the ship, studying the engine, Juliette familiarized herself with the ship's computer system.

"Have you seen Dr. Violet again?" Noah asked when Juliette stepped back out into the garage in search of some extra wires.

Juliette hesitated. "Yeah. Earlier today." She cleared her throat. "I, uh, the doctor said I had a seizure."

"What?" Noah slid out from beneath the ship, bumping his forehead on the bottom of the ship in his haste to get out. His eyes were wide, filled with concern.

"I'm fine," Juliette quickly added. "I think. Dr. Violet said they were able to stop it before anything irreversible happened."

Noah didn't look appeased. "Have you ever had one before?"

Juliette shook her head. "I don't think so."

"What sparked it? The seizure."

"I don't know for sure, but I noticed when I went to give Odette her tablet, I don't know, it felt like I was being attacked from the inside. Like someone was stabbing me, in my head, in my chest. It hurt, it physically hurt. Things started to go black, but Odette was expecting it, though, because she sent me right to the infirmary."

Noah could only blink, his brows furrowed in concern. "Dr. Violet didn't say anything about it?"

"No, not really. I know she knows what's going on, but she won't tell me, and Odette's behind it. The doctor's been giving me different colored solutions, and then she does a bunch of different tests—monitors on my head, my chest, checking my heart, seeing if my blood pressure rises or falls."

Noah heaved a sigh. He dropped back to the ground to continue working. "What's her name?"

"Dr. Violet's?" Juliette paused at the counter along one of the walls, looking through the mess of drawers and cabinets. "Seas, doesn't anyone organize any of this stuff?"

"Yes to the first, no to the second."

Juliette shrugged. "I only know her as Dr. Violet." Finding a handful of wires that might work for her purpose, she paused beside the ship. She typed "Dr. Violet" into her search engine, and about three thousand results came up. She narrowed her search and found her on the second page. "It says she was employed originally in House Armament as a research scientist."

"A research scientist?" Noah asked, his voice muffled.

"Yeah, she specialized in neuroscience." Juliette frowned to herself. "How did she end up as a…whatever kind of doctor injects people with mystery serums?"

Noah's brows sank. "No idea. But we have a name. Marie Violet."

Marie Violet. Juliette committed the name to memory, climbing back into the cockpit where she spent the next several hours going over what was left of the ship's computer system.

Chapter Fifteen

At Noah's insistence, Juliette returned to her room at three in the morning to try and get some sleep. He could tell she was exhausted, and because he didn't know what Dr. Violet was doing to her, he was afraid that a lack of sleep would only worsen the effects.

He couldn't get past her having a seizure.

"There's still so much to do," she said, shaking her head as they walked back to her room. "I need to get the ship's computer system built. I need to set it up with new software that wouldn't be traceable and need to look into who Marie Violet is and what in the skies she's doing to me."

Noah inwardly shuddered. "We'll have time, but if you collapse from exhaustion, then it will make things a whole lot harder." He pulled her door open but hesitated. "Are you sure you're okay? About, you know…the seizure thing?"

Juliette shot him a half-hearted smile. There were circles beneath her eyes, and her dark hair made her skin look even paler. She looked exhausted. "I think so. I feel fine, anyway."

Noah licked his lips. "If you start to not feel fine, let me know."

Juliette nodded.

Noah jerked his chin toward her bed. "Get some sleep. I'll see you tomorrow."

Juliette reluctantly disappeared inside her room. Noah hurried back down to his and collapsed into bed. He fell asleep after only a few minutes, his dreams filled with ship parts and machinery.

He slept through his alarm and barely made it to the training room on time, still blinking the sleep from his eyes.

"You look like death," Mason said as he walked in.

Noah shot him a thumbs-up. "Thanks. Always appreciate a confidence boost."

"Are you excited?"

Noah blinked.

"About Armament? The assessment test?"

"Right." Noah shook his head. "Sorry, I spaced out. Yeah, yeah, I'm excited." Seas, he'd completely forgotten about the assessment test. He'd known it was coming for weeks, and once he returned, he'd be placed in a permanent position on the royal guard. He finished his last school class last Friday, and this was the final step in securing the job he would have for the rest of his life.

If he were to stay at the palace.

Noah hesitated, pulling his gloves over his hands and then wiggling his fingers. "Hey, can I ask you a weird question?"

Mason's eyebrows shot up. "Yeah, sure."

"You're from Armament, right?"

"Yeah."

"Have you ever heard of Marie Violet?"

"No, it doesn't sound familiar. Why?"

Noah jerked his shoulders in a shrug. "No reason. I was just doing some reading, and this woman's name popped up, and I thought maybe she was well-known there or something."

"Oh, not that I know of."

Noah frowned to himself, thinking. Marie Violet wasn't his main concern, but if he could learn more about her and her specialties, he might be able to figure out what she was doing to Juliette and come up with some ways to combat it.

Training started and ended, and by eight, Noah was showered, dressed, and on his way to Juliette's room. Odette was hosting a brunch for a handful of her House leaders. Aside from the whole making-Juliette-her-test-subject-for-a-strange-doctor, Odette had been oddly civil toward Juliette.

Noah didn't trust it. She was never this civil, even when their mother was alive. She was planning something; Noah was sure of it.

Juliette was pacing the length of the hallway outside her room when he rounded the corner. Her dark hair was piled on top of her head in shiny curls. A few pieces had come free and hung around her face, and she was wearing a dark purple, floor-length dress with sleeves that stopped at her elbow. She had always been pretty, but somehow she had become even more so, seemingly overnight.

Noah didn't realize he'd stopped walking until Juliette turned around and met his gaze, shaking him from his stupor.

"I was jittery and wanted to walk," she said with a partial laugh, knotting her hands together. Her eyes were especially bright, but there was a haziness to them. She was still the most beautiful girl he'd ever seen.

Noah forced a nod. "Ready?"

"I am," she replied, smoothing her hands down her front and then starting down the corridor. There was something off about her movements. She was walking slower than she normally did, and she didn't seem entirely *there*.

Thank the skies Odette was preoccupied when Juliette walked in, speaking with Lord Galvan, who oversaw House Galvan that was responsible for the country's electricity conduction.

Odette was wearing a dark red dress, made of a stiff brocade and had a plunging neckline. Her hair hung down her back, and her black crown was perfectly arranged on the top of her head. Everything about her was the polar opposite of Juliette.

Breakfast started, and Noah took up position beside the window. From this vantage point, he had a view of the entire room and both entrances.

"I have been in communication with Viktor Yeltsin, the president of Russia. He hasn't said anything outright, but I have high hopes that a peace treaty will be signed by the end of next year," Odette announced.

A collective gasp went around the table. Everyone started talking at the same time, praising Odette's cleverness, speculating that once the peace treaty was signed, forming alliances wouldn't be far behind. Odette didn't put an end to the chatter, no doubt thriving on being so highly exalted.

"Still won't let us see your beautiful daughter?" Lord Apatite asked, one of his eyebrows arched.

Juliette visibly tensed, her gaze darting to Odette, who froze.

Seconds stretched across the room in a blanket of tension.

"I beg your pardon?" Odette finally asked.

If Noah didn't know better, he would think Odette was hurt. Rumors had been floating around Demetria for a decade and a half that Odette had gotten pregnant sixteen years ago and kept her daughter hidden.

The term *The Lost Princess* was coined, people insisting Odette was hiding her daughter from the public eye until she was of age or Odette was crowned queen.

Odette's coronation came and went with nothing. The only person she was hiding was Juliette, and it was because she hated her.

"Apologies, Your Majesty. I couldn't resist," Lord Apatite added with a laugh.

Juliette didn't say a word, though her eyes flickered up to Noah for a split second. Noah barely shook his head, thinking he was an exceptionally brave man.

Odette looked down at her plate as she cut into her meat. "Natasha, see this gentleman out of the palace. I will appoint a new House Head by the end of the day."

"Your Majesty, I'm so sorry, I was only trying to—"

"I suggest you stop flapping your lips if you wish your wife and son to live to see tomorrow." Odette didn't stop eating. Didn't give any indication she was rattled.

Lord Apatite blinked. He stood up, bowed, and walked with Natasha out of the room.

"I have been in communication with the royal family from France," Odette continued, addressing the rest of the table, "and have invited them to visit Demetria in December. I'm hoping to begin trade deals with them when the war is over, and thought there was no better way to establish a solid relationship than by meeting them in person," she added, waving at one of the footmen to bring her another glass of wine.

Before anyone had the chance to reply, the chandelier above the table rattled. The hanging crystals tinkled against each other, and the ground rumbled beneath them.

Noah waited for the quake to die down. When it started to grow more intense, he took a step closer to Juliette, ready to yank her back and shield her should the need arise.

"It's just a quake, get back," Odette hissed.

Noah obediently took a step back, as did Odette's guard who had also moved closer. Juliette glanced at Noah, shooting him a silent *thank you*, before turning back to breakfast.

Chapter Sixteen

As soon as breakfast was over, and after Odette moved into the library with the House leaders, Noah walked with Juliette back to her wing. He forgot to tell her he was going out of the capital to take his assessment test, and in light of everything going on with Dr. Violet and Odette and their growing plans to run away, he was worried. The timing couldn't have been worse. He knew he'd only be gone for a week, and in all reality, there wasn't much he could do to protect Juliette from Odette while he was there anyway, but he still didn't like the idea of leaving with so much going on.

Noah sighed. He hated it here. Hated it with a passion.

"I think I'll be able to finally start building the ship's new computer," she whispered as they neared her private study.

Noah instinctively cast a discreet glance around. "Great."

"Collecting parts will be a bit of a challenge, but I have a few old tablets I don't use that often. I'll just pull from there and then tell Odette they started malfunctioning."

"Don't get yourself in trouble. If you need something, write it down and I'll see about going into town and getting it."

Juliette grinned. “Thanks. I also figured something out about Dr. Violet.” She closed the door after them, making Noah just the tiniest bit uncomfortable. He shouldn’t have been in here, alone with her in a closed room. “We know she was only recently relocated here, within the past year. She’d been studying in Armament for almost ten years, neuroscience and the like. There was a report from Atworth last year, a study done on the effects of subliminal frequencies that were applied to the soldiers in training. There wasn’t much of a boost in productivity, but there was *some*. Dr. Violet took the findings and worked on applying them in heavier frequencies to amply the effects.”

Noah nodded along.

“About that time, Odette requested her to come to the palace for some additional research on how the thought processes of our brains impact what we’re physically capable of.”

Noah almost frowned, not sure he understood.

“I’m not entirely sure what that means,” she added, grimacing. “But that’s where she originated.”

“What would she be doing here? And why is she seeing you?”

Juliette shook her head, slowly. “I don’t know. The only thing I can think of is Odette wanted to fund her studies and she wanted an easy test subject. Which, honestly, isn’t the worst thing I thought could be happening.”

“No, I suppose not. Except you said she’s been giving you shots. Drugs. What does that have to do with the brain’s power over the body?”

Juliette reluctantly shrugged. “It might have nothing to do with it, they might be two different studies. I just…wanted to share what I learned in case something stood out to you that didn't occur to me."

"Thanks, I'll be thinking about it. Speaking of Armament, I'm going there for a week or so in a few days."

Juliette looked up. "What? Why?"

"For an assessment test, nothing serious," he added quickly. "My last one, thank the seas, which means no more school. Plus, it will give me the chance to do some more looking into Dr. Violet. Maybe there's someone there who knows more than whatever we could find on the Nexus."

Juliette hedged. "When will you get back?"

"In about a week. Probably less, but they estimate high."

She chewed the edge of her thumbnail, and Noah saw her smile. He could tell she was working to keep her face neutral, and he wondered if she was worried about him leaving. He knew why *he* was, but from her point of view, his presence didn't do anything for her. He couldn't save her from Odette, and he couldn't protect her from Dr. Violet.

"I'll have access to the Nexus, so we'll be able to stay in touch and keep each other up-to-date with what we find. If you can, keep working on the ship, but please be careful. If Odette, or one of her people, saw you poking around out there, it would bring up questions."

"Of course. By the time you get back, I'll have a working computer system ready to be installed, and then I can do whatever I can to help with the engine."

"Perfect." Noah would also hopefully have the chance to make a few running-away related purchases, like bulk food items. He didn't want to do anything in the capital where there was a greater chance of someone noticing something was amiss.

Noah nudged her. "But don't be a stranger. Send me pictures of whatever it is you're doing throughout the day. I don't want to get homesick."

Juliette almost scoffed. "You won't get homesick."

You can be homesick for a person, Noah thought. He kept it to himself. "We'll celebrate when I get back," he instead voiced aloud. "I may have a stash of cacao truffles hidden."

Juliette's eyes popped open. The only time she was supposed to have anything sweet was one day a year—on her birthday.

"You have truffles?"

"I do. To be enjoyed upon my return *and* successful assignments for the both of us," he added, holding up a finger.

"Can I have just one? Please? It can be an early birthday present!"

"Sorry. You have to wait."

Juliette sighed, frowning.

"Besides, your birthday's not for a while," Noah said with an eye roll.

"I know; I said *early* birthday present."

"No way. It's not even a big birthday either."

Juliette scowled. "Easy for you to say. Philip at least gets you a cupcake."

"I gave you my frosting!"

Juliette laughed, but the smile almost immediately dropped from her face. "What if you do really well in the test and you qualify for a position higher than a guard? Will you at least get to come back and say goodbye? I'm sure we could still plan to get away—if, you know, you want to still go—but it might take a bit longer."

Noah drew back. "What are you talking about? I'll go, take the test, and be back as a guard. We'll keep planning."

She scoffed. "You're smart. You're going to place high. You're going to be the rarity that gets to move up."

"Even if that were the case, I'd throw the exam. If you think I'd stay in this place one day longer than I have to, you're wrong. We're getting out of here, together."

Juliette visibly relaxed, the grin turning a little less forced. "We still need to decide *where* we're going," she added, almost wistfully.

Noah shrugged. "Name a few places that pique your interest."

A smile tilted the corner of her mouth. "The beach."

"The beach. That'd be fun. Do you know how to swim?"

Juliette shook her head. "No."

"I hear it's easy to learn."

"Okay, then I want to go to the beach. In California!"

Noah smirked. California. "Sure, why not?"

"Or maybe Australia? We could do some scuba diving in the coral reefs?"

"That'd be fun. Oh, and we could go camping."

Juliette laughed. Her grin was infectious. "Camping? With tents?"

"Why not? I saw a show where they went camping,

and it looked fun. Out in the middle of nowhere and cooking over a fire, sleeping in tents, going stargazing. I have a lifetime of adventures to live up to."

"Oh seas, I've never even seen stars in real life." She smiled. "Okay, camping has been added to the list."

Noah smiled, excitement bubbling in his stomach. He glanced at his watch, jerking a thumb behind him. "I should get going. I'll see you later?"

Juliette nodded, gracing him with a smile.

Chapter Seventeen

By the time dinner rolled around, Juliette's stomach was in knots, and she wasn't hungry. The House Leaders were still there, and she didn't want to skip out. Odette would probably think something was wrong and send her to the infirmary for no reason again. Juliette's head had been hurting all day, even after taking some pain relievers; the last thing she wanted was to go back to Dr. Violet.

Taking her seat beside Odette, Juliette looked around the room at the faces in front of her. Noah's shift had ended, so it was Luis who walked her to the dining room and was standing at the door. She hardly ever spoke to Luis, since he mostly worked the night shift.

Juliette sipped at her water. She knew each of the Lords, and single Lady, by name, their Houses, and what they contributed to the capital city of Anadia. She knew from the hours of listening in to their conferences hundreds of miles away. She knew about Lady Luxe having an affair. She knew Lord Apatite's daughter had just moved to live on a farm with her husband. She knew the former Lord Canyons just passed away in a car accident that seemed a little too convenient to be a true accident. She knew far too much about their personal lives and made her uncomfortable.

All through dinner, as much as she tried to pay

attention to the conversation around her, the only thing she could think about was Noah leaving. She would have plenty to do in his absence, but him not being there made her nervous. At least with two of them, they could watch each other's backs. Thankfully she'd still be able to nex't him and keep him updated.

As the first course was brought out, Juliette's eyes wandered to the window. She thought about looking up at the sky and being able to see stars. Or feeling sand on her bare toes. She'd never been swimming before, but if she and Noah learned, she could see the two of them spending hours on the beach.

As the dinner dragged on and there seemed to be no end to dinner in sight, the headache in the back of her head grew. She wanted to learn more about Dr. Violet and why she was here at the palace, but she also needed to pay attention to what Odette and her House Leaders were talking about so she could write up a report in case Odette sprang it on her. She'd done it before, and not that she needed an excuse now that she was queen, Juliette thought it better safe than sorry.

She was also supposed to have another doctor's appointment tomorrow, and already she was trying to think of a way to get out of it. Dr. Violet and the mystery of her being brought to the palace had lit a spark of curiosity that she couldn't ignore.

"Are we boring you, Your Highness?" Lord Canyons asked, smiling politely as he turned toward Juliette.

Juliette shook her head, calling up a smile. "No, I just have a lot on my mind."

"Pay her no mind, Lord Canyons, she tires easily. Juliette, you may go upstairs," Odette said, waving a hand toward the door.

"Thank the seas," she replied with a sweet smile, eliciting a series of polite laughs from around the table. Juliette stood up and then stepped through the opened door, ignoring the glare Odette cast her. With a relieved sigh, she happily retreated to the safety of her room and kicked off her shoes.

Juliette curled up beneath her blankets and stuffed one of the pillows behind her, reaching for her computer. She pulled up the saved tabs she had on Dr. Violet, but she'd read the same pages so many times she had them memorized. There was nothing new hidden anywhere.

She would see Dr. Violet tomorrow, and while she wasn't looking forward to it in any way, she held on to the hope that she would be able to learn something else about her. Either about why she came to the palace, or what she was doing now that she was there.

Juliette switched tablets, doing some more setup for the ship's computer. It would be fairly simple, but she wanted to be able to have Nexus access through the ship itself, which would help her better block their signals.

Juliette's tablet chimed, and she picked it up, grinning when she saw Noah's name flashing up at her.

–You awake?–

Juliette quickly typed back a reply. *–Yep…why?–*

–Just asking.–

She smiled to herself, her fingers hesitating over the keypad. She wanted to tell him she was going to miss him so much and she couldn't wait for him to get back. She wanted to know if, now they were on the road to not having titles and roles to play, if his feelings toward her went beyond friendship. If he thought of her as more than a friend, if he fell asleep dreaming about her as much as she did him.

Instead, she typed, *–send me pictures from the train when you board?–*

–Of course.–

Juliette talked with him for a while longer, but she found it hard to come up with things to say. A thought would pop into her head, only to fade out again. She wasn't sure why her eyes started to well up, and she tried to tell herself she was just sad at him leaving, however short a time it would be. She couldn't remember the last time he'd been away. For as long as her memories stretched, he was always there.

It was a week. He'd be gone for a week, not a year. She would do everything she could to ready the ship, including cleaning out the interior and making it suitable to live in. She didn't have any money of her own to spend, and as much as she hated to make Noah pony up all the expenses, she knew there was no way around it.

Once they were out of the country and she got a job and was working, she'd pay him back.

When Noah stopped sending messages, Juliette figured he went to sleep, so she sank back down against her pillows and pulled up some of the recent news reports from across the country. She checked that the shipment of produce Atworth had sent was on time for delivery, then switched over to House Luxe and put another order in for Odette.

A shadow of movement outside the window caught her attention, and she almost let out a yelp of surprise as a figure appeared over the balcony.

Juliette leapt up, reaching for the cord hanging beside her bed that would call for one of the maids to come.

The figure stepped from the shadows, tapping on her glass.

"Seas, Noah, you almost gave me a heart attack!" Juliette hissed, crossing the room and unlatching the window.

Noah almost fell headfirst onto the ground but managed to catch himself. "The guy on the Nexus show I was watching made that look way cooler."

Juliette almost laughed. Seeing him in sweats and a hoodie made her insides tremble, though she wasn't sure why. "What kinds of shows are you watching?"

"Fun ones. Watch out." He waved her away as he climbed in the window.

"There's a door—" She stopped talking as Noah swung a leg over.

"I know, I got your balconies mixed up." He stood up and smiled. Most of the shoes Juliette wore had at least a little bit of heel, but standing barefoot next to him, she realized how tall he'd gotten. Tall and beautiful and perfect.

"Cards?" he asked, holding up a deck.

Cards. A card game. Juliette tried to remember how to breathe. "Yeah, that sounds fun," she finally replied, stepping back and moving to a clear space on the ground.

They played several games, talking about a myriad of subjects—Noah's upcoming exam, Juliette's findings from the various Houses, her progress on the ship's computer, Noah's excitement at getting to build an engine.

"Jeez, you're good at this." Noah sighed after their fifth game.

Juliette shot him a smug smile. There were so few things she was good at—let alone *better* at than him—it always made her feel excited when he was impressed with her. "What time do you leave tomorrow morning?"

"The train leaves at six."

"That's early."

"I know." He yawned. "Speaking of, I should probably head back to my room and get some sleep."

Juliette tossed her cards onto the deck as Noah swept them all up, then tucked them into his pocket. She licked her lips. "Could I go with you to the station tomorrow morning?" she asked, handing him a stray card that had gotten stuck beneath the bed.

"You'll be awake at six?" Noah asked doubtfully, his eyebrows shooting up.

Juliette easily nodded, not seeing the need to mention she didn't sleep well most nights anyway. "I'm an early riser."

Noah's smile warmed, just a little. "I'd love that. I'll send you a nex't when I'm leaving."

As soon as Noah left, Juliette set her alarm for five thirty so she would have time to get dressed and meet him at the station by six. She'd never seen a train up close before. Odette had a private one that had a station in the back of the palace, but the train itself was kept somewhere else unless Odette needed it.

She went to sleep and thankfully didn't wake up again until her alarm went off. Maybe it was talking to Noah minutes before going to bed, but she didn't have a single nightmare. Hurrying into her closet, she pulled a thick, floor-length dress over her head and then shook out her hair while waiting for Noah to nex't her.

Odette was still asleep when he messaged her that he was ready, so it was easy for her to slip away outside. Philip insisted she bring a guard to walk her back since the station was a good two miles from the palace.

"Remember, send me plenty of nex'ts throughout the week. Pictures and/or videos are a bonus," Noah said as they neared the boarding ramp.

Juliette shoved her hands into her coat pockets, the cold making her shiver.

"And…" He pulled out a small paper bag from his pocket and dumped the contents into his hand. Two chocolate lumps fell into his palm. "I thought we could have half now and the other half later."

With a grin, she took one of them, and he took the other. She popped it into her mouth and reveled in the bitter-turned-sweet taste of chocolate.

Noah seemed to hesitate, his hand reaching for her wrist. "Be careful. Make sure you eat and get lots of sleep," he said, a shadow crossing his face.

"I will," she promised.

Noah took a step toward her, sending Juliette's heart rate through the roof, and wrapped his arms around her in a hug. Her own arms automatically moved around him. He'd hugged her before, but it seemed like it had been a while. Juliette didn't realize until now how much she missed it. How much more it meant to her now than it did when she was younger.

Noah pulled away, tucking a piece of hair behind her ear and managing a smile.

Juliette took a step back, watching as he walked

down the stretch of concrete and into the train. She waited until the entirety of the vehicle had disappeared from her line of sight before letting the strained smile drop from her face. Something squeezed at her chest, making it hard to breathe.

The moment she stepped back inside the palace, a guard was waiting to tell her that Odette wanted to speak to her.

Juliette tensed. She walked with the guard to the library, where Odette had a spreading of books on the table in front of her.

"I am taking a train to House Apatite and will be gone about a month," Odette said without looking up from the holo-table she was leaning over. "I need to see about appointing a new House Head, and I'd rather do it in person."

Juliette stamped down the rise of excitement bubbling in her chest. A whole month in the palace with no Odette to worry about? It was almost too good to be true. She could easily build the ship's computer and probably even get the entire inside ready to leave.

"I expect you to finish the tasks I sent to your tablet by the time I return."

"Of course." Seas, if Odette was leaving for a month, and Noah would be back in a week, they could probably get the ship ready to leave before her return! Leaving would be so much easier without having to worry about her. "Then…have a good trip."

"You'll be confined until I return, and you will use that time to listen to speeches and lectures from the French king and his cabinet. I want to know everything about their political and financial standpoint, as well as the economic affairs of their capital."

Juliette barely registered what Odette said. "Confined? Where?"

"I've had your study converted into a...shall we say, holding cell? The windows have been sealed, and the door locks from the outside. You'll have meals brought to you, and Dr. Violet will be coming to you for continued surveillance."

No. No, no, no— "What? Why can't I work in my room? You'll be gone, so it's not like I'll be in your way."

Odette heaved a dramatic sigh. "Not that I must defend my actions to you, but I can't trust you to roam freely around the palace while I'm away. Not when you've displayed so much defiance and rebellion. I might come home and have you gone, and then where would we be?"

Juliette tensed, but Odette didn't seem to have any real idea Juliette was planning on leaving.

"Besides, I prefer it when you do your work without the risk of someone looking over your shoulder."

"I can work in my normal room without someone looking over my shoulder," Juliette suggested. She set her jaw, blinking her eyes clear. She couldn't be locked away, not when there was so much to do.

Odette rolled her eyes. "It's only a month, you'll be fine. There's plenty of food inside, and the staff here will bring you fresh food. Dr. Violet will come visit you once a week to continue her research—"

Odette kept talking, but Juliette stopped listening. She would lose an entire month of work. She couldn't do anything to the ship, and Noah would come back and have to wait three more weeks for their plan to continue.

Noah wasn't here. Juliette could fight back without the fear of him being punished. She could lunge for Odette. She'd just made the decision to at least try, when Odette looked up at one of the guards standing nearby and cocked her head to the side. "Take her."

Juliette felt a hand wrap around her arm and tug her into the corridor. "Let me go!" She wrenched her arm free.

"Don't start!" Odette snapped, finally looking up. "I'm not in the mood."

"I can walk myself; you don't need to—"

Odette turned, thrusting her elbowing into Juliette's stomach.

Juliette doubled over, but the guards holding her kept her upright. A cough choked its way out.

Odette grabbed a fistful of her hair, yanking her around and shoving her against the wall. "I said I'm not in the mood. That doesn't mean I won't do what it takes to remind you who's in control," Odette hissed.

Juliette groaned, the back of her brain flaring in a sharp pain. Odette let her go, and she turned around.

"Now." Odette looked at one of the guards. "Take her to her study and lock the door."

Juliette didn't fight. The guard pushed her through the door. The part of her scalp Odette grabbed stung. She must have scratched her.

Computers and trans-screens lined the wall over a small desk in what had formerly been her study. There was a small bed in the corner, a desk beneath what used to be the windows, and a washroom.

The rest of the room was empty save for a metal cabinet with food and water.

Juliette hesitated at the door, the confinement and darkness and thickness looming in front of her. Her throat tightened, and her palms grew clammy.

The guard pushed her inside, closing the door before she had the chance to finish her thought.

Juliette slammed her hands on the door, pounding against it with her palm, screaming to be released. The cold steel barely made a sound.

Drawing a shaky inhale, Juliette sank to the ground and wrapped her arms around her legs, burying her face in her knees. Her chest squeezed, frustration bringing tears to her eyes.

Juliette propped her chin on her knees, letting the air in her lungs out in a steadying sigh. Just because she was trapped didn't mean she was helpless. She had tasks from Odette that needed to be done. She could learn more about Dr. Violet. Noah would still be sending her information, and she could piggyback on whatever he learned.

With a shaky sigh, blinking her eyes clear, Juliette pushed herself up and started on her work.

Chapter Eighteen

Odette watched the palace come into view, her shuttle nearing the small landing pad outside the palace. As soon as it touched down and she was cleared to disembark, Odette stood up and started down the black metal stairs.

Natasha was already waiting for her, and for a split second, guilt pricked Odette's mind. She never invited Natasha to ride in the main part of the ship with her, instead letting her ride in the cockpit with the pilot. The guilty feeling passed.

"I'd like to speak with Dr. Violet," Odette said, unbuttoning the front of her cloak as she walked and handing it to a maid who appeared at her side.

"She's in the infirmary."

Odette nodded once, starting in that direction. Dr. Violet was sitting behind a desk in the far corner, where Odette had instructed her to do her work. She didn't want anyone else getting wind of her proposed weapon until there was something to tell.

Dr. Violet stood up as soon as Odette neared. "Your Majesty. How was your trip?"

"Fine. Report."

Dr. Violet hesitated. "If you'd like to step into a private room?"

Odette bristled. She started into the nearest room, waiting for Dr. Violet and Natasha to follow.

"One of the biggest setbacks I've experienced with the princess is her physical size. She's small."

Odette waved a hand for Dr. Violet to continue. "Yes, I know, that's one of the reasons I want to use her in the first place. If she can be functional as a weapon, then anyone can."

There was another reason, arguably more important, but Odette kept that to herself for the time being.

"Exactly. Given that, I've been doing some research on the latent potential of the human body, seeing how I could implement that into the serum. If it works, it will enhance her muscle strength, provide her with added strength and speed, and heighten her reflexes."

Odette almost drew back, stunned. It was too good to be true, surely.

"I am still struggling to activate the serum. It's been in her system for almost two months now, and she still hasn't shown full potential."

Odette tried not to sigh. "How much *has* she shown?"

Dr. Violet hesitated. "Very little. Our bodies release different neurotransmitters that aid the brain in communicating with the rest of the body, via the central nervous system. The serum is activated by the release of norepinephrine, which is the fight-or-flight response. I've been unable to get the princess to have that kind of neurological reaction on her own, thus rendering the serum ineffective."

Odette worked her jaw. "Then what if we created a series of injections that targeted those neurotransmitters? Wouldn't that give us the ability to activate and deactivate the serum at will?"

"Yes, in theory. Which has been my main focus at this point, but if the princess's body doesn't react to it, we're in the same position we're in now."

"The fight-or-flight response is something that occurs when you're scared, correct?"

"Scared, sometimes even angry."

"And you can't get that reaction from her? She's so easily angered; I would think it would be simple."

"I have been unsuccessful," Dr. Violet repeated. She almost smirked. "Perhaps now that you're back, you'll be able to help."

Odette straightened. "I'm sure I could," she replied, speaking with more confidence than she felt. Juliette was starting to grow immune to Odette's threats.

Well, that was about to change.

"I've developed a few different serums, all at different strengths. We'll introduce the first serum at the lowest strength and see how her brain reacts to it. If it's successful, we'll go on to the next level, until we can't go any higher. Then from there, we'll work on generating that fear reaction," Dr. Violet continued.

Odette pressed her glossy lips together, digging her fingernails into her palms and drawing a steading breath. She took half a step forward, lowering her voice. "Is it possible to create a similar effect on a subject whose brain is…underdeveloped?"

Dr. Violet's eyebrows twitched. "What do you mean?"

"Could the serum be applied, but instead of being used to arouse feelings of hatred and destruction, could it force the brain to regenerate itself? If the serum dictates what the body does," she added, almost hesitantly.

Dr. Violet blinked. "I…I don't know, Your Majesty. It would depend on the subject, on the state of her brain, of her growth—"

"The princess's size and weight, approximately."

"Is there someone specific you have in mind?" Dr. Violet looked at Odette over the rim of her glasses.

"Perhaps. Answer my question."

"I don't know, Your Majesty. I can't know, not without having a better understanding of the situation, however hypothetical it may be."

Odette cleared her throat. "I will come back with more answers, but I would appreciate it if you would look into the different ways the serum could be used when applied differently."

Dr. Violet seemed confused, but she nodded. "Of course."

Chapter Nineteen

Juliette drew her knees to her chest, wrapping her arms around her legs. She tried to focus her thoughts on something. *Anything*. Nothing seemed to stick long enough to hold her attention. Her head hurt so much she couldn't keep her eyes open.

The air around her was cold and dark, but a tap on the screen of her tablet said it was almost eight in the morning. With a shaky sigh, she stretched out onto her back and stared up at the ceiling. Her blanket had ended up tangled around her, and she worked to get it straightened.

She didn't think she'd ever felt this empty, this blank. Her eyes burned, but the urge to cry wasn't there. If anything, she was just plain tired and would have loved to get some decent sleep.

True to Odette's word, Dr. Violet had been coming to see her. Odette said she would only come once a week, but she'd come eight times already, and Juliette had been locked up for a little less than a month. She had the same, brain-prickling sensation every time she was injected. It went away after a few hours, but Juliette wasn't spared from having nightmares.

She really hoped Noah had been able to get his ship repaired in her absence. She hadn't been able to send or receive any external communications, and it had been driving her insane. Noah wouldn't know why she wasn't answering, and she couldn't take any of what he learned and expand on it. She hadn't been able to do any work on the ship's computer or clean the inside or look into purchasing supplies for their trip.

Eat something. You need food. She hadn't eaten in over twelve hours, and despite her stomach gnawing at her, nothing sounded appealing. There were plenty of snacks here and even some juices, but that would require getting up, and she'd finally managed to get warm.

Something rattled outside the heavy metal door. Juliette's heart leapt to her throat, but she didn't move. The door creaked open. Juliette glanced at the clock again, frowning. Breakfast was here early.

The door creaked open with a thud. Brightness flooded the room, and Juliette squinted, her eyes finally watering.

Two guards stood outside, but a woman cloaked in black stepped in.

Natasha. She dipped her head in a bow. "Your Highness. Her Majesty returned from Canyons last night and has ordered your release. I'm to take you back to your room."

Juliette blinked. She pushed herself up, gathering her two portable tablets and favorite hoodie from the small bed. She kept her jaw clenched, refusing to let Natasha see how cold she was.

Natasha walked with Juliette back to her room—her real room. The one where the windows opened into fresh air, and the bed had more than one blanket. The one where Noah had climbed up onto the balcony and played cards with her, where they used to fall asleep together watching TV.

"Your maids will be up tomorrow morning," Natasha added softly. She walked in with Juliette but motioned for the guards with her to stay outside before closing the door. "There's some fresh breakfast there if you're hungry, and I had some clean clothes brought in as well. I don't know if you remember, but Odette's birthday celebration is in a few days."

Juliette almost chortled. Odette and her stupid, frivolous parties.

Natasha took a step forward. "Are you okay?"

Juliette met Natasha's gaze. "I've been locked up for a month with no one but a needle-wielding doctor."

"I'm so sorry, Juliette," Natasha whispered.

Juliette's eyebrows twitched. She shook her head. "It's not your fault."

Natasha looked like she might say something else, but she didn't. She swallowed. Licked her lips. "Eat something and then get some rest."

"Thank you. Is…is Noah back?" She hadn't heard from him the entire time she'd been locked away. Odette had restricted her communication abilities for the duration of her imprisonment.

"He got back from Armament a few weeks ago, but he's not here now."

Juliette's heart stilled.

"He's fine," Natasha quickly added. "He took a piloting assignment for one of the House Leaders, but he should be back in a few days or so."

Juliette let out another shaky sigh. He was safe, at least.

Alone, Juliette sank down at her desk where some food had been left. Fluffy scrambled eggs, toast and jam, and what looked to be buttered beans. Steam was rising off the plate, curling into the air. She probably should have waited for it to cool off, but she was too hungry.

Juliette groaned. She hadn't had anything decent to eat in a month. Her workroom-turned-prison-cell had a decent supply of food, but it was all freeze-dried or dehydrated. Nonperishables.

She took her plate and pulled open the curtains at the window that opened onto one of her balconies. The sun was hidden, as always, but she could still soak up some radiant light. She shivered, taking another bite and relishing in the feeling of hot, fresh food.

While eating, she fished her tablet out of her pocket and sent another nex't to Noah. Her first one had gone undelivered, and she worried something was wrong with her tablet. If he was out of the country, though, it might not be able to get through until he came home. She just assumed he was somewhere in another House, but maybe he flew out of the country.

With a shaky exhale, Juliette checked on the status of Odette's birthday party. Everyone who was someone in Demetria was invited, well over three hundred people.

At some point, a maid came in with a brand-new dress straight from House Luxe. It was beautiful. So beautiful, Juliette was afraid to touch it for fear of ruining it.

Juliette shivered, snapping her tablet off. As soon as she finished her breakfast, she took a shower and then put on the clothes from Natasha. They were soft and smelled new.

Juliette's tablet pinged, and she glanced at it, her heart leaping to her throat. It wasn't Noah, much to her disappointment, but an itinerary for Odette's birthday.

Throughout the rest of the day, Juliette picked up her room. It wasn't terribly messy, because she'd been gone for so long, but it gave her something to do.

Finally, at the end of the day, Juliette climbed into her bed and relished in the comfort her blankets always brought. Her sheets still smelled clean. They were washed right before she was locked up, and the faintest hint of the laundry detergent lingered.

Juliette worked her jaw, bunching one of the pillows beneath her and forcing her eyes closed.

Chapter Twenty

Juliette had just finished getting dressed when her bedroom door opened and a guard walked in.

She should have expected it.

"Her Majesty has requested to speak with you," he said.

Juliette reached for her tablet in case it was another assignment. The guard stepped back out into the corridor and walked her toward Odette's wing of the palace, but instead of turning up the staircase toward her conference room, he started down.

"Where are we going?" she asked.

"The infirmary."

Juliette stopped short. "Why? Dr. Violet came to see me two days ago."

The guard didn't stop moving, grabbing her arm and pulling her forward. "I have my orders, Princess."

Juliette struggled to yank her arm free. "You might be taking orders from Odette, but I'm still your princess, and you will not touch me."

The guard almost smirked.

Odette wasn't there this time, and Juliette was able to go into the room alone. She held on to a sliver of hope that maybe, just maybe, she would get to see Dr. Greene. Maybe today was just a normal, routine checkup. Maybe Dr. Violet realized the drugs she was giving Juliette and the constant blood withdrawals were taking a toll on her mind and body.

But then Dr. Violet walked in with a tray of vials, and that hope evaporated.

"Go ahead and get undressed and then get on the table."

Juliette thought to refuse, but she wanted to get out of there as quickly as possible, so she did as she was told, setting her tablet down on the counter and then taking her warm and comfortable clothes off. She reached for the hospital gown that was left out and slipped it over her arms.

Dr. Violet started with the basics—checking Juliette's heartbeat, blood pressure, height, weight, and lung capacity.

"I'm going to take a blood sample and then give you a separate injection."

Juliette's fingers went cold, and the edges of her vision started to swim. She swallowed, blinking her eyes clear. Two needles. Just two needles.

"You'll be fine, don't start."

Juliette chewed her already bleeding lip, wishing she wasn't so afraid of needles. She involuntarily winced when Dr. Violet reached for her arm.

"Don't do that," Dr. Violet snapped. "You have to hold still, or it will take longer."

"I know," Juliette snapped right back. "You could be a little nicer, you know. It won't kill you, contrary to what Odette says."

Dr. Violet leveled a glare at her, but she drew a vial full of blood and then retreated. Juliette pressed her other hand to the needle wound, her head swimming. Stars speckled her vision.

Juliette tried to keep her voice neutral. "Why do

you always take so much blood?"

"For tests. I have to make sure the injections I'm giving you aren't causing any negative effects."

"What do those injections do?" Juliette asked with a casual shrug. "I mean, clearly you know more than me, so…" she trailed off, feigning innocent curiosity.

Dr. Violet was in no mood to chat. "Alright, here's the second one."

Juliette yanked her arm back. "What are the injections for?" she asked. "You can answer one question."

Dr. Violet reached for her arm, and Juliette shoved her back. The needle clattered to the floor. "Princess!"

Juliette swallowed her fear. No doubt this would be reported to Odette. "What are you injecting me with? What's Odette doing? I know you transferred from Armament and you started as a research scientist. What are you doing to me?"

Dr. Violet huffed, her face reddening. "You make this so much harder on yourself. Guards!"

Juliette's throat tightened. "Please, just tell me what's going on. We both know I won't be able to do anything to stop it, but at least let me *know*," she whispered.

For a split second, Dr. Violet seemed to consider it, but then the door opened, and two guards walked in.

Juliette tried not to resist, knowing it would hurt more and take longer, but her body betrayed her. The two guards pinned her down, and she struggled against them. Her muscles clenched, and it took three tries for the needle to find a vein. A dull ache was drained into her blood. She couldn't help the few tears that leaked onto her face.

“You really don’t like needles, do you?” Dr. Violet said, shaking her head. She tapped on her tablet for an agonizingly long time before motioning to the guards, who took their hands from Juliette’s arms and legs, leaving imprints on her skin.

“You’re finished for now.”

Juliette leapt from the table. Her legs wobbled, and she almost fell. Pulling her dress over her head and brushing the flecks of dirt that had gathered along the hem, Juliette pulled the door open and stepped outside. She sagged against the wall, pausing to catch her breath and giving her heart the chance to settle.

Chapter Twenty-One

Noah flipped a switch, adjusting the cruising altitude on the ship as they neared Demetrian territory. The engines changed their pitch, and there was the slightest change in pressure, causing his ears to pop. He glanced at his tablet, but there were no messages from Juliette. He knew she was probably still in her prison, but he hoped her lack of communication was because she was busy, not because something more serious was wrong.

He checked the ship's computer. He had about thirty minutes until he'd need to manually fly, so he set the ship on autopilot and stood up. It felt good to stretch his legs, and Atticus, his one and only passenger, didn't ask that he confine himself to the cockpit. He couldn't imagine being a pilot for someone and not being allowed to move around every now and then.

It was almost seven in the morning, Demetria time, so Atticus was probably asleep in his cabin. Noah would have loved to get some rest as well, but he wouldn't have enough time. He couldn't land on autopilot, and they would be touching down within the next hour.

Instead, he crept into the galley and helped himself to an early morning snack. His eating and sleeping patterns had been thrown off the past week, hopefully it wouldn't take too long to get back into a normal routine.

While enjoying his short break, he tried once again to send a nex't to Juliette. With a sigh, he leaned back against the wall. He closed his eyes for what felt like a second, only to startle awake at the ship's gentle chime. Jogging back to the cockpit, he began the entry procedures that would allow him to reenter Demetria. There were only two gates into and out of the country.

One was in the capital, Anadia, and the other was in Fatir, at the opposite end of the country. Since Atticus lived in Atworth, which was close to the center, he said he didn't mind entering through the Anadian entrance and then taking a train back home.

Since it was Noah's job to follow orders, he made no arguments. And truthfully, that arrangement suited him just fine, since it would save him almost a full day of travel.

He liked Atticus. He was nice and reminded him a lot of Mason. Noah would have enjoyed himself a lot more getting to fly oversees, but he was eager to get back to the palace and find out what was going on with Juliette. He didn't know the details of her being locked away, but knowing Odette, she was reveling in Juliette's misery.

It felt like forever, but by eight o'clock, Noah had docked in the palace hangar, made sure that Atticus was escorted to his train, and he was officially free for the rest of the day. He ran straight to his room in the palace sublevels, showered, and changed into a fresh uniform. He wanted to see Juliette, but he wasn't about to go running around the palace in jeans and a T-shirt.

At least not in broad daylight.

Footsteps thudded around the corner. "Noah, thank

the seas you're back," Mason said, his shoulders dropping.

Noah immediately stiffened, his fingers turning to ice. "What happened? Is she okay?"

"She's fine, as far as I know. She was released from the room yesterday, and she went to the infirmary right away. The queen's birthday is later today, and she'll be in attendance."

The air in Noah's lungs escaped in a sigh.

"The doctor's been seeing her, several times a week," Mason continued, his voice dropping. "I don't know what happens, or why. Yesterday she had to bring in two guards to keep Juliette down."

Noah swallowed, the taste in his mouth turning sour. "What time does the queen's party start?"

"Eleven. Juliette's been holed up in her room, I don't think you'll get to her before then."

Noah thumped a fist on the wall, then glanced at his watch. It was just now eight thirty, which gave him about two and a half hours to kill. He might be able to sneak into the party as a guard and at least let her know that he was back.

Chapter Twenty-Two

Juliette took a deep breath in, stretching her lungs, then letting the air out with a sigh. Clenching her hands into fists, she dug her fingernails into her palms. Her foot started tapping the side of her vanity. Within minutes, she'd get to go outside. It felt like it had been ages since she'd been in the gardens. She tried to imagine the air cold against her cheeks and the smell of roses surrounding her.

Peace. Comfort. Happiness.

Noah.

Juliette licked her lips, studying herself in the mirror. She willed the dark circles under her eyes to fade away, willed some color to rise to her cheeks. She reached her arms back, tugging and twisting her mane of dark curls into a simple half-updo.

Satisfied, and hoping Odette wouldn't scrutinize her too much, Juliette stood up and crossed her room where a small silver chest was settled on a simple shelf. Opening the lid, she pulled out a handful of the butterfly clips she'd been collecting over the years, arranging them in her hair in a way that mimicked a tiara. She used to have a tiara of her own, one her mother gave to her when she turned thirteen, but Odette took it away when their mother died. She said Juliette didn't need a crown and that she should be grateful Odette let her stay at the palace instead of turning her out onto the streets where a worthless piece of trash like her belonged.

Juliette tried to smile at her reflection, turning so she could see the back of her hair that hung just below her shoulder blades. It actually didn't look that bad. Her dress—floor length, white chiffon, with silver snowflakes along the hem that faded up toward her waist—swished around her ankles as she turned. She loved the dress. It made her feel like an actual princess, even though it was simple in comparison to anything Odette wore.

Juliette sank down at the window's ledge, drawing her knees to her chest and smiling out at the forest beyond the palace. She hadn't seen Odette in almost a month, and if it wouldn't have been for Dr. Violet, that month would have been a much sweeter time.

Chewing her lip, she turned her head toward the door. She wasn't sure when exactly Noah was getting home. She shouldn't have been hoping he would be on duty this morning, but she was. He might have smiled, if they were alone. He might have told her she looked nice or even hugged her.

She hoped he would be getting home soon so she could feel a sense of normalcy. She wouldn't be feeling like her own mind was turning against her, not if he were here. She would have had the promise of running away to hold on to, the warmth of a boy she was very much in love with.

Her eyes welled up, and she tried to blink them clear. She missed him so much it physically hurt, and she hadn't realized until now just how *much* she missed him.

When there was a knock at her door, a stranger

walked in. He must have been one of Odette's because Juliette didn't recognize him at all.

"Are you ready, Your Highness?" he asked, hands clasped behind his back. There was no expression on his face. He may as well have been made of stone. She wondered what his reaction would have been if she were to hug him.

Juliette stood up, smiling. "Yeah. Thank you." She smoothed the front of her dress, walking out into the corridor behind the guard.

As she neared Odette's wing, which she had to pass through in order to get to the gardens, Juliette cast a glance around. The corridors had been newly redecorated, boasting of swirled marble walls and thick red carpets, elegant paintings of the royal family's ancestors, and crystal chandeliers that sparkled in the light. A guard was stationed every twenty paces, each one standing straight and tall with no signs of life. They could have been statues.

An entourage of people rounded the corner, and Juliette instinctively tensed, struggling to stamp down the jitters that threatened to show as she caught sight of her sister. She froze, but the guard behind her gripped her arm and forced her forward.

Odette rounded the corner. She was dressed in a flowing dress of shimmering gold fabric that hugged her in all the right places, her auburn hair cascading down her shoulders in billowing curls with her magnificent black crown set with black diamonds upon her head. She looked every inch a queen.

Juliette felt her face reflexively contort into a scowl, and she had to consciously smooth it away. She didn't want to greet Odette. She didn't even want to look at her. What she wanted to do was shove her away, elbow her in the ribs and see how *she* liked it. She wanted to stab her with half a dozen needles and pump her veins full of drugs.

"Wipe that look off your face before I do it for you," Odette snapped.

Juliette clenched her jaw. She wasn't in the mood to deal with a fight. "Happy Birthday," she muttered.

Odette smiled, patting Juliette on the side of her face. Her fingers closed around Juliette's jaw like a trap as she turned her head from side to side. "You look pale. Are you feeling all right?"

Juliette tried to glare, tried to bring some kind of emotion to her face even if it was only irritation.

Odette raised her eyebrows.

"As fine as to be expected after spending a month in prison."

"Good."

Juliette cleared her throat.

"Come along." With a sweep of her hand, Odette floated down the corridor with her ring of attendants fluttering around her, forcing Juliette out of the cluster of people.

Continuing down the corridor, trailing after Odette, Juliette's heart started pounding harder and harder in her chest the closer they got to the grand double doors that would open out to a crowd of hundreds of people. Hundreds…of…people. And not one of them was the one she wanted to see.

Juliette kept her hands hanging at her sides, stepping forward when one of Odette's attendants waved her to do so.

"What's wrong with you? Why are you

so…lethargic? My skies, you'd think you were being sent to your death, not a party."

What's the difference? Juliette thought to herself, clenching her hands into fists and trying to settle the trembling in her arms. She exhaled shortly, shaking the hair that had fallen over her shoulders as she stood a little straighter. She liked the idea of social events more than the events themselves.

As Odette came to a pause in front of two opaque glass-paneled doors, white curtains fluttering, Juliette checked that her dress was hanging properly and hadn't gotten caught on anything. Much to her chagrin, she was mildly curious to see the gardens. Odette always spared no expense when it came to her parties.

Fanfares thundered from outside, startling Juliette and announcing Odette's arrival. The doors were flung open. Applause and cheers of congratulations filled the air.

Odette's smile had lost all hints of its forgery as she strutted gracefully down the gold-lace pathway toward the dining area that had been erected in the gardens. Black and gold brocade ribbons were woven through the white trees, shimmering tassels with teardrop diamonds of all different colors at the end dangled from branches, and red lace tablecloths fluttered in the warm breeze. The air itself sparkled.

Juliette glanced at Odette's retreating back, thinking how funny it would be if she shoved her forward in front of all her guests and watched her fall on her perfect face.

Odette dove right into the throng of people, greeting the House Leaders and members of her court. There were a few other political leaders and ambassadors Juliette recognized when she tore her eyes from the trees.

Once the luncheon was announced and people began to wander to their designated tables, waiters trickled around the edges with trays of food and drinks in their arms.

Juliette moved toward her seat, the one beside Odette. After she took her place, course after course was brought out—Bluefin tuna, prawns drowning in a butter-garlic sauce served with risotto, smoked potatoes, lobster bisque, and various kinds of white crackers.

Juliette heard corks popping from champagne bottles. Odette laughed at something someone said, flashing her perfect smile and raising her glass when someone else proposed a toast in her honor, congratulating her for another successful year reigning as queen. Silverware clinked against fine porcelain. Voices danced in the air in a symphony of chaos.

As the minutes progressed, more food was brought and more people continued to pour and swirl around her—praising Odette, gushing about her accomplishments, asking her questions, wishing her a happy birthday.

If Juliette hadn't been so out of it, she would have been nauseated. She wondered how anyone could praise her so much. Even the House leaders who were on her good side, didn't they see the negligence of her reign? How she had been depleting supplies from other Houses to cushion her own spending?

And they all had to be okay with it because if they did anything to resist her, they'd be removed and possibly killed.

Someone walked up to Odette, a man not much older than her. Odette giggled at something he said, her hand brushing his shoulder as a seductive smile crept onto her face. The young man smiled back, leaning over and whispering something to her.

Juliette grimaced. It wasn't hard to guess who her companion would be that night. Kneeling down in front of her, the man kissed the back of her hand and winked as he turned away, a card in his hands.

The man's eyes flickered to Juliette, and he wiggled his eyebrows at her.

Juliette thought to warn him away, but Odette turned her head and shot her a look that could kill.

Juliette shot her a glare right back. She crossed her arms over her chest, glancing around at the gardens. One of the diamonds dangling from the trees caught her attention, and she tilted her head to the side, wondering if it was real. It sparkled, turning delicately around in the faint breeze.

Another plate was set in front of her. Prawns sauteed in butter, Italian risotto, grilled vegetables, potatoes, and herb rolls.

"Your Highness, it's so good to see you!"

Juliette looked up, her mouth full of risotto, as someone approached the table.

Lady Luxe, dressed in a glittering gold gown that hugged her curves and offset her deep, velvet complexion.

Juliette never met her in person before, but she was one of the longest-standing House Heads since Odette had been crowned queen, and the only female House Leader.

Juliette swallowed the food in her mouth, not sure

if she was supposed to stand and greet her or stay where she was. She glanced at Odette, who seemed irritated someone was talking to Juliette.

"Thank you," she finally said, staying seated. Her eyelids had grown oddly heavy. Blinking took a concentrated effort. "It's good to see you, Lady Luxe. I trust everything is well back home? Not that I'd expect anything less, given that Luxe is one of the better looked after Houses because of the resources you provide." She didn't think she'd actually said that out loud until Odette tensed beside her.

"Juliette," she hissed.

"What? It's true, isn't it? Luxe gives you your pretty dresses, so they're given second pick of food and supplies while houses like Fatir and Apatite are overlooked because they don't flatter you."

"Juliette!" Odette whispered sharply again. She plastered a smile on her face.

Juliette thought to say she was sorry, she didn't mean to say any of that out loud. She wasn't sure why she couldn't seem to concentrate on what she was thinking. But then she didn't want to apologize, because she wasn't sorry. It was true, everything she was saying.

But Odette was already standing up. She grabbed Juliette's arm, said something about needing a moment with her sister, and then walked back inside.

Juliette's stomach rolled, and she numbly shook her head. "I'm sorry—"

The doors were closed behind them, and Odette backhanded Juliette in her face. The guard with her wrapped his hand around Juliette's arm, keeping her from being thrown to the side.

"You will behave yourself!" Odette was seething, her eyes dark and stormy. "I don't know what you're doing, or what game you're playing, but I will *not* tolerate any more of your defiance, do you understand?"

Before Juliette could reply, Odette shoved her farther down the corridor, shouting at the two guards with her to hold Juliette still.

Juliette barely managed to push one of them away before the other grabbed her and forced her against the wall. In her peripherals, Juliette could just make out Odette being handed her leather stick, the same one she used to beat Juliette with since she was a child.

Fear settled in Juliette's stomach. She heard the *whoosh* of the stick a tenth of a second before she felt it. Pain ripped across her back, searing into her skin. The thin fabric of her dress did little to dampen the pain. Around lash eight, Odette paused to catch her breath. The anticipation was almost as bad as the whipping itself, Juliette realized. She counted nine more before the guards pinning her let her go, and she collapsed to the ground.

Odette must have been angrier than she let on, because the welts she left behind started to bleed.

Odette appeared in Juliette's face, her hands grasping her chin. "You will learn to fear me the way you should, do you understand?"

Just another whipping. The bruises would fade. The welts would heal. The pain would recede.

It made her sick, but Juliette nodded. She kept the glare off her face. She forced her eyes to the ground. There were other ways to be strong. She reminded herself of the lesson she had learned a long time ago.

Odette straightened. "Good. I've been far too gracious with you, and it's starting to show. Not anymore." Spinning away, Odette disappeared back outside.

Alone, Juliette didn't even try and stifle a grimace. She groaned, pushing against the wall to stand back up, fixing her dress so it didn't hang off her shoulders. Pausing to catch her breath, she made her way to the back of the palace and outside again.

Tripping over a seedling, she traipsed through the overgrown bushes and shrubs toward the outside of the guards' entrance. There were some dorms along the outside of the palace itself, but most of them moved deeper within and didn't have windows.

Noah's did.

She pushed open the metal door, walking down a short flight of stairs and jogging along a line of doors until she came to the end, then took the corridor that branched off to the right, then down a flight of stairs.

The second-level garage was just as unorganized and messy as it was the first time Juliette came down, and she wondered if she and Noah were the only ones who used it.

Noah's ship was still tucked in the back corner, the box of tools under the cockpit. Juliette yanked the door open and pulled herself inside, ignoring the way her back throbbed. The door swung shut behind her, and the dank smell of musty air greeted her nostrils. It was cold inside, but she didn't care.

Sinking down on the bed inside the one and only room, she forced air in and out of her lungs. She clenched her shaking hands into fists until her knuckles turned white.

Juliette choked on a cough. She imagined she wasn't here, in Demetria, in the palace. She imagined she was a human being too big to hold down.

No, she was somewhere far, far away. A warm beach with the sun on her face, or a cabin in the woods with raindrops hitting the ceiling. She and Noah got away.

He hadn't held her in far too long, and she missed the security of his arms. As much as she *hated* confined spaces, she hadn't ever felt safer than when he was holding her. That was the only time she was ever safe. The only time the world around her disappeared and she didn't have any reason to be afraid.

Juliette swallowed against the tightness of her throat, refusing to cry. She would not give Odette the satisfaction. Carefully loosening the top of her dress, Juliette sank down until she was lying down in the worn and faded but terribly soft blankets. They didn't smell bad, just old.

Bringing them around her neck and shoulders, Juliette squeezed her eyes shut until her heart started to settle down, until the throbbing in her back started to go away. She stifled a sigh, fatigue creeping over her, bringing with the smallest bit of peace.

Sometimes she wished she would just go to sleep and not wake up again.

"Did you have a nightmare, butterfly?"

Juliette blinked her eyes open, sucking in a startled breath. Darkness surrounded her. She wasn't sure how long she had been there; it could have been minutes, or it could have been hours.

Lifting her head, she blinked. The air in her lungs escaped in a gasp. The guard standing in the doorway was tall, taller than her. His dark blond hair hung past his jaw, the jacket of his uniform fit better through his shoulders than it did before he left. A pair of pale green eyes that never failed to captivate every fiber of her being looked at her like she was *something*.

How did he still look so perfect after just four weeks, while she felt like she was falling to pieces?

Swallowing despite the dryness in her throat, Juliette's eyes filled with moisture. Noah moved into the room, sinking down beside the bed until he was eye level with her. She was foolish to hope he didn't notice the bruising on her back, however faint they were.

"Sleeping on the job again?" he asked, smoothing some of the hair away from her face.

That single touch threatened to undo her. She almost smiled. "I got tired."

"Understandable." His eyes skirted her back, but only for a moment. "I've got some antiseptic back in my quarters."

Juliette managed a nod, but she didn't move. "I'm glad you're home."

"Me too."

Noah's fingers worked through her hair, and for several minutes neither of them moved. Juliette could have fallen asleep.

"Come on, let's get you back to your room," Noah finally whispered.

Juliette stood up, walking with him back out toward the cockpit. He helped her to the garage down, and Juliette made her way into the main corridors of the palace, ever aware of the steady presence just behind her.

Chapter Twenty-Three

Alone in his room beneath the palace, Noah heaved a tired sigh. He was exhausted and wanting nothing more than to collapse into bed and sleep for a week.

He had hoped Juliette being in the comfort of her *actual* room would allow her a decent night's sleep. She looked exhausted, no doubt a result of not only Dr. Violet's work, but the stress of being in a confined space, trapped.

He had to remind himself that she was strong. Much stronger than he gave her credit for, and certainly stronger than Odette gave her credit for.

Tugging on a pair of worn and comfortable sweatpants, Noah pulled a T-shirt over his head and then sank down onto his bed.

Noah grabbed the bottle of antiseptic from his medicine cabinet and started up to the third level of the palace. Odette was no doubt in bed by now, giving him the chance to go to Juliette without risk of her walking in on them. There was no guard outside of Juliette's room. Luis must have either worked a different shift or been moved.

Noah paused at the door, knocking softly.

The door immediately opened. Juliette blinked, surprised. A smile warmed her face, and she waved him inside.

Noah paused, glancing back toward the closest

camera mounted in the corner of the hallway.

"What are you doing here?" she asked, still smiling. She was wearing a navy sweatshirt that was too big, and her sleeve-covered hands were fiddling with the ends of her hair. The hoodie had been Noah's at one point, though he couldn't remember how she ended up with it. The royal crest on the left side had long since faded.

Noah stepped in, glad she had the live security feed on one of her computers. They'd know if someone was coming. He held up the tube of cream.

"It's not that bad anymore," she said, twisting the ends of her hair into knots. "There wasn't even much blood, and it's scabbed over."

Noah hesitated. "Are you sure?"

"Yeah." She smiled, but it looked strained. "I'm sorry I was so out of it when you got back."

Noah almost scoffed, but he masked it with a cough. He set the bottle of antiseptic down on the small table by the door and took a step closer to her, cradling her face.

Juliette's breath hitched.

"It's okay to not be okay," he whispered. She wasn't okay, despite the brave façade she put on, and he knew that.

Her blue eyes sparkled. "I…I've missed you," she whispered. Despite the rawness behind her eyes, her tone didn't waver. "Seas, Noah, I've missed you so much."

Noah pressed his lips together in a smile. "I've missed you too." He carefully pulled her into a hug, aware not to hold her too tightly.

"I've felt…not myself lately," she murmured, so

softly he almost didn't hear. Her blue eyes sparkled with added moisture. "I don't like being locked up or seeing Dr. Violet. I don't know what Odette's doing to me, but I can feel it in my system."

Noah let the air in his lungs out in a steadying exhale. "You won't have to live with it much longer."

"I know. I just…want you to know if I'm acting weird, or different, it's…it's not on purpose."

Noah forced a nod, hating that she felt she had to justify her natural reactions to Odette's abuse.

"Your face'll freeze like that," she said with half a laugh, poking his forehead.

Noah relaxed from his frown, barely managing to smile. He pulled her back into a hug, wrapping his arms around her and wanting to apologize over and over for not being able to save her. For not being able to really and truly protect her.

"I've been doing push-ups every day," she added.

Noah almost laughed. "Oh yeah?"

"I'm up to twenty regular, plus five on my knees."

"Arctic skies."

Juliette grinned, pleased with herself. Noah saw a little bit of her old self shine through and relaxed the tiniest bit. "You'll have to show me pull-ups again next time I come to the gym with you."

"Definitely."

Juliette looked like she wanted to say something but seemed to change her mind.

"What?"

"Nothing. Sorry. I can't seem to turn my mind off."

Noah licked his lips, thinking it was time for a subject change. "So now that I'm back home and you're free, we can keep working on the ship."

At that, Juliette brightened. "Yes! I wasn't able to do a whole lot, but was able to map out a plan, so I'll be able to start building right away and then get it installed by the end of the week. Hopefully."

"Great! I was able to get some freeze-dried food that I stashed in there earlier today. It doesn't taste all that great, but it's compact and inexpensive. I want to get some more, just to be safe, so I thought I'd go to town on my next day off."

Juliette set his tablet down. She looked back at him and smiled, then shoved her hands into the pocket of her hoodie. "So, where'd you go when you were away?"

Noah smirked. "America."

A giddy smile crept onto Juliette's face, her eyes widening. "You flew to America? Over the ocean?"

"I did. I got you something," he added, reaching for the postcard he'd tucked into his back pocket.

Juliette's smile shifted as she took it from him. Her eyes scanned the bright colors of a mock sunset. "It's beautiful! You were here?"

"Around there, yes. It's called the Golden Gate Bridge. Guess where it is?"

"California?"

Noah nodded.

"It's beautiful! What do you think? Is it a good place to relocate?"

"Absolutely."

"Did you see the stars?"

"I did. There were *so* many of them, it was insane. I hadn't ever seen the Milky Way in real life." He sank down against the end of her bed, pulling up a series of photos he'd taken on his tablet. "I tried to get a picture, but it doesn't quite do it justice." He flipped the screen around and handed it to her. As she took it, his gaze wandered to her hair that was spilling over her shoulder. The pieces around her face had fallen from the braid and hung in loose curls. He fought against the urge to play with them or tuck them behind her ear.

"It's so…beautiful," she murmured, smiling. "I can't believe you were this close! And for a whole *month*?"

"It was closer to two weeks. Atticus wanted to get back to the clinic he's been working at as soon as possible, so he doubled up on a lot of the lectures."

Juliette tilted her head. "Atticus?"

"Atworth. Lord Atworth's son. He's a medical student, and he just started his third year of residency. There was some medical conference in America he wanted to attend."

"In *America*? There wasn't anything closer?"

"Guess not. Which worked out perfectly for me because I haven't ever flown that far for that long and thought it would make good practice. Plus, I was able to get to see how the gates work up close and in person."

"Was it doable? Flying that far for that long?"

"Oh totally." Noah drew a leg up and laced his hands together around his knee. "It was actually kind of relaxing."

"Were you scared to fly over the ocean?"

"No."

"Not even a little?" she asked doubtfully, her eyes narrowing.

"*No*. Why would I be scared?"

"I don't know, because it's over water and there's no place to make an emergency landing."

"Oh. Well, no. I wasn't scared, and we didn't need to make an emergency landing."

"How long did it take?"

"Almost eleven hours."

Juliette's eyes widened. "Eleven hours *straight*?"

"As you just pointed out, there are no ports in the ocean, so we had to keep going until we reached land." He shrugged. "But I was piloting a Trinity, so it was much more comfortable and way roomier than the ship Phil gave me, and I was able to set autopilot for a few hours to catch up on some sleep."

"I've never been inside a Trinity, but I've seen pictures."

"It was pretty cool. Atticus was really nice and hung out with me a lot in the cockpit."

Juliette smiled.

"He plays a mean game of Trolls, too."

Juliette laughed. Still grinning, her eyes wandered back to the postcard in her hand. "Did you find any good camping spots?"

"Nah, I thought I'd wait for you to help me look."

Juliette's laugh was a little forced, but at least it was genuine.

Noah wanted so very badly to leave right then and there. To take off, to fly away and never come back to this frozen prison.

Juliette was in danger—more danger, perhaps than he acknowledged—and they needed to get away.

Soon.

"Hey, how did you get down to the garage, anyway?" he asked. He still didn't even have all the pathways committed to memory; most of the time he used the map on his data tablet. Getting from the main area of the palace was like walking through a maze.

Juliette wiggled her eyebrows. She held up her arm with her wristlet strapped around it. “I created a map of all the servants’ passages and hidden corridors of the palace.”

“Oh?” he asked, turning so he could look at her better.

“I figured since I’ve been spending more time there recently, I may as well learn the lay of the land. I had to walk up and down every single hallway and level so it would track where I went,” she added with another shrug. “It took me almost two months, minus the four weeks I was locked up.”

Noah’s eyebrows shot up, impressed. “You’ve become quite the acclaimed programmer.”

Juliette’s grin broadened. She bit her lower lip, still smiling. “Odette’s been giving me a lot of assignments lately. That’s mainly why I was in my study for so long, according to her. They keep getting harder. I like the challenge, though; it’s good. And it’s something I’m good at,” she added, no hint of arrogance in her tone. Just pure fact.

Noah nudged her arm. “Your turn. What have you been doing in your workroom? Tell me everything.”

“There’s not much to tell, really. I set up a new security line for Odette, which was honestly kind of fun because I hadn’t ever set up a whole new security line before. I’ve only ever altered or changed them. I practiced tapping into international communication lines without having it traced back to me. Oh, the king of France is coming for a visit in the next few weeks, I think, with his wife and son, Prince Rene.”

Noah tilted his head.

"I don't know why. I just heard Odette talking to Natasha about it. My guess is she wants to work on multiple alliances, and since Russia is being hesitant, she wants to take advantage of whatever she can get." Juliette shrugged.

"France, though? Why?"

"No idea. I would have thought she would want a country that holds a little more influence over the rest of the world leaders, but maybe she knows something I don't."

"Maybe."

"From what I gathered, France doesn't have anything she would want. They have money, but not enough to sustain them *and* Demetria, and we don't have any major exports they'd be interested in, so it's not like we'd be trading with them."

"Hm."

Juliette pursed her lips. "Also, the dome has been weakening with all the quakes, and Odette's worried it's just going to get worse and worse. Maybe France is the only one who will help, I don't know."

"When are they coming?"

"The end of the week." Juliette paused, her eyes wandering off. "I've never met a royal from another country. Wonder what it'll be like."

"Me either, the royals here are bad enough," Noah said with a mock grimace.

Juliette laughed.

They talked for another hour or so before Noah noticed her eyes starting to blink slower. He glanced at his wristlet, seeing it was almost twelve thirty. "I should get back to my room and get in some sleep before tomorrow."

"Of course." Juliette stood up with him, hesitating before giving him another hug.

Noah held her for several seconds, waiting until she let go first. They walked to the door together, but Noah paused. Juliette deactivated the security cameras, giving him the chance to get back to the guards' wing without being spotted.

"We're going to get out of here, Jules," he said, lowering his voice.

"I know." Juliette opened the door, gracing him with another smile. "What I wouldn't give to somehow see Odette's reaction to finding us both gone."

Noah almost laughed. He took a step back into the hallway, and Juliette closed the door after him.

The sconces along the wall had dimmed to almost nothing, and the sky outside was pitch black. Having had the rare chance to view the sky without clouds or snow in the way, Noah itched to see it again. Walking back to his room, Noah collapsed onto his bed and fell asleep.

Chapter Twenty-Four

Odette drew a steadying breath, glancing down at her data tablet as one of her maids brushed through her hair. A report had just come in from Dr. Dean, one of her scientists in charge of the electrified dome that encapsulated the entire country. Evidently, a small part of it had wavered, leaving a two-and-a-half-foot gap open for almost a minute. The temperature in the surrounding area dropped twenty degrees.

Again.

The dome was able to reset itself, closing the gap, but those issues had been happening more and more recently. Left unattended, Demetria was once again in danger. What was worse, this was the fifth crack in as many years. They kept being repaired and fixed only for another part of the dome to weaken.

When Odette had started taking on more responsibilities after the death of her parents, she considered initiating a project to replace the whole dome bit by bit, but the entire country's money combined couldn't even pay for it.

That wasn't a viable option. As much as she wanted to build Demetria to the point of being self-sustaining, she knew she would need to better utilize her country's resources to get Demetria where she wanted it to be. It was something her parents should have been doing all along. They'd wasted so much valuable time getting involved in the war they had no business being a part of.

If she could perfect her soldier serum and solidify Demetria's army, that would at least solidify them as a country, which would make it safe to open trading routes with other countries. More money would be coming in, and then she would be able to redirect some funds toward the dome.

Dr. Violet assured her that getting Juliette's brain to release the fight-or-flight reaction was the key to the serum working, it would just take some time to figure out how to activate it at will. She had also done some minor tests on how different doses, combined with different activators, would change the reaction, but without more information, she could only theorize so much.

Meaning she still had no idea if the serum could be used to target other areas of the body.

Odette had been tempted to tell her *everything* but talked herself out of it. She would wait to see how Juliette reacted to it first. Then, if it was able to accomplish one extreme, it might be able to accomplish the other extreme.

Pressing her lips together, Odette looked back down at the report from Dr. Violet. She thought—hoped—since her mother was gone, Juliette's combined fear of Odette and general sense of guilt would cause her to experience the feeling of being afraid much more easily. Perhaps Odette had been too harsh on her as a child. She was learning not to be afraid, getting used to the punishments.

Odette thumped a fist on her vanity. Every time she took a step forward, something happened that forced her another step, or two, back. It was infuriating, and she had no one to blame but herself. She could feel the hope of its success slipping through her fingers like tiny grains of sand.

Working her jaw, Odette stood up and moved to the window. As was habit, she tried to see through the dome high above her but couldn't. All she could see was the bright white clouds mixed with snow flurries.

Looking back down at her tablet, she almost smiled. King Philippe and his family had agreed to come visit Demetria. France was such a small, peaceful country, she wasn't concerned about the strength of *their* military. She may as well open up relations with them right away.

She was rather surprised to learn, over her conversations with the French family, that the prince was unspoken for, and King Philippe was eager to establish an alliance of marriage with Juliette once both she and his son, Prince Rene, were of age.

Odette wasn't sure about that idea, thinking Juliette might not live to be "of age," but she didn't refuse King Philippe. Not right away, at least. No, it was better to keep her options open. Juliette might survive the testing, and then Odette would have an easy way to get rid of her once and for all. Let her go to France and ruin their lives, instead of Odette's.

"Your Majesty?"

Odette glanced to the side, snapping her tablet off, casting a glare at the maid standing by the door. She forgot she wasn't alone. "What?"

"Would you…" The maid nervously cleared her throat. "Like assistance getting dressed?"

"Well, that dress isn't going to put itself on, now, is

it?" Odette asked, standing up and sliding her silky robe off.

While her three maids slid the stunning brocade dress through her arms and laced the corset tightly up her back, thoughts continued to swirl around in her head.

King Philippe and his family were on their way to Demetria this very minute to discuss the intended wedding contract. If Odette decided to sign the papers, then Juliette would be set to marry Prince Rene in two years, right after her eighteenth birthday.

Odette's attention darted to her reflection in the mirror—to her porcelain skin and chocolate hair that hung in perfect spirals down her back and stopped at her waist, and dark brown eyes—reflexively smiling.

With any luck, if Dr. Violet was able to come through, by the time the soldier serum was working, Juliette would be sent off to France and be gone for good. One solution would fix two problems.

Possibly three.

Chapter Twenty-Five

Noah was awake well before six. He wasn't sure he'd be able to get any sleep, but somehow, he did. His shift started at eight, so he hit the gym, took a quick shower, and then changed into fresh clothes.

Checking that his door was locked, he sank down at the small desk and propped his tablet up. He'd never been through the gates of Demetria before two weeks ago. His trip to America was a literal godsend and gave him the chance to see how the gates were operated.

His thoughts had been so focused on getting the ship ready for flight that he hadn't given much thought to the process of actually leaving the country when the time came. To the best of his knowledge, people were allowed to leave Demetria without documentation or authorization. It was getting in that was trickier.

Juliette's affinity for computers and hacking would come in handy, should something change, but as of right now, he wasn't anticipating the gates being an issue.

He pulled up the data he'd collected while away and started to read over it. The gates were mechanized, both by computers and by registered personnel. There were only certain times cargo and passenger ships were allowed through, and it was about a thirty-minute process for them to be opened.

So far it seemed like an easy ordeal, the problem he

had was what to do *after*. He'd been working for a little over two years, so while he had a decent chunk of money saved, he knew it wouldn't be enough for two people to live on for very long. Which meant he needed to be looking for another job that he could jump right into as soon as they reached whatever country they ended up going to.

He didn't doubt Juliette would be willing to work as well, which would help. She could easily get a job working for a security company.

Seas, he couldn't believe they were another step closer to leaving the palace. Leaving the *country*. They only had one chance, so they needed to make it count.

Noah ran his hands down his legs and then leaned back, his eyes wandering to the side as his mind started to churn over this string of thoughts. It really wasn't so impossible, the idea of running away. It would only be dangerous if he were foolish in his preparations to leave. But if he were careful—*more* than careful—it should be easy.

Getting supplies stocked so far hadn't been an issue. He would continue to purchase things, gradually, that he could hide on board.

With a sigh, Noah stood up and started down to the communal kitchen for something to eat.

"Hey, have you been sleeping for a full day, or what?" Mason asked, walking up behind him and smacking his shoulder. "I haven't seen you since you got back."

The corner of Noah's mouth tilted in a smile. "Yeah, well, I needed to catch up on as much sleep as I could before I started work again."

"So how was it? Flying overseas?"

"Amazing. A little strange going through the gates. Felt almost illegal, but seas, it was such a great experience."

Mason almost laughed.

Noah made himself something to eat and then retreated back into his room where he pored over the rest of his notes and then started compiling his thoughts and ideas.

Chewing the inside of his cheek, Noah did a quick search on the housing places he'd found in California, then compared them with some of the places he found in Australia. Australia was a little more affordable, and unfortunately at this point, they needed to go with practicality. They could always relocate down the line.

Chapter Twenty-Six

Juliette folded her legs in front of her, leaning back against her fluffy pillows. There had always been something appealing about the idea of having coffee in bed, but she wasn't allowed to have coffee. Instead, she savored the first few minutes of the morning, warm and comfortable with her thick, soft blanket wrapped around her. The thought of getting to see Noah again was just the motivation she needed to get up and start the day, even though, to the best of her knowledge, she didn't have anything to do.

She slid out of bed and pulled open her closet doors, surveying the dozens of dresses hanging in front of her. All of them were soft, pastel colors. Like a sea of flowers. Nothing at all like the bold colors Odette wore, which was just fine with Juliette.

"She won't let me out in public, but still cares about what I wear," Juliette muttered to herself, shaking her head and pulling out a floor-length, sea-green dress. The sleeves were cinched at the wrists, and the waist was gathered with a simple tie.

Sitting down at her vanity, she began the tedious process of brushing through her hair, working the knots and tangles free until it hung in loose waves. She should have asked Noah when he would start working again. She just assumed he'd be starting right away, but maybe he didn't.

Juliette studied herself in the mirror, trying to call up a smile. She hoped seeing Noah last night would snap her out of whatever funk she'd been in for the past few weeks, but there was still a hollowness in her chest. Something still felt…*off.*

Stepping out into the hallway, Juliette fixed the sleeves around her wrists as she started forward. A shadow caught her attention, and she almost jumped at seeing two of Odette's guards starting toward her.

"You're wanted in the medical wing, Your Highness," one of them said.

Juliette clenched her hands into fists. She thought to push back, to fight, to resist them when they would no doubt pick her up. But what would that do? It would tire her out and force Dr. Violet to put her to sleep again.

Besides, Juliette wanted to sneak away at some point to work on the ship since she was free to roam the palace again, so she'd need all her physical strength and mental capacity she could muster.

"Fine." She steeled herself, starting down the corridor toward the medical wing.

As she walked, her eyes wandered toward the windows, at the brightening sky. She used to always hope the sun would shine bright enough to break through the clouds and melt the snow.

Natasha was waiting for Juliette just outside the infirmary. Her hair was slicked back in a tight bun at the nape of her neck, and her floor-length cloak hardly moved when she walked. It must have been heavy. So much of Odette's palace décor was black. That extended even to Natasha.

Juliette neared the infirmary, and the blood drained

from her fingers, turning her hands to blocks of ice. She glanced at Natasha, whose face was partially hidden behind her brocade cloak.

"Your Highness," Natasha murmured, offering Juliette a sympathetic smile. She cocked her head to the side. "Your sister filled me in on everything."

Juliette blinked. Tilted her head. Filled her in on what?

The sliding glass doors hissed open as Natasha led her back through the maze of corridors to her usual room. A table lined with tissue paper was sprawled out in the middle. A row of cabinets, counters, and computers lined one of the walls.

It was the same room she'd been in for years, yet there was something different about it. Something darker.

Juliette sank down onto the table and folded her hands together, tapping the back of her foot against the metal legs. She glanced at Natasha, who, as she often was, was typing furiously away on her tablet.

"Do you know what she's doing today?" Juliette asked, fingering the blunt ends of her hair.

"I don't, I'm sorry." Natasha's face softened into a smile.

Juliette frowned to herself. Natasha didn't usually come with her, at least not to see Dr. Violet. Something told Juliette that couldn't be good. Something must be about to happen, and Odette was probably too busy to see to it herself.

"Are you glad Noah's back?" Natasha asked.

Juliette didn't look away from her hands, knotted in her lap. "Yes." Natasha was the only person she had ever heard call Noah by his first name. Odette always referred to the guards by their last names.

Dr. Violet walked in not two moments later, a tablet in her hand and a stylus pen behind her ear. Her eyes landed on Natasha, and she paused uncertainly before shifting her attention to Juliette. "Take your clothes off."

"Why? I can roll my sleeve up for shots."

"We're taking measurements today, now do as you're told," Dr. Violet snapped.

"Excuse me." Natasha stood up, her eyes dark and stormy. "You will speak to Her Highness with the respect she is owed."

Juliette blinked, surprised.

Dr. Violet looked equally taken aback. "I have orders from Her Majesty—"

"I am Her Majesty's second-in-command, and you will speak to Her Highness with respect and professionalism. Do we have an understanding, Doctor?"

The muscles in Dr. Violet's jaw flexed. "What would you propose I do when she refuses to cooperate?"

"If that should happen, which it doesn't appear to be at the moment," Natasha added with a glance at Juliette. There was something behind her eyes. A warning? "Then I would advise you to call Her Majesty, since you have no authority over the princess."

For a brief moment, Juliette wondered if Natasha just wanted to get Juliette in trouble, but then the implication of her words sank in. With Natasha here, if Juliette cooperated, she would be treated better. Either way she would be forced to undergo Dr. Violet's testing, but unless Juliette gave Dr. Violet cause to call in Odette, Natasha's presence would keep her in check.

That, if nothing else, gave Juliette motivation to cooperate. She couldn't retaliate against Odette, but she could steal Dr. Violet's hold over her. She could make her call her *Highness* and *Princess*.

Juliette turned an expectant eye toward Dr. Violet, delicately arching her eyebrows.

"If you would undress, *Your Highness*, we can proceed."

"Such manners. I feel so spoiled." Juliette untied the ribbon around her waist and then slid her arms from the sleeves, gathering the soft material and setting it on the chair beside Natasha. She stifled a shiver, wrapping her arms around herself and hating with a passion the feeling of vulnerability.

"Stand up straight," Dr. Violet said.

Juliette did as she was told, her eyes wandering to the far wall as Dr. Violet measured her waist, shoulders, and hips, then her height from head to toe. Her body twitched, wanting to fight back, wanting to shove the doctor's hands away.

"Still won't tell me what Odette's planning?" Juliette asked.

"That I cannot. No matter how much I'm threatened." Dr. Violet said the latter portion with a glare at Natasha, but Natasha was innocently writing on her tablet again. "No change in height or measurements. You may sit back down."

Juliette dropped back onto the table. Maybe today was just going to be another day of measurements. No shots or needles or strange liquids to drink. No reason to fight back.

Dr. Violet readied a black box with a light attached

to it, and a groove to rest on Juliette's nose.

"Why do you always check my eyes?" she asked, knowing even as she spoke her question would be unanswered.

Dr. Violet grabbed Juliette's chin, shining a bright light into Juliette's eyes. "Just seeing how much your pupils dilate."

Juliette tried not to flinch as tears welled up in her eyes and trailed down the sides of her face. She had to concentrate on keeping her eyes open, but it was hard. *Dilate*. She'd have to look that word up later and see what it meant.

"Are you going to give me a shot? Or take a blood sample?"

"I don't know why you always ask, since we do it every time."

Something flickered in Juliette's chest. "Just hoping, I suppose," she snapped. She swallowed against the tightness of her throat, forcing a deep breath in. She glanced around. She could make a break for the door and run. The only way she'd be able to evade the guards who were sure to chase after her was if she got into one of the hidden passageways.

Dr. Violet held a stethoscope to Juliette's back. "Take a deep breath in."

Juliette inhaled and exhaled. There was a wall opening closer to her wing, she knew, and she was pretty sure the painting in the hallway just outside the infirmary opened into a stairwell.

Juliette watched Dr. Violet tap around on her tablet. A holographic image of her skeletal form appeared, but Dr. Violet waved it away. She set her tablet down, then turned to the computer on the counter.

Juliette leaned over, just catching the words printed on the screen.

Height, growth stunted: 158.496 centimeters
Weight, stabilized: 47.628 kilograms
Martin-Schultz scale: 1c
Fitzpatrick scale: Type I, score: 0

Growth stunted?

"Here."

Juliette jumped. She took the cup of blue liquid, staring down at it for a few seconds. She downed the contents in a single gulp. It didn't taste like anything, but she still shivered. She had to turn away and bite the inside of her cheek to keep from groaning as a series of needles were thrust into the underside of her arm. It seemed like each one hurt worse than the last.

"What are all those?" Natasha asked, her eyes narrowed and her eyebrows sunken on her forehead.

"Do you want a detailed ingredient list?" Dr. Violet drawled.

Natasha arched her eyebrows, waiting.

"They're stimulants to monitor her brain activity, the next step in our process."

Process? Does that mean there's an end in sight? Juliette wondered. "Is that why I always get dizzy?" she asked aloud.

Dr. Violet scoffed. "You get dizzy because you don't like needles."

Juliette's eyes narrowed, a retort bubbling in the back of her throat.

Natasha held something out to her, a small rubber ball. "Squeeze it, it'll help," she whispered.

Juliette snapped her eyes up to Natasha. She wasn't sure what she knew, but she knew something. Juliette took the ball and threw it across the room. "I don't need a *ball*," she murmured, emphasizing each word carefully. Natasha had always been nice to her, but if she knew something Juliette didn't and was keeping silent, she was just as bad as Odette.

"Alright, Your Highness." There was pain in Natasha's eyes, but Juliette didn't care. Her chest started to ache, the realization that everyone in the palace, except for Noah, was against her. Everyone was more than happy to ignore her and the constant abuse Odette put her through.

"Did you take the optical tests I gave you?" Dr. Violet asked.

When Juliette was locked in her workroom, Dr. Violet gave her some "homework"—different kinds of reading and spelling tests, IQ evaluations, and brain games.

Juliette hesitated. She did them, but only because she was told that for every item she did, that meant one full meal for the day. But now, with the threat of going hungry gone, she didn't want to give Dr. Violet the satisfaction.

"I have the answers on my tablet," she finally replied, nodding to her folded dress.

Dr. Violet was silent as she transferred the information from Juliette's tablet to her own. "I have a new task for you. This—" She handed Juliette a small chip, black and shiny. "—is loaded with some binaural beats I'd like you to listen to for at least three hours a day. You can do it while you sleep if you'd prefer, and you can multitask while listening."

Juliette took the chip, turning it in her hand. “What are binaural beats?”

“They are an auditory illusion your brain creates when you listen to two different pure-tone sine waves at the same time. Use your headphones to listen to it.”

“What does it do?”

“Bit of a long answer, but it can help balance your brainwave frequencies.”

Juliette felt her eyebrows twitch. “Is there something wrong with my brainwave frequencies?”

Dr. Violet didn’t look up from the tablet she was studying. “Do you think panic attacks are normal?”

Juliette shrank back, and she could feel heat climb to her cheeks. “I haven’t had a panic attack since I was eight.”

“Then let’s keep it that way. You can go. Make sure you eat something.”

Juliette jumped down from the table, grabbing her dress. She shot a glance at Natasha, then stepped through the door without waiting for her.

Chapter Twenty-Seven

Juliette leaned against the wall, sinking her head into her hands and forcing air in and out of her lungs. She slid to the ground, wrapping her arms around her knees. It was over, and she survived. She didn't panic or start to feel like she was going to pass out.

It was a victory, albeit a small one.

Glancing to the side, she saw Noah rounding the corner, moving straight toward her.

"Is your shift just starting?" Juliette asked, glad that her voice didn't shake. She pushed herself up and started toward him.

"Yes," he said, the smallest hint of a smile tugging the corner of his mouth.

Juliette breathed a sigh of relief. "I just want to run to my room and then we can go to my study."

Noah didn't make a reply. He'd been much quieter lately when he was on duty, and Juliette was afraid he was starting to regret being on her personal guard instead of a rotation.

Juliette started down the corridor. She hated walking in front of him. It just served as another reminder that no matter what she felt toward him, there was a wedge between them.

Once she tried to deliberately slow down so he could catch up to her, but it didn't work. He slowed down as well for all of six seconds before nudging her to pick up the pace.

"Odette's been being sent various gifts from the Houses, but she's throwing most of them away recently," Juliette said, keeping her voice low. "I've been sneaking them back into my room and repurposing them, making all kinds of jewelry. It's actually pretty cool, all the things people send her. I've been distributing the more useful things to the maids and guards, and recently some of them have picked up on it and started helping me accumulate everything that's being thrown away. We have a whole system going. I thought once we're, you know, not here anymore, I could sell them on the side and bring in a little extra money."

"That's a good idea. I hope you're being careful, though," Noah said, keeping his voice down so that none of the other guards they passed would overhear. "If Odette knew you were taking things from her, she would be furious."

Juliette almost rolled her eyes. "What doesn't make her furious? Besides, I'm only taking the things she's throwing away. But I am being careful."

One of the things she discovered over the past few years was that she liked to sew. She had made countless sweaters and scarves, gifting them to her team of servants and sending them home with things for siblings and parents. The items from Luxe wouldn't be of any use to anyone, so Juliette had been tucking those off to the side to take when she and Noah left.

A few months ago, she started making a cloak out of the most beautiful material she'd ever seen. She gave up on it after only a few days. If she finished it, she would be able to sell it, either in Demetria, or after they'd left. It wouldn't be much, but it was something she could do to contribute. She hated not having a way of earning some steady income.

Walking with her to her room, Noah held the door open, and Juliette walked inside. Her cloak, or rather the pieces that would eventually *be* her cloak, were scattered all around her room in patches of shimmering white that looked like ice. Hurrying through, she gathered the pieces and stuffed them into her shoulder bag.

Slipping back out into the hallway, she smiled at seeing Noah waiting patiently against the wall. His face warmed when he saw her, and her heart did a little flip. She bumped the doorframe, almost losing her bag. Heat flared in her cheeks.

Noah's eyebrows shot up, amusement crossing his face.

"Not a word," she mumbled, dropping his gaze. Smiling to herself, she started toward her normal study—the one with the real windows and door that was made of wood instead of steel and didn't lock from the outside.

Juliette sank to the ground in between the coffee table and the settee as Noah took up his post opposite her. Sliding the bag off her shoulder and propping it open, she pulled out the latest piece she had been working on and threaded the tiny needle. She picked up where she had left off, stitching a delicate silver butterfly along the edge of the hood.

She wished it was safe enough for her and Noah to work on the ship during the day, but given how much Odette had been calling for Juliette, Juliette worried it would land her and Noah in trouble.

No, it was safer to play stupid during the day, then disappear into the garage at night.

"Don't you get tired standing up for so long?" she asked, resting her wrists against the edge of the table to steady her hands. Her eyes flickered up to Noah.

One of Noah's shoulders twitched in a partial shrug. "Not anymore."

"How long did it take you to get used to it?"

"Honestly, I don't know. Maybe a few months?"

Juliette shook her head. She didn't think it was fair that all the guards had to stand up when they were working. Especially the ones stationed in the halls, where there wasn't even anyone to guard. They should be able to sit down and give their legs and back a break, that way if something happened and they were needed, they weren't exhausted.

She chewed her lip, furrowing her brow as she looked back at the fabric in her hands, her mind roving once again to the ship down in the second-level garage.

It took her another ten minutes to finish a single butterfly, at which point she decided to take a break from the detailed sewing so she could pin the hood to the neck of the cloak.

"I've been doing some research on different kinds of plants because I wanted to bring some on the ship. I started a garden in my room, to try some different ones out, but I had to find plants that don't need a lot of light. Roses are my favorite, but they need light, so I want to get some seeds to plant in an outdoor garden."

"Smart. What got you thinking so much about plants?"

"Plants release oxygen, so I figured since we'll be living with recycled air, at least for a little bit, it would be nice to get in some extra filtration."

"We should look into getting a special kind of light that mimics the sun so they'll live longer," Noah added. "You can start a garden until we settle somewhere."

"Oh, good idea!" Juliette knotted her thread with a yank and started backstitching the hood to the neck of the cloak. The milky white fabric was heavy in her hands, and she loved the way it rippled in the light.

Juliette grew silent for the next few minutes, concentrating on an especially difficult section of the cloak. Her hands shook a little, so she moved slower than she otherwise would have.

Juliette reached for the small scissors, snipping at the thread. Pain sliced the space between her thumb and forefinger.

"Ow—skies!" She gasped, dropping the fabric in her hand, sitting up straighter as deep crimson blood pooled in her hand.

Noah was there in an instant, kneeling in front of her and pulling an antiseptic wipe out from one of his pockets. He took her hand and gently pressed it against the cut on her finger.

Juliette winced. "Thanks. Careful, don't get blood on it," she murmured, awkwardly pushing her cloak away from her with her free hand. Her eyes darted to the wipe, turning red, and she almost smirked. "You carry those on you?"

"Yes."

"Wait, seriously?" Juliette almost laughed. "Why?"

Noah shot her a glare. "Because I'm around *you* most of the time."

"And I'm just so important you don't want to risk me getting hurt and you not being able to help me?"

Noah innocently shrugged. “More like you seem to attract falling and bumping into things like a magnet.”

Juliette frowned at him. “I do not.”

“Oh, butterfly, you are easily the most accident-prone person I have ever met.”

Juliette made a face, glancing down, suddenly aware of his hands touching hers. The tips of his fingers sent sparks of electricity up her arm. With his hands cradling hers, concentration etched on his features as he kept gentle pressure on her cut, all she could think about was how much she wanted him to lace his fingers through hers, to graze her cheeks, to knot his fist around her hair and *kiss her*. She wanted him to smile her favorite lopsided smile, pull her into his arms, and make her laugh again.

Daring to peek up at him, her heart started to beat in a way it only did when he was so close.

More than anything, she wanted him to tell her he loved her. She was pretty sure he did, at least to some extent, but that didn’t stop her from dreaming of a verbal confession, or hoping he’d finally declare it aloud and sweep her up in a way that would make her forget everything else.

Noah, completely oblivious to her inward thoughts and the way her heart was beating erratically in her chest, secured a small bandage on her cut. His eyes darted to meet hers, and the breath hitched in her lungs. For one glorious second, time seemed to freeze.

Kiss me, kiss me, kiss me—

Just as quickly as he had knelt in front of her, he stood and was back against the opposite wall.

The air in her lungs escaped in a slightly pained exhale, and her lungs burned from holding her breath.

Blinking, she sat frozen for several seconds before she forced herself to turn back to her sewing—if nothing else to give her hands something to do—the flutters in her stomach beginning to fade away.

She looked down at her hand, holding it up to him. "Thanks."

"Anytime." The smallest hint of a smile tilted one side of his mouth.

Rather abruptly, the ground beneath her started to tremble. Juliette instinctively tensed, holding the edge of the coffee table. She hated the constant earthquakes that seemed to be happening more frequently. Granted they were never severe and only lasted a few seconds, but there was something about the entire palace—the entire ground beneath them—shaking and having nowhere to run that made her anxious. She looked up at the ceiling, at the chandelier that started clinking and gently swaying.

Three…four…five…six… Juliette frowned, glancing back up. It was growing stronger. A vase from the mantel fell, crashing to the floor and sending shards of glass every way.

Noah took a step forward. "Come on, under the table."

Juliette set her cloak aside, ducking her head and sliding beneath the coffee table in front of her. Noah crouched to the ground beside her, but there wasn't room for him.

"I'm fine," he said when she waved him forward.

She glanced again at the chandelier, wondering how intense of a quake it would take for the whole thing to come crashing down.

Juliette held on to one of the legs of the table.

"Remember when we used to race during these quakes?" she asked when the shaking didn't stop.

Noah snorted. "I remember you cheating and intentionally tripping me."

"I refuse to comment on that."

Noah laughed.

The quaking finally stopped, and as soon as Juliette helped Noah get the glass cleaned up, she went right back to work on her cloak.

An hour later, an entire string of butterflies lined the hem of her hood, only visible when light struck the fabric in certain ways.

Juliette smiled, pleased with herself. She stood up, moving into the hall where a massive mirror took up an entire section of the wall. Turning her head to let the light hit it, she saw the butterflies dance and shimmer. As if they would flap their wings and fly away.

She couldn't wait to fly away with them, to break free from her glass cage and finally be free. Smiling to herself, she turned around and glanced at it from behind. Excitement made her want to laugh, seeing how beautiful it was. Without moving her head, she glanced at Noah in the mirror. His gaze was fixated straight ahead, and she felt herself deflate just a little.

"What do you think?" she asked, turning around so she could face him.

His face softened just the tiniest bit—so faint she wondered if she imagined it—and his gaze never left her face. "It's beautiful."

Juliette's grin intensified, and she bounced up on her tiptoes, hugging the cloak tighter around her. She gathered her mess of hair and pulled it to one shoulder, shoving the hood off her head and glancing at it again in the mirror. For a moment, she tried to imagine herself with wings and what it would mean to know true freedom. To be able to just fly away whenever she wanted to.

Chapter Twenty-Eight

Noah's watch vibrated. He glanced at it, his heart stilling. "Jules, Odette's on her way here."

Juliette looked up. Frowned. "Why?"

"No idea."

With a grunt of frustration, Juliette stood up and started cleaning the mess around her, stuffing everything back into her bag and then setting the bag behind the sofa where Odette wouldn't be able to see it.

Heels clicked on the tile. Noah straightened as Odette walked in.

"There you are. I've been looking for you," Odette announced.

Noah concentrated on keeping his expression blank. *Not very hard if you didn't start in her wing.*

Juliette said nothing, but Noah didn't detect any fear from her body language. She carried herself straight and tall.

Well, as tall as a just-over-five-foot girl could carry herself.

Odette was dressed in a green dress that grazed the ground when she walked and accentuated her tiny waist and full bust. There was a slit going up the side that showed one of her legs. Noah guessed it was her attempt to look sexy, provocative.

Odette heaved a sigh, glancing around her with a look of unbridled disgust. "I just received Dr. Violet's report and thought you might want to know that given your refusal to cooperate, we'll begin sedating you for as many procedures as we can."

Juliette chewed the inside of her cheek, but she didn't move. Noah saw something spark in her eyes, but she kept it reined in.

"I thought that would please you," Odette added, smiling smugly.

The muscles in Juliette's jaw worked. She glanced to the side, her eyes wandering to the window. "I couldn't care less whether or not I'm sedated or not—"

Odette slammed her closed fist into Juliette's temple, so quickly Noah almost jumped. She hit her with such strength it caused Juliette to lose her balance. "Look at me when you're talking to me," Odette said, as calmly as if she was discussing the weather.

Juliette's hand reflexively moved to the side of her head. Tears had sprung to her eyes, and she blinked them back.

Noah worked his jaw, his vision turning red.

"Right," she muttered.

Odette's eyebrows shot up, her eyes fixated on Juliette. "Really? That's it?" She crossed her arms over her chest, the start of a cruel smile tilting her lips. "No crying? No running away?"

Juliette shook her head. "No," she replied mechanically.

"What about an apology for wasting Dr. Violet's time? For making those poor guards have to step in? You make everyone around you miserable when you behave that way."

Noah's eyebrows twitched. What guards had to step in and why?

Juliette remained silent once again.

Odette laughed. She waved her hand in Juliette's general direction. "You're so…pathetic. Such a waste. And you have so much potential."

Noah's eyes narrowed ever so slightly. Odette was goading her, more so than usual. She usually didn't see Juliette unless there was a reason. To the best of his knowledge, she hadn't sought her out *strictly* to abuse her in years. The hits usually came when their paths crossed.

The air around them seemed to grow even colder than it already was. He could see the hurt in Juliette's eyes that she tried to hide.

Juliette started to say something, but Odette's hand snapped out, grabbing Juliette's arm and turning her wrist over to reveal the edge of her reddened skin. "I really wish you'd stop doing this to yourself, it looks *awful.*"

Noah had to remind himself over and over that if he said or did anything, Odette would take it out on Juliette. Him stepping up to defend her would accomplish nothing. If anything, it would only make things worse. But what was Odette doing? She was trying to get a rise out of her, intentionally. Why?

Juliette yanked her arm back. "Then leave me alone."

"I will not. You, little girl, have a few valuable traits that are just important enough for me to keep you around. But the moment you cease to be valuable, I will have no problem getting rid of you entirely."

Juliette was silent for several minutes before turning and starting to walk back out.

"Don't you walk away from me." Odette grabbed

Juliette's arm, yanking her back.

Juliette wrenched herself free, her eyes blazing. She looked like she was going to say something or lash out, but the fire quickly faded. "I was going to go to my room so I would be out of your way, since you don't seem to actually need me for anything beyond tormenting me," she said, surprisingly calm.

Odette took a measured breath, anger in her eyes. Her cheeks very slowly lost their flushed color. She licked her blood-red lips, straightening her shoulders. She started to turn away, then abruptly spun, grabbing the front of Juliette's dress and shoving her back.

Juliette stumbled, tripping over the leg of the sofa and falling to the ground.

"I have been entirely too gracious with you lately," Odette said, stepping toward her.

Noah's jaw began to ache.

Juliette slowly, deliberately, got to her feet, but she didn't react. The only indication she gave that she was still conscious of what was happening was her attempt to ward off a second blow from Odette.

"Stop it!" Juliette shrieked.

"I'll stop it when I feel like it!" Odette grabbed a fistful of Juliette's hair, pulling her to the side and punching Juliette's temple a third time.

Juliette pushed back, but with Odette's fingers wrapped through her hair, she could only make it so far. The tears in her eyes didn't spill.

Odette finally released Juliette and shoved her away. "I'll have him hold you down, if you don't stop fighting me, understand?" she asked, her chin jerking toward Noah.

Oh seas, no. There was no way Noah would do

that. He'd already determined that it didn't matter what it cost—if Odette demanded he hold Juliette down while she beat her, he'd refuse.

The muscles in Juliette's jaw flexed.

Odette's eyes flickered to Noah. Something in her expression shifted. She looked back at Juliette, then smoothed her hands down her dress. Her gaze softened as she took a step toward Noah, giving Juliette the chance to get to her feet, and rested one of her hands on his arm. He didn't flinch or give any kind of indication he noticed. Her gaze lingered on him for several seconds before finally looking back to Juliette with a wicked smirk on her burgundy lips.

"Oh, him again. At least you have good taste. I might have to borrow him one of these nights."

Juliette's face flooded with heat, her cheeks turning the brightest red Noah had ever seen. Her eyes hardened, her lips thinning. Anger clawed up her throat in a guttural roar, and she hurled the tablet across the room, lunging for her sister.

Noah's hands locked around her wrists before she had gotten close to reaching Odette, but for a split second, a look of genuine panic flashed in the queen's eyes.

"Don't you *ever* touch him again—don't you even *look* at him!" Juliette shrieked. "You stay away from him!" She bucked and fought against Noah's grip, demanding to be released and trying to pry her arms free. He held her back, but barely. She twisted against him, demanding to be released again and again. She tried to shove him away, but he snaked an arm around her waist with one arm, trying to grab her wrists with the other.

Seas, she was stronger than he thought. He almost lost one of her arms, but he managed to catch her again.

Tears were trickling down her face, and she continued screaming, demanding to be released. A tiny part of Noah wanted to let her go, let her attack Odette and give her what she deserved.

Odette laughed, her hands flying to her mouth in genuine amusement. “Aw, the little pigeon has some fire in her after all. Keep her under control and make sure she doesn’t break anything,” she sneered, never taking her eyes from Juliette and her feeble attempt to pry herself free. Though Odette’s tone was light, there was poison in her eyes as she walked past and continued through the corridor.

“Yes, Your Majesty,” Noah replied.

Juliette kept struggling, trying to push herself away from him, twisting her arms and wrists.

“Let me go!” Juliette bellowed, dropping her weight in an effort to evade him. “Noah! Let me go!”

Noah didn’t listen. His heart was in his throat, but he kept hold of her. He looked around, still trying to keep her contained without hurting her. She was so caught up in her fight to break free—fighting as hard as she could—she didn’t realize he picked her up and brought her inside another room until it was too late. He closed the door, and her screams intensified.

“No, *no*! Let me *go*! Let *GO!* I hate her, I *hate* her! She can’t…she’s—!”

“Jules, stop, please! You’re going to get us both in trouble,” he said, loud enough to be heard above her but not so loud that he was shouting.

Shaking from a dangerous combination of

adrenaline and rage, Juliette pushed against him in another attempt to escape. She must have finally realized it was useless. Her yells started to die down, and the strength in her legs waned as she realized it was a pointless fight. She stopped struggling, sobs wracking her body.

Noah waited a few seconds, making sure she wasn't tricking him into lowering his guard, before loosening his grip. He wrapped his arms around her from behind, but she pushed away from him, so he let her go.

Juliette crossed to the other side of the room, leaning back against the wall and sinking to the ground. Tears streaked her face, and sweat trickled down her back as she sobbed.

Chapter Twenty-Nine

Noah pressed back against the closed door, checking to make sure it was locked. Juliette didn't let him hold her for long before breaking away. He understood it, understood her frustration at Odette, at him for being the one to hold her back, at being trapped in this frozen prison. It did little to lessen the sting. He couldn't let her out until she'd settled down, or Odette would kill them both.

"How could she say that?!" Juliette shouted, hurling one of the pillows on the sofa across the room, knocking over a glass vase. "She's…I hate her!"

I hate her, too, Noah thought to himself, his hands shaking. He thought for sure he wasn't going to get Juliette away from Odette fast enough.

"And you just do what she says!" Juliette shot Noah a glare. He knew she was mad—mad at Odette, and even mad at him.

"What did you want me to do?" he demanded. "Let you attack her? She'll just retaliate!"

"Then let her!" Juliette had risen again, tears still making their way down her face. "She does it every day, what difference does it make?! At least if I don't always have a guard holding me back, I can show her I won't just lie down and take it!"

"Jules—"

"No! Don't! Just let me be mad, *please*." Juliette

sank back against the wall beside the fireplace. Her face was red, her cheeks blotchy. She wrapped her arms around her legs, burying her face in her knees. Her shoulder trembled. She was angry, she was frustrated. None of that did anything to lessen how beautiful she was. Lifting her head, she grabbed something from the mantel and hurled it across the room. It must have been glass, because Noah heard it shatter.

"Okay, be mad. Let me know when you're done."

Juliette looked at him, still glaring. "Don't try and make me laugh."

"I wasn't." Noah pressed his lips together. He'd never felt more trapped in his life. He hated—*hated*—that he had to listen to Odette. That he had to be one more person to control Juliette.

She shook her head. "She's such a *witch*," she muttered, brushing her face with the back of her hand. "And no one ever does anything to stop her, because no one can."

Noah scoffed his agreement.

"Why did you stop me? I could have taken her."

"I have no doubt of that, but she has guards who will stop you."

Juliette arched her eyebrows.

"More than just me," Noah amended. "She has guards who will hurt you, okay? At least all I did was get you away from her before she had the chance to do anything."

It sounded like she almost laughed. "I know what she's capable of, Noah. I've been dealing with it my whole life. I know what would have happened to me if I hurt her, and I don't care."

"And I would let you make that choice for

yourself, butterfly, but try to understand where *I'm* coming from. I'm a guard. I have no power, no value. She can replace me in a minute. If I disobey an order and stand by while the *queen* is attacked, what do you think is going to happen?"

Juliette exhaled.

Noah arched his eyebrows. "She'll go after me, she'll go after Phil, or one of the other guards here, and then she'll go after you." He sighed shortly, stamping down his own mounting frustration.

Juliette didn't reply. She swiped at her face, but tears continued to trickle down her cheeks.

"Are you going to be okay?" he asked after a few seconds of silence. The words sounded flat, empty.

Juliette shook her head. "Not if she goes after you. I'm so stupid, all this time I thought she hadn't paid any attention to you." She pressed a hand to her lips. "She sees everything."

"*This* is all she wanted; she wanted to get a rise out of you. That's it." Noah took a step toward her.

Juliette's eyes welled up. "No, it's not, and we both know it." She pushed away from the wall, pacing across the length of the room. Her hair had come out of its style, and it hung down her back in gentle waves.

Noah was silent. Juliette was right; they did both know what it was Odette wanted and how her endless string of lovers was never enough.

"Don't let her get to you," he said, emphasizing each word carefully and hoping he didn't sound too harsh. "That's what she wants. Odette *feeds* on misery. The more people are miserable, the happier she is."

Dropping onto the sofa and sinking her face into her hands, Juliette heaved a deep sigh. Noah wanted to wrap her in a hug. He wished he could hold her forever and never let her go.

"Jules, we'll be out of here soon, okay? Don't worry about what she wants or what she's after. Let her think she's winning, if that's what it takes to stay safe and unharmed."

"That's what I've been doing, but it doesn't matter." She sighed. Her eyes finally roved back over to him. "I'm sorry, Noah; I'm so sorry I put you in that position. I should have just swallowed it back, but I—I couldn't."

Noah almost smiled. He shrugged one shoulder, pressing his lips together. "For what it's worth, you're way stronger than I thought."

Juliette barely laughed.

"I mean it. I almost lost you at least twice." His hand twitched, and he once again stamped down the urge to reach for her, to hold her hand. "Don't let her win."

Juliette dashed away another tear. She wouldn't look at him. "I don't care what she says to me, but she…the way she looked at *you*."

As much as he wanted to refute it, he knew it was pointless. Odette controlled a lot at the palace. Too much, to be sure, but not everything. She couldn't control his thoughts. He and Juliette both knew all too well how Odette liked those on her personal guard to be physically strong as well as physically attractive. Decorations as much as security. Toys and playthings as well as protectors.

Noah held on to the slim hope that because he was on Juliette's guard, he would be just outside of her radar. Because truthfully, he was more concerned at how she'd try to use him to get at Juliette.

"She doesn't even think twice about me," Noah said, crossing the room and plucking a handful of tissues from a box that he handed to her. "She has her own guards she sees every day. They're way more convenient."

"Yeah, because Odette's all about convenience." Juliette dabbed at her face.

"Jules—"

"Don't let her touch you, Noah. Please," Juliette begged, her shoulders sagging. She'd never looked more defeated. "I don't care if she threatens to hurt me, but I couldn't take it if she…" She slowed, swallowing. "If she touched you."

Noah shook his head. "I won't let her."

"Promise?"

"Promise." Noah straightened his jacket, glancing up at the security camera mounted in the corner. He wasn't sure if someone was watching them right now, but he really hoped not. "Let me grab you some water."

"Why?"

"I don't know. It seems like the appropriate thing to do."

The corner of Juliette's mouth twitched. She leaned back against the sofa, taking a deep breath.

Noah grabbed a glass of water from one of the tables laden with different drinks and snacks. He often wondered why each room in the palace was stocked with small snack items, even when empty.

"Here." He handed Juliette a glass, relieved when she downed the whole thing. "Hey, will you do something for me?" he asked after neither of them said anything for a while.

Juliette looked up at him. “Anything.”

Noah glanced at the inside of her forearm where she rubbed herself when she was especially stressed. “Stop hurting yourself. Please.”

Juliette visibly tensed. Ducked her head.

“I know habits are hard to break, especially nervous habits, but I don’t want you to hurt yourself.”

She nodded, but barely. “I don’t even know I’m doing it,” she said, almost laughing. She glanced down at her arm and shrugged one shoulder. “Some people bite their fingernails. Me? I scratch my wrist.”

“Bite your fingernails.”

Juliette smiled, a genuine smile, before setting the glass down and wrapping her arms around him.

He hugged her back, squeezing her in a quick pulse before releasing her. He straightened his jacket, casting another glance up at the camera in the corner. Its sensor light blinked lazily at him.

Juliette took a deep breath and let it out. She wiped her face with her hands, then shook her fingers through her hair. Back to being a princess and a guard. She turned and glanced at herself in the mirror hanging over the fireplace, taking a moment to fix her hair and straighten her dress.

Chapter Thirty

"House Armament is reporting an eight percent increase in training productivity, and because of House Galvan's increased work hours, they were able to up their electrical conduction and distribution by *twelve percent.*"

Odette sighed, staring out at the window at the glimmering streets below. She glanced down at the back of her hand where a faint pink scratch was puffing up. "And House Atworth?" she asked.

"No change, Your Majesty," Natasha said, lowering her voice in sympathetic frustration.

Odette sighed. "Let's reduce the school age then. Start drafting anyone over the age of thirteen. Children have more energy than adults, we can utilize that. And really, how much schooling do farmers need?"

"Yes, Your Majesty." Natasha made rapid notes on her data tablet in front of her.

"What else?"

"House Luxe has been unaffected. They recently sent you an entire cache of jewelry as a show of appreciation for your continued generosity."

Odette scoffed. " 'Appreciation.' "

"As they claim, Majesty."

"More like manipulation." She waved a hand in the air. "Is there anything else?" She arched her back, bringing a hand beneath her chin and refocusing her gaze through the window. The image of Juliette's outburst kept replaying in her mind. One minute she was as meek and insignificant as a bug, and the next she was an angry, vicious little firecracker.

Natasha hesitated for a long enough stretch that Odette's attention was piqued. "There have been…protests."

Odette raised her eyebrows, waiting for an elaboration.

"Against the extended work hours with Atworth. There have been declines in health, and with the recent crack, the temperatures have dropped, so it's been harder to be out as long."

Odette scoffed. "Atworth is overpopulated as it is. Maybe with fewer bodies, we'll see fewer quakes. Send three more brigades of soldiers, and make sure those work hours are enforced by whatever means necessary. And reduce their pay for disobedience," she added, noting that the added withholdings would cushion her finances for the palace.

"Yes, Your Majesty."

"And make sure none of this is released. With my ongoing negotiations with France, the last thing I need is a report that we're falling apart." Odette turned her attention to her own tablet and started ruffling through the various reports that she had been receiving since the increase of quakes across Demetria. Glancing up at the holo-map still projecting where Natasha was, she shook her head.

Years of her own time and energy had been spent on ensuring her people, her country, would flourish. Yet these quakes continued to weaken the country's foundation. The shield continued to malfunction.

Without a source of a larger income, Odette could do very little. As soon as her team of scientists would finish with their blasted reports, Odette could formulate the next steps.

"Natasha?"

"Yes, My Queen?"

"I know it's still a month, but have you started working on the Winter Ball?"

Natasha straightened. "Yes. I have some things started that I can always change or cancel if you have a different idea or want to cancel it altogether."

Odette scoffed. "Skies no. I like having parties every few months. It gives my people something to look forward to in these troubling and uncertain times."

Natasha dipped her head. "Absolutely. Would you still like to keep our previously discussed date?"

Odette sighed. "Natasha I am far too busy to remember every little detail. What date had we talked about?"

"The twenty-first of December. The Winter Solstice."

Odette grinned. She almost laughed. "Perfect! Whatever you need from the Houses, you have my full authorization to get it."

Natasha's face warmed into a smile. "Yes, Your Majesty." She bowed respectfully.

"That will be all."

With another bow, Natasha gathered her data tablets and motioned for the guard with her to follow.

Smiling to herself, Odette waved away the map and chanced to glance back at her feed of rotating security feeds.

Her attention was instantly grabbed by one of the

cameras from the music room.

Juliette and her guard. She was obviously angry, and it looked like she was yelling at him. The guard had his back to the door, and no matter how much Juliette cried, he didn't move. She had been expecting Juliette's reaction. Hoping for it, even. But what really caught Odette's attention was the look on the guard's face. Concern, maybe? Worry? Or perhaps it was closer to infatuation.

A snarl bubbled in Odette's throat. He hadn't so much as *looked* at her, and that irritated her more than she thought it would. Every guard in the palace would look at her. When she wanted some fun, they were all too willing to oblige her entertainment. All too willing to flirt back or risk a daring touch. To spend the night with her. All except that one.

Whatever. Let Juliette have her stupid guard.

Odette had bigger things to worry about than her ridiculous sister.

No, her ridiculous *adopted* sister. Why her parents thought it a good idea to bring in a crying baby found at the palace kitchen's doorstep was beyond her.

It was embarrassing. It was a *waste* of palace resources to spend them on a street rat, one who carried no royal blood in her veins. Odette lost respect for both her parents when that happened. They hadn't even considered the fact that the war was already claiming the majority of their attention. They barely acknowledged Odette's presence, and then suddenly there was a wild, untamed child running around the palace.

By the time Odette could have set the record straight, after her parents were finally gone, it was too late. Somehow it was worse to have people thinking a commoner was living in the palace than it was to endure Juliette's behavior.

Odette looked down at the scratch on her hand, the corner of her mouth tilting in a smile, replaying her interaction with Juliette. Juliette's reaction was a shock, to say the least. She had let Odette physically assault her with barely a grimace, but the minute she touched *him*, she turned into a little monster.

Filling her lungs with air, Odette leaned her head back. She'd found her trigger. Noah being threatened. Juliette cared more for his well-being than she did for her own. It was so simple; Odette should have thought about it a long time ago.

Odette chewed her lip, her eyes drifting to the side. Hope, for the first time in forever, flickered in her mind.

Chapter Thirty-One

Natasha stuffed her hand deeper into her pocket, picking at a loose hangnail, pacing back and forth in front of the window, pausing every few seconds to glance through it.

The French royal family was due to arrive at any moment, and per Odette's instruction, she wanted Natasha to greet them and escort them to their rooms so they would have the chance to refresh themselves before meeting Odette.

Pain pricked her cuticle. She must have made herself bleed again. Her heart hadn't stopped racing since she'd left Juliette in the infirmary. The backs of her eyes stung, and she had to blink them clear.

She hadn't realized, until recently, the extent of Odette's plans for her mystery project, or how much of that project revolved around Juliette. It was no secret that Odette wasn't fond of Juliette, but Natasha never imagined she could be so cruel. It was too much to stand, but Natasha couldn't do anything to stop it. As her duties with Odette had grown, she found there was less and less time to sneak off and check on Juliette or make sure she'd eaten or was warm or had clothes that fit her.

At least she still had Noah, and thank the seas that boy had a good head on his shoulders.

A beep from her tablet startled Natasha. She

glanced at it, relief washing through her at the alert that a ship was approaching the palace. She checked their credentials and then granted them access to the palace hangar.

With a short sigh, Natasha started out into the corridor. On the way, she checked that her cloak was buttoned and her hair was still tucked neatly in its bun. She used to wear her hair down all the time. One time someone complimented it, and ever since then Odette had asked that she wear it pinned back and hidden. She said it looked more professional, but Natasha often wondered, perhaps a little vainly, if Odette liked being the only "pretty" one in the palace. Even if the only thing Natasha had going for her was her hair.

It didn't matter. Natasha had grown to appreciate wearing her hood. It gave her a sense of camouflage, even though it probably made her stand out even more.

As soon as she and her guards entered the hangar, Natasha waited for the king's ship to finish the landing procedures. After what felt like hours, the steel stairs lowered onto the ground just as two figures appeared.

Natasha called up her most welcoming smile. "Your Majesty. Your Highness," she said, dipping her head in a semi-bow. Her eyebrows twitched in a frown, noticing the queen wasn't there. She might have still been on the ship, or perhaps she didn't come at all.

The prince barely nodded once, his eyes glancing around him.

"My name is Natasha Prya. I am Her Royal Majesty's second-in-command, and I will escort you to your rooms."

"Thank you," King Philippe replied. "I apologize for my wife; she became suddenly ill before we left and was unable to make the journey."

"Not to worry." Natasha smiled. "I hope she gets well soon."

Leading the way back into the palace, Natasha walked with them up a magnificent, twisting stairwell and through a corridor until the two guards with her pushed open a set of dark, wooden double doors.

"Prince Rene, Your Majesty, allow me to introduce Her Royal Majesty Queen Odette."

Odette was standing at a long table in front of the window. Her hair glistened in the pale light. Her dark eyes sparkled, and she smiled a close-lipped smile.

King Philippe stepped forward and took the queen's outstretched hand.

"Your Majesty."

"King Philippe. I'm so pleased to finally meet you."

"Likewise."

Odette turned to Prince Rene and smiled. "Your Highness."

Rene managed a smile, though he looked annoyed.

Odette turned to one of the footmen standing at the room's perimeter, and he slipped from the room. "I won't take up too much of your time; I know you've both had a long and exhausting trip, but I wanted to be the first to welcome you to Demetria."

"Thank you, Your Majesty. Your country is truly remarkable, and I look forward to seeing it in person," Philippe replied.

Odette laughed. "I'm glad you approve. I asked for dinner to be ready a little early tonight; I assumed you'd be hungry for some *real* food."

"That was considerate of you, thank you, Your

Majesty."

"Odette, please."

Natasha felt for her tablet, ready to pull it out in case the king of prince wanted something specific—either in terms of dietary restrictions or a request for special room accommodations.

"Odette. Thank you." His father smiled.

Odette looked at Natasha, slightly jerking her chin. "Natasha will show you each to your chambers. Please don't hesitate to ask for anything."

Rene turned, almost walking out before Natasha before seeming to think better of it. He slowed, letting her take the lead again, and then followed her.

"Your Majesty, please let me know if there is anything I can do for you," Natasha said, pausing in front of a door.

"Thank you, you have been very kind," the king murmured, walking through the door when one of the guards held it open.

"Your room is just down the corridor, Your Highness."

"Fantastic."

Natasha started to say something else to try and make him feel more at ease, but Juliette's voice caught her attention. Rene stopped, whipping his head around. A scowl crossed his face.

"Princess Juliette," Natasha whispered just as she stepped into view. Juliette was talking to someone, her eyes red-rimmed. She lightly smacked Noah's shoulder, a hint of a smile crossing her face. She grabbed his arm to try and stop him, but he didn't look even a little slowed down.

They both stopped short when they saw Natasha

and the prince.

Juliette's eyes widened. Noah's expression morphed into a blank slate.

For half a second Rene stood there, not sure what to say or do, before Natasha stepped forward.

"Princess Juliette, allow me to present His Royal Highness Prince Rene of the French Union."

Juliette looked surprised, glancing first from Rene back to Natasha. "Prince Rene?" she repeated, her eyebrows arching. A smile crept onto her face.

Natasha tried to stifle a smile of her own.

"As she said," Rene muttered.

The smile dropped from Natasha's face.

Juliette dipped her head and lowered her gaze. "Welcome to Demetria."

"A pleasure to make your acquaintance," Rene deadpanned.

"Likewise." She straightened, smiling. "I hope you have a pleasant trip," she added, stammering just a little as if she weren't sure what to say.

Rene barely nodded. Natasha continued down the corridor, and Rene followed.

"*That's* Odette's sister?" Rene asked, jerking a thumb to the side.

"She is." Natasha smiled, though she worried her eyes would betray her brimming anger.

"She seems…off." Rene shook his head. "And to think my father wants me to marry her."

"As Her Majesty said, if there's anything you need or would like, please let me know," Natasha said, her eyes hardening. What she wanted to tell him was that Juliette was the strongest person she knew. That she did so much to defy Odette in small ways, like being nice to the servants and making sure their family members were getting enough food and clothing rations.

Rene slipped through the door, closing it behind him.

Chapter Thirty-Two

Noah, sitting beneath his ship with an array of tools around him, ran a tired hand through his hair. He stifled a yawn and glanced at the digital clock mounted above the door. He almost got up to turn the TV on, thinking some mental stimulation might help him wake up a little more, but he changed his mind. The last thing he needed was to be distracted by what was going on throughout the country.

The past couple days had been the longest forty-eight hours he could remember. He had been walking around on eggshells since Juliette's outburst, waiting with bated breath for Odette to retaliate, to strike back against Juliette in a way that would leave her half-dead.

Two whole days passed, and nothing happened. Odette hadn't ordered her back to the infirmary, and to the best of his knowledge, she hadn't beaten her again.

Noah heaved a sigh, standing up and arching his back in a stretch. He stooped for one of Mason's books sprawled out on the ground, cross-referencing the photo with the part of the engine he was working on.

From what he understood of this specific ship, it was mostly solar powered, but there was a separate fuel line to use as a backup. Most fuel ships had been outlawed in Demetria because of pollution concerns, but this was such an old model that still had the option for fuel.

Noah thought that he would slowly purchase as much fuel as they could store, just to have in case of an emergency. The radiant light from the dome was strong enough to charge the solar panels, but if they needed to stop somewhere and it was raining, he didn't want to be stranded.

Noah rubbed his temple, a headache beginning to bloom behind his eyes. His ears perked up as soft footsteps echoed through the vast hanger, and he glanced at his wristlet again. It was just now midnight.

"I thought you went to bed?" he asked, craning around the side of the ship, his eyebrows twitching as Juliette walked down. She was wearing his sweatshirt again. The sleeves had stretched out, probably because she constantly bunched them in her fists, and the color was starting to fade.

"I did, but I couldn't sleep," she said, walking past him and climbing up on the pile of crates off to the side. She picked up one of the tools he had shoved into a box and twirled it around her finger. "Besides, I miss you," she added. "Everything's been so weird lately, I feel like it's been a while since we've just sat and *talked*."

Noah's shoulder twitched. "You shouldn't say things like that," he said, shooting her a half-hearted glare.

"Why not?"

Noah hesitated. "Someone might hear you," he said, emphasizing the *someone* so she'd know he meant Odette.

Juliette scowled, and Noah looked away, annoyed that even scowling she managed to rattle the inside of his sternum.

"We should cool it a little. At least in public," he

added, fumbling with a rusted bolt. "I shouldn't be talking to you so casually *ever,* on or off duty, and I'd bet my right arm your sister will be paying extra close attention to you. And me." He glanced up at her, his heart twisting at seeing the pain written on her face. "Right now, that's the last thing we need."

"That's fair. Sorry."

He sighed, trying to stamp out the frustration in his tone and afraid she would think he was upset at *her*. "No, I'm sorry. I've been on edge the past few days and am probably overreacting; you're fine."

Juliette pressed her lips together in a smile. She straightened, jerking her chin to the ship. "I think I'm going to try and start working on this blasted computer."

Noah nodded once. "Sounds good."

Juliette climbed into the cockpit, and Noah could hear her moving around. "How's the engine looking?" she asked.

"So far so good. I'm actually getting into it. It's starting to get fun," he added with a laugh.

Juliette was silent for a while, giving Noah the chance to tackle getting the fuel line replaced. He had a small canister of it that he emptied into the tank, testing the line to make sure the fuel ran through without leaking. Good.

Noah wiped his hands off on the grease-soiled rag, shoving out from beneath the ship. "How fares it up there?" he asked, walking around to the open door and folding his arms over the threshold.

Juliette was sitting on the ground beneath the control panel, a stylus tucked behind her ear. "Not great. I think the operating systems aren't compatible because the computer works fine when I plug it into my tablet, but the ship isn't responding. I might need to rewire the ship."

Noah pressed his lips together. "I don't know what that means, but is there anything I can do to help?"

Juliette shook her head. "No, I don't think so." She shook her hair away from her face, pushing herself up. "I tucked some spare parts down here last time. I might be able to do it really quickly."

Noah stepped back so she could jump to the ground, watching as she crossed to the opposite side of the garage and started digging through a box.

"It's freezing down here," she muttered, coming back with a handful of different colored wires.

"I know. Speaking of, I need to remember to check the ship's heating and cooling units. My sweatshirt's on the sofa inside if you want it."

"Oh thanks."

"I'll need that one back though," he called after she disappeared inside the ship.

Juliette laughed. "Fair enough."

For a while, they both worked in silence. Noah kept thinking of things to tell her or ask her, but every time he popped his head into the cockpit and saw her brows furrowed in concentration, he changed his mind.

Juliette abruptly let out a cry.

Noah leapt up, darting to the cockpit. "Are you okay?"

"Yes! Sorry, I got it! It's turning on!" Juliette was grinning, craning her neck to look up at the inner workings of the ship's computer.

Noah relaxed into a smile. "Really?"

"Yes. Which means we'll be able to plot a course,

we should have internet access, and it will give me the ability to conceal the ship from radars, should we need to."

Noah sagged against the doorframe. "You're amazing."

Juliette looked at him, still grinning. The grin turned sheepish, and she quickly looked away. "Oh seas, my heart's racing." She pressed a hand to her chest, still smiling.

"Where's a TV in the living area, did you—"

"I saw that. It's old, which figures, but I thought I could plug in one of my tablets and we could use it basically as a monitor. I don't think we'll need it, but just in case I want to outfit it with the ability to."

"Smart."

Juliette sighed, happy. "Will you teach me to fly?" she asked, craning her neck to look at the rest of the ship.

"Why; you don't trust my flying capabilities?"

Juliette almost smiled. "Of course I do. I just thought we should take turns, that way you aren't stuck in here the whole time."

Noah jerked his shoulders. "Sure, I'll teach you."

Juliette grinned.

Noah looked back at the parts in his hands, fumbling with them and trying to keep his hands busy and his thoughts distracted. He blinked, several times, in an effort to clear the burning that had settled in his eyes. "Maybe we should call it for the night? It's getting late."

In his peripherals, he saw Juliette drop her gaze. "Yeah, you're probably right," she said with a sigh. She jumped back to the ground, bunching the sleeves of her hoodie in her hands. She tried to smile, but it faltered.

"Hey," Noah reached for her wrist. He swiveled around on the crate. "We can keep going if you want, it was just a suggestion."

"I know, but you're right. We both need sleep."

Noah studied her face. "What's going on?"

Juliette drew a shaky inhale. "I don't know. I haven't been sleeping well recently. Whatever Dr. Violet is doing hasn't changed, but each time I go see her, I feel like…like I'm losing a part of myself." Her voice broke on the last word, her eyes sparkling with tears. "I know I'm being dramatic, but—"

"You're not being dramatic," Noah said softly, standing up.

"Every time I go, she gives me the same four injections. But the past month, she's been switching it up, just a little, and giving me these strange 'homework assignments' that mess with my head and…it's like I can feel my mind…my brain, changing. The way I think about things, the way I react."

A rock settled in Noah's stomach. "What—what do you mean?"

"I don't know, I can't explain it." She swiped at her cheek, dashing a tear that leaked onto her face. "I just…" She licked her lips, looking right at him. "It's like my body is reacting to things before my mind has the chance to process what it is I'm reacting *to*."

Noah nodded again, slowly.

Juliette let out a shaky exhale. "I was thinking we could leave the night of the winter ball. It's a month away, and that should give us plenty of time to finish the ship and get everything ready to go. Plus, with all the guests coming and going, it will be an added distraction for Odette and her security detail."

Noah licked his lips, then pressed them together. "That should work. A month is cutting it a little close, but I think we can pull it off."

Juliette relaxed into a smile.

Noah pulled her into a quick hug, his hand cradling the back of her head. He felt her arms around his waist.

"Thank you," she murmured against him.

Noah let her go. "Let's say we take a quick peek inside, and I'll give you a short tour of the cockpit?"

Juliette dabbed at the corner of her eyes, then relaxed into a smile. "Sounds good. You said this was Philip's?"

"Technically it was both of ours. It was our dad's, and then Phil didn't want it, so he said I could just have it."

"I'm sorry Philip had to leave."

Noah shrugged. "I think honestly it will be good for both of us."

Juliette paused. Put a hand on Noah's arm. "Are you okay leaving him? I know you two aren't especially close, but if you need more time to think about it, we can hold off."

"Thanks. But no, let's keep planning. Phil being in Fatir will protect him from Odette, and once we're free and clear, I'll reach out to him."

Juliette smiled. "Okay. But if you change your mind, it's okay."

Noah squeezed her hand in a quick pulse.

As they continued through the short corridor, Noah felt her slide her hand into his. Instead of pulling away, like he should have done, he laced his fingers through hers as they walked into the narrow cockpit.

After giving her a basic tour of the control panel and dashboard, as well as the overhead dials, Noah had her repeat everything he said and even gave her a quiz after he had gone over everything a few times. She picked up surprisingly fast and even made a few educated guesses about the unnamed levers.

"Alright, time for a fake test flight." Noah dropped into the copilot's seat, patting the pilot's chair beside him. "What's the first thing you do before takeoff?"

Juliette sank down beside him. Ticking off her fingers, she said, "Make sure the entry hatch is sealed, check the fuel levels, and raise the jet blast deflector."

"Perfect." He started to say something else when his wristlet pinged, telling him it was midnight. Glancing back at Juliette, he saw a flicker of nervousness cross her face. He knew the look. The look of dread at needing to go to her room, being by herself, trying to sleep.

"Do you want to come to the gym tomorrow morning?" he asked, wishing there was more he could do for her *right now*.

Juliette nodded. Glancing back up at him, time seemed to freeze, just for a moment. The air around them tingled with tension and unspoken words.

Noah didn't drop her gaze like he normally would have. He didn't mask his face into one of stone or stand up and say it was time to go. In that single glorious, precious moment, it was just Noah and Juliette.

Not a princess and a guard.

Noah's heart leapt against his ribs. His hand moved on its own accord, grazing her jaw, trailing down her neck. He saw her swallow, her eyes trained on his.

"Try and sleep, if you can," he murmured. "I'm

always just a nex't away."

"Thanks." Juliette smiled, but it didn't reach her eyes. He could see the loneliness in her face where there had once been excitement. The spark that used to light her whole personality had dimmed, and he would have given anything to get it back.

Noah stood up, and she followed. After locking the hatch and shoving the boxes of tools and spare parts beneath the belly of the ship, Noah grabbed his zip-up hoodie and slung it over his shoulder. She didn't even bother saying he didn't need to walk her back to her room.

"Good night, butterfly."

"Good night, Noah."

Chapter Thirty-Three

With Juliette once again safely in her room, Noah returned to the garage and finished cleaning the mess he'd made. It was already past midnight, but he'd managed to snap some pictures of the inner workings of his ship that he could then continue studying in the privacy of his room. He needed to purchase some new parts, but he was hoping to be able to find them used.

He wasn't aware of any junkyards in the capital, but it wouldn't hurt to look.

Noah groaned, kicking one of the wheels of his ship as he passed. He slung his sweatshirt over his shoulder, snapping the garage lights off and then taking the stairs two at a time up to the ground level.

"I thought you stopped working night shifts?" Mason said, pausing as Noah passed the kitchen.

"I was in the garage."

"Ah." He must have been finishing a shift. "How's Ju—the princess?"

"Fine," Noah said, a little too sharply even for his ears. He cleared his throat. "She's fine."

"Glad to have a little more freedom, I bet," Mason added with a scoff.

Noah didn't bother to reply. He kept on toward his room but slowed. Mason was a fairly decent mechanic. He'd repaired several of the palace ships before; he *might* know a way to disable the tracking equipment.

Unfortunately, that would require telling him at least some of his intended plan, and Noah wasn't quite that desperate.

But, he might be able to discreetly pick his brain.

"Hey." Noah paused. "I've been working on that old ship, trying to get the engine running again. It seems to be going well, but I can't figure out some of the more detailed mechanics. Don't suppose you could give me some pointers?"

"Yeah, of course. Did those books not help?"

"They did, but because the ship is old, there are some gaps." Noah waved a hand in the air. "It's not the end of the world, but if you *know* what to do, it would help if I could learn that way."

"Oh sure. I traded shifts with David, so I'm free. Do you want to go now, or are you headed to bed?"

Noah hesitated. It had been a long, tiring day, he had another long, tiring day ahead of him tomorrow. Unfortunately, Mason worked most nights, so there might not be another chance in the near future.

"Yeah, now would be perfect," Noah finally said. He would have plenty of time to catch up on sleep once he and Juliette were away.

They walked back out to the garage, and as Mason gave Noah a basic rundown of things he mostly knew, Noah took detailed notes.

"This panel houses the tracking units, and there are three different ones," Mason said, tapping a small metal box off to the side of the interior control panel.

"Oh, it's inside? I thought the tracking equipment was outside."

"No, not with these older models." Mason shook his head.

If that were the case, then Juliette probably either already took care of it or would know how to.

"I'd give you a tour of the inside, but we need special clearance to open them up because the opening is tagged and will send an alert to Aaryn," Mason added.

Noah deflated, but he tried to hide it. "I'm assuming that's so it can't be tampered with?"

"Correct."

"So how would you fix it if something was damaged?" Noah asked, feigning confusion.

"You just get permission from Aaryn. He'll give you a time slot, and then he can override the alert."

That sounded like something Juliette might be able to do. Noah chewed the inside of his cheek, thinking to let her know of the danger just in case she didn't know.

Mason kept going, oblivious to the additional obstacle he unknowingly threw in Noah's path. For the most part, Noah was able to keep up, jotting down as much information as he could as quickly as possible.

By the time Mason said he was going to turn in, it was almost one thirty. Noah was so wired he wanted to review all the things Mason had shown him and cross-reference them with what he'd been piecing together from Nexus research.

He stayed in the garage, propping his tablet up and being careful with his word choices when he made a search. From what he understood, a lot of the control boxes of his specific ship's year and model were recalled due to mechanical issues.

Specifically, with the black-box trackers.

Noah's heart did a little hiccup, and he had to read the same paragraph three times before his brain was able to make sense of it.

There was an issue with *his ship's tracking equipment*. He tried not to get too excited, thinking it couldn't be that easy. But if that was the case, then his job just got a whole lot easier.

Disabling a faulty part would be so much easier to take care of *and* talk himself out of trouble if he got caught.

Chapter Thirty-Four

Juliette was awake early, after tossing and turning for what felt like hours. Nightmares plagued her dreams, and she didn't feel much more rested than she did last night. Glancing at her wristlet, seeing it was only *seven*, she turned back onto her pillow to wait for the eight o'clock trumpets. She stared up at the ceiling, trying to call up what happened yesterday. Her mind drew a blank, and she couldn't for the life of her wrap her thoughts around anything that had occurred.

With a sigh, Juliette pressed a hand to her eyes, trying to remember the latest thing that happened. Odette's birthday party was recent. A week ago? Two weeks?

Noah was home, that she remembered.

How long had it been since she'd seen Dr. Violet? A few days?

Taking a deep breath in and letting it out slowly, Juliette slid out from beneath her blankets and grabbed her hoodie from the back of her desk chair. She yanked it over her head and flung her door open, slipping out into the corridor.

"I'm just going to pace up and down the hallway," she told the guard outside her room. It was Luis today. She hadn't seen Mason in a while, she realized. She thought for a second to tell Noah she was awake early, in case he wanted to come up now, but she changed her mind. He'd been so busy lately, working extra night shifts and spending so much time in the gym, she didn't want to disturb him any more than she already had.

Odette's favorite seamstress was coming today for the first fitting of a new dress, and she would be taking Juliette's measurements as well.

Juliette almost smiled, taking another deep breath and letting it out. A brand-new, custom-made dress. It was so unlike Odette, to do something nice for Juliette. Going out of her way to have a dress specially made was odd, for more than one reason.

Juliette paused at the end of the corridor, turning so she could jog back. The guard outside her room had turned so he could watch her. There were supposed to be four guards stationed in her hallway at night, but it had been a while since she had more than one since Odette had dwindled Juliette's personal guard to fill in her own gaps.

On her second jog down, Juliette slowed, continuing past her room to the massive bay window at the other end of the hallway. The drapes were drawn, so she moved one aside and peered through.

Sighing, she pressed her back against the window frame and then took off running as fast as she could to the other end. It felt good to run; she hadn't done it in forever, and she didn't realize how much energy she had pent up.

Slamming into the opposite wall, she turned and ran right back. She continued with her workout for another minute before slowing down. Her heart was pumping madly in her chest, and it was getting hard to breathe.

She pressed a hand to her chest, her heart

squeezing with every inhale. She sagged against the wall, trying to catch her breath.

"Juliette—what's wrong? Are you okay?"

Juliette looked up, relaxing into a smile at seeing Noah coming toward her. "Yeah. I'm just more out of shape than I realized."

He slowed, his eyebrows twitching in a frown. He straightened, clasping his hands behind his back and standing straighter. As soon as Luis disappeared, having been relieved, Noah took a step closer.

"How'd you sleep?"

"Not great. I woke up early and couldn't go back to sleep, so I thought I'd burn off some energy," she replied. "Sorry, did I push the button again?" She glanced down at the watch around her wrist. She programmed the watch a while ago to send her location just to Noah, thinking if Odette ever locked her away somewhere she would have a way of letting him know where she was.

"You must have, but it's fine."

"Well, now that you're here, I need to ask your opinion on something." With an excited grin, Juliette darted into her room and grabbed her data tablet. "I have a list of dress options I wanted to show you and see what you think. I keep changing my mind on which one is my favorite, so I need a second opinion."

"Jules?"

"Hm?"

When Noah hesitated, Juliette looked up from her tablet. "You're not dressed yet," he said.

Glancing down at her hoodie and nightdress that hit mid-thigh, Juliette frowned. "You've seen me in my nightgown before."

"Not that one. And not in public," he replied softly.

Juliette scowled, confused at how the hallway outside her bedroom was considered public. With a shrug, she walked back into her room and yanked her sweatshirt over her head, flinging it onto her bed.

Stepping into her closet, Juliette tugged on her favorite dress—a soft, gauzy, pale pink one that was worn to the perfect softness and seemed to float through the air if she moved fast enough. The bottoms of the sleeves were starting to fray, but she didn't mind.

Starting back out into the corridor and standing in front of Noah, Juliette opened her first option—a yellow dress with a sweetheart neckline, strapless, floor length, and a sheer, glitter overlay.

"Okay, what do you think?" Holding up her screen, she started to add something, but Noah was already shaking his head.

"No."

"Really? Why?"

Noah looked at the dress, then at Juliette, as if visualizing it on her. "I don't think yellow would be a good color for you."

"Okay, that makes sense." Juliette flipped to the next one. And the next one, and the next one. The fifth one, her personal favorite, was made of a pale pink material and had a wide skirt that looked like it would swish beautifully around her feet. The waist was a snug, corset-style bodice, and thin, diamond-studded straps went across the shoulders and crossed in the back. It was only a sketch, so she could probably request some minor changes to it if she wanted to.

Noah barely smiled. "I like that one."

Juliette pressed her lips together. "It's my favorite. I'll show it to Madame Miller when she's finished with Odette, but it should be simple enough." She shrugged to herself. "Especially compared to Odette's. I have some jewels from Luxe—I think I told you about that, right?—so I thought I could wear some of the jewelry I've been making." She sighed, feeling once again like someone was squeezing her heart, making it hard to breathe.

"Breakfast is ready, if you're hungry."

Juliette almost groaned. "Starving." She filled her lungs with air, chucking her data tablet back into her room and then starting down the corridor again.

After a quick breakfast, during which Odette said nothing, Juliette headed to her private study where she could be confident no one would catch her by surprise. She pulled up some information on Noah's type of ship, familiarizing herself with how the tracking equipment worked.

When Madam Miller arrived at the palace, Juliette reluctantly joined Odette in her sitting room. She hoped to have her fitting done without Odette there, but she shouldn't have expected it.

Standing in a forest of fabric drapings, lace samples, and strings of glittering beads and gems all sent from House Luxe, Juliette sank to the ground at the edge of the room where she would be out of the way. She tried not to look at Odette when she could avoid it, her mind once again roving back to the problem of getting the ship's tracking equipment disabled.

"This is the silk I specified?" Odette asked, turning on the pedestal to study herself from a different angle. "It feels different than I was expecting."

"Yes, Your Majesty, it's the same. Lady Luxe had it imported from France. If you like, I can have some other samples brought in for you to inspect?"

Odette shook her head. "As long as this is the one I specified, it's fine. You like it?" she asked, catching Juliette's eyes in the mirror. She spread her arms out, turning in a circle. "You're such an *expert* seamstress, let's hear your input."

Juliette cleared her throat, picking up on the hint of mockery in Odette's tone but determined to ignore it. Studying her sister's dress, made of champagne silk and rose diamonds that glittered across her entire bodice and accentuated her full bust, a small smile tickled her lips. "I'm sure it will be beautiful."

Odette's smile faltered. Her eyes narrowed. "I wondered, since Madame Miller has so many commissions for the ball, if *you* would be able to finish my dress?"

Juliette blinked. Madame Miller's eyes widened in surprise, and she looked from Odette to Juliette with a look of confusion.

Odette barked out a laugh. "Oh, I could barely get through that with a straight face. As if I would ever ask *you* to finish my dress."

Despite the harshness of her words, Juliette relaxed. There was no way she would ever voluntarily make Odette a dress.

Straightening, Odette turned back to the mirror and studied herself once again. "I'm afraid I will be needing Madame Miller for much longer than I expected, so it looks like you will have to find something presentable on your own as far as a gown is concerned."

Juliette blinked. Frowned. Opened her mouth to

ask what that meant when it clicked. No new, custom-made dress. She shouldn't have been surprised. "Yes, of course. I'm sure I can find a dress already made." Thankfully she had plenty of time, though she wasn't sure it mattered. All the time in the world would be useless if she didn't have the resources to find a dress. She chewed her lip, choosing her words carefully. "I wonder if I might have some credit with the shops in Demetria—"

"Absolutely not! You think I would trust you to handle *credit*? You can barely handle getting dressed in the morning." Odette lifted the top layer of her dress with a pleased smile. Her eyes snapped to meet Juliette's again, and this time they were filled with venom. "Perhaps if you were wiser with your time and didn't waste the house gifts on those useless *projects* of yours, you would have enough material to have a dress made."

Juliette clenched her jaw.

Odette smirked. "You think I didn't know you'd been saving all the things I've been throwing away? You will have to figure something out as far as a dress is concerned without my help. But you will not be permitted to come dressed in an old gown or one that falls short of my expectations."

Juliette dipped her head once. "Fine. I didn't want to go to the ball anyway."

Odette waved a hand in the air, unbothered.

Juliette slipped back out into the corridor. She was silent as she and Noah walked toward her study, telling herself she wasn't that disappointed. Sure, she'd been looking forward to having a new dress and getting to go to a fancy dinner, but in reality, no one would ask her to dance, and it would be an anxiety-filled night, knowing Odette would be watching her.

Watching the ball from the balconies would be just as much fun, she thought. She could *pretend* she was wearing the most beautiful gown in the world and imagine dancing with Noah.

Gathering up the pieces of her partially finished earrings, Juliette let the light catch the glittering facets.

"Have I mentioned before how much I loathe your sister?" Noah asked as he fell into step behind Juliette.

"You may have, a time or two." Juliette pressed her lips together in a smile.

Chapter Thirty-Five

"Do you actually have a final destination in mind, Jules? Or are you training to go on a hike?"

Juliette cast a scowl over her shoulder. "I want…to show you something," she panted, continuing up, up, up the spiraling stairwell to the level that would overlook straight down into the ballroom.

Noah wasn't quite sure what the little balcony was used for. He heaved a dramatic sigh, almost smiling when Juliette had to pause to catch her breath.

"You might want to consider jogging down the halls more often," he said, trying to keep from laughing.

Juliette shot him a glare, and this time he couldn't keep in a laugh. "I was thinking, since, well—you heard what Odette said, right? About me not going to the ball?"

"I did." Since she had mentioned leaving the palace that night, he assumed that meant missing the ball altogether. Odette banning her from attending was perfect.

"I thought instead of staying in my room, you and I could watch everyone arriving and dancing from up here," Juliette was saying, gesturing to the ballroom below. This high up the light was significantly dimmer and no guards were stationed around since the only stairwell was connected to the great hall and there was just one small window. "It will be easy to sneak up some food, we could have our own buffet, and we can try to guess who is who, or who's going to mess up the dances, or eat the most food…" She trailed off, her smile wavering as she glanced at Noah.

Noah worked to keep the confused frown off his face. She wanted to leave *after* the ball? He took a step forward, resting his forearms on the banister, studying the room below. Chances were that every guard in the palace would be on duty that night, including himself. He was counting on Juliette being able to override his shift so that no one would notice his absence.

His arm bumped against her shoulder, and she turned to look up at him.

"We could do something else, if you don't want to watch a boring dance," she said with a wave of her hand. "Or if you wanted some time to yourself, that's cool too. I've certainly monopolized enough of your time to last the rest of eternity." She laughed, but it sounded forced. Shrugging nonchalantly, she added, "I don't really care."

"No, I think it would be fun to watch," Noah replied, stammering just a little. "You had mentioned leaving that night, were you thinking you'd want to go after?"

Juliette tilted her head. "Leaving?"

Noah almost laughed. "The palace. Remember? The ship we've been working on? Going camping in California, swimming…"

It looked like Juliette might laugh as well. "What ship?"

Noah blinked. Opened his mouth and then closed it again. He drew a steadying breath, worry burrowing in his heart. "Our ship. The one…you know, the one

Philip gave me."

"Philip gave you a ship?"

Noah could only stand frozen. She wasn't messing around with him. She had no idea what he was talking about, even though the night before she'd been out on the ship working with him. "Yes. He gave me an old ship that we've been working on repairing," he said, slowly, saying a silent prayer that she'd burst out in laughter and tease him for being so gullible.

Juliette opened her mouth. Paused. Understanding flooded her expression, and she slapped a hand over her mouth. "Oh my—yes, of course! The ship. Seas, I'm so sorry, I don't know what's wrong with me this morning."

Noah breathed the smallest sigh of relief.

Juliette cleared her throat. Her hands trembled as she worked them through her hair. "I'm so sorry, I can't believe—seas, I didn't…that was weird." She tried to laugh.

"It's fine. We all have brain hiccups." Noah shrugged, then risked a subject change. "I talked to Mason yesterday—don't worry, I didn't tell him anything—but he mentioned that the tracking equipment for the ship is built into the system and needs special authorization for it to be disabled. I thought maybe if you were familiar with the inner workings, you'd be able to override the access code so we can disable it without anyone noticing."

"I'm sure I could," Juliette replied.

"Good." Noah was still mildly concerned, but he said nothing. She remembered now, and that was what mattered. "But, I mean, if you want to go after the ball so we can watch it, it's up to you," he added, once again looking out over the banister into the ballroom below.

Juliette firmly shook her head. “No way, I want to leave as soon as we can, and I couldn’t care less about Odette’s stupid ball.”

Noah breathed a sigh of relief. The sooner they were away—the sooner she wasn’t being injected with mystery solutions—the better.

“Happy Birthday, by the way,” he said, bumping her arm.

Juliette smiled, but it was delayed. “You remembered.”

“Of course. And I’ve been waiting *all* day to have you alone for a few minutes.” Noah reached into his pocket and pulled out a small box tied off with a blue ribbon, the back of his mind wondering if she had also forgotten it was her birthday.

“Can I open it now?” she asked when he handed it to her.

“As opposed to next Tuesday?”

With an excited grin, Juliette slid her finger beneath the fold and tore off the paper, lifting the lid. Inside the crisp white box was a necklace. A small pendant with a single rose etched on its round surface hung from a gold chain that glittered in the dim light.

Her lips parted. Carefully lifting it from the box and letting its shiny surface catch the light, Juliette bit the edge of her lip to keep from grinning so broadly. “Noah, it’s *beautiful*. Is that a rose?”

“Mm-hm. I saw it in this little pop-up stand in California and thought you might like it.”

“I do! It’s beautiful. Thank you so much.”

Noah smiled.

Setting the box down on the edge of the banister, Juliette unclasped it.

"May I?"

She handed it to him and then turned around.

Noah then carefully clasped it around her neck, making sure not to catch it on her hair. The pendant stopped just below her collarbone. She grinned up at him.

"Do I do it justice?"

Noah almost laughed. "I think *it* does *you* justice, yes."

"Thank you. Really. It's…I love it."

Noah dipped his head before pointedly looking back out over the ballroom.

She leaned her head on his arm, grinning out over the ballroom. "I can't wait to be out of here."

"Me either," he murmured. "Me either."

Chapter Thirty-Six

Juliette tugged her shoes on, laced them up, and then knotted her hair on the top of her head. Staring toward the door, she pulled it open and stopped short.

"Ah, good timing." Odette grinned, appearing around the corner.

Juliette set her face in determination and squared her shoulders. She had planned on spending the morning with Noah in the gym. Odette coming to *Juliette's* wing couldn't have been good news.

Once they got to the infirmary, after Juliette fought to get free the entire time, Odette took her place against the wall, leaning back with a look of unbridled satisfaction.

Juliette was once again tied down to the table, and only then did she give herself permission to stop fighting. She tried to ignore the seemingly dozens of vials and needles lined up in a metal cart. She tried not to watch Dr. Violet. She kept her eyes glued to the wall opposite her, masking her face into one of stone. She imagined her and Noah down in the gym, tangled together at the end of her bed, him telling her to take things slow and not push herself.

"Alright, Princess, first one," Dr. Violet's voice said.

Juliette's eyes slid closed, and she tried to harness some of that inner strength, even if it only was in her imagination. She told herself she would start training more consistently in the gym with Noah, she'd push herself to go more consistently so Odette wouldn't be able to *ever* touch her without backup.

Juliette heard Odette breathing, heard the soft rustle of fabric as if she were shifting her weight from one leg to another.

Ignoring Odette, Juliette licked her lips. She could feel her self-control, as if it were a tangible piece of string, but she knew it would take the slightest distraction for her to break down in tears or fall into a panic attack. Another pinch made her jump, and she involuntarily jerked back, ripping one of the restraints out of the bed and knocking something to the ground.

"Princess!" Dr. Violet groaned, stooping to the ground for one of the vials that had been resting on the tray beside her.

Juliette tore her eyes from the wall, glancing at Dr. Violet and then at Odette. Then down at her arm that she ripped free. Before she could think about it, she yanked one of her legs up, thrust the heel of her foot into the tray, sending it skittering across the room and crashing into the wall.

Odette flew back. "What's wrong with you?"

"What's wrong with *me*?" Juliette repeated. "What's wrong with *you*?"

Dr. Violet waved one of the guards in, and Juliette drove her entire body into his stomach. It didn't have the same effect as it did in her dream, but the guard was surprised enough to stumble back.

"That's enough! Stop it this instant!" Odette raised her hand, either to slap Juliette or grab her hair.

Juliette caught Odette's wrist mid-swing, driving a

fist into her ribs. The air was forced from Odette's lungs, and she stumbled back, her eyes blazing.

"Why don't *you* come in here and let them stick you with needles then if it's so easy!" Juliette shouted, shoving against Odette and putting just enough distance between them for Juliette to straighten.

Odette almost laughed. "I'm not a worthless little imp, otherwise I probably would."

Juliette didn't take the glare from her face. She wasn't worthless.

Odette glared right back. "Get on with it," she said, shifting her eyes to Dr. Violet. "I don't care what you have to do to her."

Juliette clenched her jaw, wishing she could shove Dr. Violet away from her and tell her to never touch her again. But even if she did that, there were more guards outside at Odette's beck and call who would be more than happy to hold Juliette down.

"I'll need to prepare more of the solution, so I won't be able to finish today," Dr. Violet said, hesitating.

Odette let out a grunt of frustration, wheeling on Juliette. "You little brat! Why can't you do something as simple as hold still and cooperate?!"

Juliette held Odette's gaze. "Because I don't want to be your human guinea pig! None of this makes sense, and everything hurts all the time! I can't concentrate on anything for more than a few seconds, and—"

Odette grabbed Juliette's shoulders, yanking her forward and shoving her into the wall.

"Your Majesty, I must warn you against agitating her!" Dr. Violet cried.

Juliette's eyebrows twitched in a confused frown,

but it seemed to make sense to Odette.

Odette straightened, smoothing the front of her dress. She stepped around Dr. Violet, eyeing Juliette with pure hatred. “You may have escaped punishment this time, but I will not tolerate anything less than obedience from you.”

Juliette lifted her chin.

Chapter Thirty-Seven

Juliette didn't stop running. Her hair flew out behind her like a dark flag, and tears streamed down her face in an endless, gushing river. Her heart was racing inside her chest, slamming against her ribs in a desperate effort to break free. She paused in front of one of the palace's many paintings and yanked hard on the frame. The hidden door swung open, and Juliette darted inside, closing the frame after her. She tripped going up the narrow stairs, catching her hand on the edge of the step.

Pain shot up her arm, but she hardly noticed.

Shoving herself back up, Juliette dashed at the tears clogging her vision and kept moving up the stairs. She didn't make it to the top level of the palace before she had to stop, the sobs wracking her body making it impossible to keep walking. Sinking onto the stairs, cloaked in darkness, Juliette collapsed into herself. She let her frustration and anger and pain out in gut-wrenching sobs, hating Odette for putting her through this, hating herself for not being strong enough to stand up to her, hating the guards at the palace who did whatever she said without question.

Anger clawed its way up her throat. She screamed until her lungs burned from lack of oxygen, until her entire body was shaking so hard she thought she might vibrate through the ground.

With another ear-splitting shriek, Juliette slammed her hand into the inside wall. Again and again, until her knuckles bled. The stone stared blankly back at her, and for a moment she found it cruelly ironic. Odette wouldn't be moved, no matter how hard Juliette pushed back. She could fight until her body was broken, and it wouldn't matter.

Another scream ripped its way out, tearing the insides of her throat, coating it with blood. She shoved herself up from the stairs, darting the rest of the way up to the small room she'd taken to hiding in recently.

There were a few loose boards she'd noticed before. She yanked on them, as hard as she could, reveling in the sound of splintering. One of the boards came loose much easier than the others, and she hurled it across the room. A cloud of dust rose in its wake, but she didn't pause long enough to notice.

Something pricked her fingers, and Juliette looked down to see a splinter had lodged itself in her hand, crimson blood pooling in her palm. She was still shaking, so it took several tries for her to get it out.

By the time she did, her whole hand was smeared with blood. Seas, it was so much blood.

Blood and pain and needles and nightmares.

Juliette sagged against the wall, sliding until she was a puddle on the ground. She wrapped her arms around her legs, crying into her dress and trying to force air into her lungs.

Chapter Thirty-Eight

Odette couldn't remember the last time she was this angry. She could have smacked Juliette. She *should* have smacked Juliette until she'd learned her lesson, given her a beating she wouldn't forget so the stupid girl would *cooperate* and not break into fits every time she got a little scared.

Odette wouldn't have hesitated if she thought it would have done anything, but as it was, the number of tantrums Juliette had been having was already getting too frequent. Another punishment would probably only add to that, and Odette couldn't take the risk.

At least during dinner, Juliette finished her plate and even asked for seconds.

Good. Dr. Violet had expressed repeated concerns that Juliette wasn't eating enough. Odette wasn't sure how that was possible. She saw Juliette without clothes on and was rather surprised at the beginning of muscle definition she could see. The serum must have been working better than she realized.

"If you're finished you should get some sleep. I'm sure you're winded from that little scene today," Odette said, shooting Juliette a mock smile.

Juliette looked up but didn't move. "Little scene? You mean my reacting to your goons holding me down and injecting me with needles?"

Odette shoved away from the table and started

toward the door before her frustration reached a boiling point and she *did* strike out and whip Juliette. "You could at least apologize."

"For what?"

Odette barked out a laugh. "For that display at the lab today! Seas, it was embarrassing for *me*, to have to be told that you couldn't handle a few innocent injections and then watch you fly into a fit about it."

Juliette scoffed. Her eyes flashed. "It wasn't a fit; I couldn't help it. Trust me, if I could avoid being at your mercy, I would."

Odette could only blink. Juliette spoke with such conviction, such confidence. Odette started to say something else, but Juliette flung her napkin onto her plate, stood up, and started for the door.

"You think you can talk to me like that and get away with it?" Odette grabbed Juliette's arm and yanked her back. She told herself to stop, this wasn't good. She couldn't hurt Juliette, not when she needed her alive and well.

Juliette jerked her arm free, taking a step back, her eyebrows darting to one of the guards posted at the door. Her eyebrows had sunk lower on her forehead, and there was hatred in her eyes.

Odette's mind filled with rage, all thoughts of reason flying out of her mind. She moved to grab Juliette, thinking to order the guards to come help.

Juliette yelled, making a lunge for Odette. She would have knocked her to the ground if Odette hadn't grabbed one of the dining room chairs and intercepted her.

"Guards!"

Juliette had kicked the chair aside, her hands

finding Odette's throat. Odette screamed, doing anything and everything to get Juliette off her, but she was surprisingly spry. As slippery and slimy as a snake.

Two guards yanked Juliette up, holding her back even while she kept fighting against them.

"You're out of your mind," Odette growled. Another guard helped her up, but she didn't give him a second glance, stepping closer to Juliette who was growing angrier by the moment.

"And you're a fraud," Juliette hissed. "I'm not your punching bag to take your frustration out on!" she cried, her face red.

"You're exactly what I tell you you are," Odette seethed. She gripped Juliette's chin, digging her nails into her skin, then smacked her face with her other hand. "When I want to hit something, you're a punching bag. When I want to laugh at something, you're the royal jester. When I have a project, you're my pin cushion."

Juliette whipped her leg up, kneeing Odette in her stomach with such force it brought tears to Odette's eyes. The wind was knocked from Odette's lungs, and she coughed several times.

"No, I'm not," Juliette spat. "I know you hate me, and if I did something to you, then I have the right to know. But I know that's not it. I know you're so miserable you have to make everyone around you miserable, and I know you were so desperate for the throne you laced our parents' drink—"

"*My* parents!" Odette snapped. "They're not your parents. You were found on the palace doorsteps—unloved and abandoned!"

Juliette froze.

"They should have left you there to die." Odette choked on another cough, her stomach starting to ache. She was going to kill Juliette. She'd never wished for her death more than she did right now.

But she couldn't kill her. She needed her, at least for now.

"I want you to love me," Juliette said again, calmer this time. "That's all I *ever* wanted, regardless of our blood relation, but you're incapable of that."

"I'm incapable of loving *you.*"

There. The tiniest bit of hurt flickered in Juliette's eyes, but it disappeared just as quickly as it came. She made another attempt to break free, but the guards held her back, steel traps clamped around her arms.

Odette could feel her rage boiling within her, growing hotter and hotter. She couldn't contain it. She drove her fist as hard as she could into Juliette's face, striking one of her eyes. When the guard holding Juliette let go, she stumbled to the ground, giving Odette purchase to rain anger down on her.

Juliette was smaller, but she pushed back, harder than Odette had been expecting. It had been a while since Juliette had fought back like this. Odette had gotten used to guards helping. For the first time in a while, Juliette fought back, and she fought back hard. She bucked and squirmed and screeched, even when Odette had the guards hold her again.

"Take her to her room, lock her there."

Odette, panting, wiped her mouth with the back of her hand. She watched Juliette be pulled away until she'd disappeared down the corridor before sinking down onto a chair and holding her side. Juliette's kick must have bruised a rib.

"Your Majesty, are you well?" one of the guards asked.

"Do I look well? I was just attacked!"

Natasha appeared in the doorway, concern etched onto her otherwise serene face. "Let me help you back to your room," she said, stooping to put an arm around Odette. "Would you like me to have a bath prepared for you?"

"No, I need to see a doctor—a real one. I will also have to speak with Dr. Violet about increasing Juliette's medication or putting her under sedation when we're not working on her."

"I believe, Your Majesty, we briefly looked into that when we first started our research, and Dr. Violet was concerned it would affect her abilities. Less movement would lead to muscle deterioration, and lack of mental stimulation would—"

"Yes, yes, I remember," Odette snapped. "I meant sedate her during her procedures." Seas, if she didn't hit something, she might explode. She almost wanted to hit Natasha, though she had no idea why. She certainly hadn't done anything.

Odette closed her eyes, took a deep breath, and counted to ten. *Let it go*, she told herself. *Juliette will pay. I just need to give it time. We'll see who gets the last laugh.*

With that as her only comfort, Odette stood up and started back to her room.

Chapter Thirty-Nine

Noah shoved the last bit of his sandwich into his mouth before stooping for the box on the ground and stashing it into the small compartment of his ship. This was the last of the food rations he would be able to fit, which was fine. He wasn't anticipating needing more than enough for two weeks of travel time.

His wristlet vibrated, and he glanced at it, Juliette's name flashing up at him.

–I just hit Odette!!!–

He had to read it twice, thinking she must have mistyped something. He started to type a response, three times, but didn't know what to say. He finally ended up going with a simple, *–What?–*

Noah shuddered. Seas, if she *actually* hit Odette, she wouldn't be alive to tell the tale. She must have meant something else. He stood up, glancing at his message again, but she hadn't responded yet. She was probably teasing him.

With an eye roll, Noah started back inside. As soon as he walked in, he noticed right away something was off. There was an air of electricity in the halls, and guards walked quickly past each other, talking. Some smiling, others looking worried.

"Hey, what's happening?" Noah asked, pausing beside Mason.

"Where've you been? Juliette just went after

Odette!"

Noah blinked. "What?"

"At dinner, I was on my way back to the dorms, so I just heard the tail end of what happened, but she attacked her."

"*Attacked—*?"

"Yes! Odette was irritated at something again, and Juliette was able to fight back before Odette's guards intercepted. They both went to their rooms, but supposedly Juliette punched her." Mason raked a hand through his hair. Smirked in disbelief. "Seas, what I wouldn't have given to see that."

Noah took off down the corridor, grabbing his jacket on his way up the stairs toward the palace hallways.

Not so surprisingly, there weren't any guards outside Juliette's room.

"Jules? Hey, you in there?" he asked, knocking.

"Yes!" Juliette's voice immediately replied, pulling the door open.

"When you said you *hit* Odette, I thought you were kidding," he said, suddenly breathless.

Juliette was holding a rag to her face, and she was grinning so broadly it looked painful. "No! I was serious! I am serious."

"Did she do this to you?" he asked, studying her face. He could already see a bruise developing on her eye.

Juliette lowered the rag, no doubt damp with cold water. "Yeah, but you should have seen what I did to her! I swear I heard a rib crack when I kicked her."

Noah walked into the bathroom and grabbed another washcloth, running it beneath the faucet. "Kicked—?"

"She was so surprised I didn't just stand there, but I didn't care. I just kept going. I mean, she always has a few hands to help her, so it was somewhat of an unfair fight, but is anything with Odette ever fair?" She paused to take in a few breaths.

"Here, trade," Noah said with a shaky smile, handing Juliette the new rag and taking the old one.

"Thanks. But *seas*, you should have seen her face!"

Noah tossed the cloth in the laundry chute, not quite sure what to say or do. He raked his hands through his hair, still trying to wrap his mind around the fact that Juliette had *hit* Odette. She must have caught her guards by surprise if she was able to get close enough to strike.

Seas, he was so proud of her.

Juliette sank down onto the end of her bed, smiling through whatever pain she was in. She drew one of her knees up, pulling her dress up just enough to examine it. The faintest bruise was beginning to bloom.

"It felt so good, Noah. I know it was probably really stupid, and she'll make me pay for it again later but…" She pressed a hand to her forehead, looking up at him. "Just to have that satisfaction of letting her know I'm not as weak as she thinks. I *can* fight back, and she does bleed. She's not invincible."

Noah swallowed, surprised at how fast his heart was racing. His mouth twitched in a smile. "You'll have to pull up the security footage and show me," he said.

Juliette almost laughed.

"Are you hurt anywhere else?"

She shook her head. "I mean, a little, but I'm fine.

It was worth it." She almost laughed, her voice growing soft as if she were thinking out loud. Her eyes focused on him once again. "I want to keep working out with you in the gym, is that okay? I don't care if she has to bring in help, I want to be stronger than her. Strong enough to fight back."

"You can come to the gym as often as you want." Another smile tugged at Noah's mouth, and his eyes darted back to her. She'd definitely have a black eye, but he suspected it would be the first Odette injury she would wear with pride.

****

Noah was awake before five.

By seven, he was antsy and eager to get in a workout. Thankfully as soon as he came out of his room, Juliette appeared at the end of the corridor. He smiled, noticing her eye had darkened even more. She didn't seem fazed.

"Hey, Princess. Heard you have a mean right hook," one of the other guards said as they passed. He and the other two guards with him held up a hand and she high-fived them all.

Noah stifled a grimace, but Juliette grinned. "What kind of protein drink do you want?" he asked, pausing by the kitchen fridge.

"Strawberry."

Noah grabbed two drinks—one chocolate, one strawberry—and pointed her toward a quiet corner of the gym where they spent the next hour. Not at all to his surprise, she kept up the entire time and even wanted to keep going. There was something about her being down here that seemed to lift her spirits, and no doubt her encounter with Odette last night had given her a wave of motivation.

"Let's work our way up to a longer time; you don't want to overdo it." Noah laughed.

Juliette reluctantly agreed, downing the rest of her drink.

"How's your knee?"

"Oh, good. I walked around on it a little yesterday, and it seems to be getting better."

"Good." Noah smiled. "Feel like some real breakfast?"

"I thought the drink was breakfast?"

Noah shrugged one shoulder. "It's more of a supplement. What do you feel like?"

Juliette shifted her lips. "I don't know. Nothing specific."

"I'll make what I usually do, and if you want some, you can share with me."

"Works for me," Juliette replied, a smile tugging at her lips. She walked with Noah to the small kitchen, leaning over the island and content to watch him or the other guys working out.

"Can you do a pull-up yet?"

Noah glanced over his shoulder, frowning at Graham, another guard, who was talking to Juliette.

Juliette shook her head. "No."

"Want to try?" Graham jerked a thumb behind him.

"Leave her alone," said Noah.

"Stop being such a jerk, or she'll hit *you* next."

Noah shot Juliette a glare when she laughed. She slid off the barstool and walked back to the gym area and let Graham show her how to do a pull-up. Mason and Luis nearby paused to watch, as did Davis and a few others.

Graham showed her how to hold on to the bar and was poised to help her pull herself up, but she didn't need any help.

"You got guns, Princess." Graham laughed when Juliette did two full pull-ups before dropping to the ground.

Juliette grinned, smacking Graham's hand when he held it up for a high-five. She then trotted back toward Noah.

"Here." Noah slid her plate across the table, sitting opposite her.

She was still grinning, almost mischievously.

"What?"

Juliette shrugged. "Nothing. I just like it down here."

Noah couldn't help smiling. He was just glad she was happy, for the moment.

"When do you work on your ship?" Juliette asked.

Noah shrugged. "Just whenever I find the time."

Juliette took a few bites here and there in between some more random questions and thoughts before Noah finished eating.

"Alright, let me walk you back to your room so you can get dressed."

Juliette nodded, eagerly falling into step beside him and walking with more confidence than Noah had ever seen in her.

Chapter Forty

Juliette twisted her hair around her fingers, brushing the ends along her lips and glancing around the room. There was a fire in the fireplace, and it crackled against the stillness of the air. She glanced up at Odette, surrounded by a handful of guards, military personnel, and Natasha.

"I hope you're paying attention," Odette snapped, glancing her way.

Juliette jumped, immediately straightening.

"What did I just say?"

"That you hoped I'm paying attention," Juliette deadpanned, thanking her lucky seas she thought to glance up at the same moment Odette asked her.

Odette's eyes narrowed. "I meant before that."

"Oh." Juliette glanced down at her tablet. "That you were wanting additional guards sent to House Atworth because there have been—"

"Good. Just keep paying attention."

Juliette pressed her lips together, working to keep a glare off her face. *You don't have to tell me every five minutes. Just go about your business and leave me alone*.

Turning back to one of her military men, a man named Sergeant Glass, Odette gestured to him. "Please continue."

"Yes, Your Majesty. As I was saying, our resources across Demetria are continuing to thrive. We were originally concerned that Fatir was thinning out—"

"Which is why we rerouted resources from Hastings and Canyons, I know." Odette waved a hand in the air. "I know that our resources are *not* dwindling and that we still are able to function. What are our options as of right now to repair the dome?"

"That's…difficult to say," someone else said. A woman, who looked much older than Odette. "I know you're hesitant to reach out to other countries for assistance—"

Odette firmly shook her head. "No, I will not reach out to anyone until I can be sure of certain other—" She stopped herself, her eyes skirting to Juliette.

Juliette frowned. She thought Odette was trying to secure an alliance with France, presumably because she needed financial help. There must have been more to it than that.

She watched with borderline admiration as Odette's face contorted into concentration, mulling over her options. How could she be so thoughtful, so concerned for the well-being of her country, yet so cruel and inhumane to Juliette? Her own sister.

"Natasha? I don't suppose you have anything?" Odette asked, pinching the bridge of her nose with her fingers.

"I do, Your Majesty." Natasha straightened in her seat. "It won't be an immediate solution and will require some long-term investment, but in my international communications, I've discovered that several countries are interested in more of our resources. Demetria is home to several minerals that are either not found in other regions of the world or are only available in limited quantities. Copper-bearing plutons and petroleum reserves, for example. Japan, specifically, is very much interested in funding our mining of zinc. I know it's a trace mineral, but with the right teams we can harvest those minerals backed by Japan, and deal with them."

Odette was already shaking her head. "Japan's money isn't enough."

One of the other women in the cabinet leaned forward. "Is there a reason you don't want to reach out to France before—?"

"Do *not* question me!" Odette all but shrieked.

Juliette jumped, almost knocking over the glass of water on the ground beside her, glancing up at Odette. Seas, did she have to be so dramatic?

"Shut up!" Odette snapped her attention to Juliette. Her eyes were filled with venom.

Juliette froze, though she hadn't said a word. A sharp pain stabbed at the back of her brain, and she winced. Panic started to claw up her throat that she swallowed back down.

Odette hurled her tablet against the far wall with a guttural scream, shoving a maid who chanced to be passing by against the wall. "All of you get out! This meeting is over! I'll figure out how to save Demetria by myself!" Odette's head spun around toward Juliette. "Get out of my sight, you worthless girl!"

Juliette's sternum trembled. There were so many people in the room, but that wouldn't stop Odette from whipping her. Snatching her tablet, Juliette darted through the door. None of the guards followed her.

In the conference room, she could hear Odette still yelling obscenities at guards or the people with her. Something crashed, it sounded like glass shattering.

Juliette slowed, pausing in one of the nooks to catch her breath. She listened for footsteps but heard only silence. Pinpricks tickled the back of her head, and her vision blurred. Juliette crushed her eyes shut, willing the feeling to go away.

Pain fades, she told herself, already preparing for Odette to come after her. Pain faded; it was temporary. She would be out of here soon and would never have to deal with Odette again.

Footsteps echoed off the marble walls, and a rock dropped in Juliette's stomach. She could hear Odette's voice, the low rumble of at least two other guards with her. Setting her jaw, Juliette took off again. She would *not* let Odette hit her when she'd done nothing wrong and had only been doing what she was told. Odette could figure out her own security problems.

Darting into her room, she grabbed Noah's hoodie, put on the simplest dress she could find, and tugged on a pair of lace-up boots that were too big before shoving back through her door and taking off through the back way.

The corridor spit her out into the hall just above the library, which had fewer guards. Not that any of them on duty would try and stop her. Most of them were more than willing to turn the other way when she wanted to be by herself or go on a forbidden adventure. Or when Odette was hitting her.

Only when she was outside the palace walls and in the familiarity of the woods—her woods—did Juliette dare to slow down.

Her tablet was inside. She couldn't override the security code at the back gate. She couldn't run. She was trapped.

Juliette blinked, turning her face toward the sky. She blinked against the tears building, wanting to scream in frustration for all the good it would have done. Glancing around, she wrapped her arms around herself, too terrified to stop moving even though she knew it was pointless to try and hide.

She sighed to herself, looking back up at the top of the dome as she ran. She tried to imagine what Noah's picture of stars would look like in real life.

She couldn't wait until the night of the ball; she needed to leave now. She needed to find Noah, and they needed to leave. Forget the ship, they could make it on foot.

She had just worked up enough courage to move closer to the gates, thinking she could see how many guards were posted there, when something grabbed her arm and spun her around. A sob rose in her throat.

"What in the known universe are you doing out here?" Noah demanded.

Juliette's heart was slamming against her ribs, and it took her a few seconds to catch her breath. "I…I just…"

He raised his eyebrows.

Juliette swallowed against the tightness of her throat. He couldn't know Odette was mad, he hated it when she got mad. "I just…wanted to look around," she murmured.

"Look around?"

Juliette managed a shaky nod, praying he couldn't see the panic on her face.

"Why?"

"Just…because. I wanted to look at the city and see the lights from up here."

The muscles in his jaw worked, and his eyes darted to the city. "It's dark outside, Jules." He sounded relieved, but his voice was low. "You shouldn't come out here alone."

"I know." Juliette looked around, waiting for more guards to appear. Her nerves settled the slightest bit when there was no movement in the darkness. Noah would have known if Odette ordered her to be found.

"I just wanted to go outside," Juliette said again. "I thought maybe if I got away for a little bit, I could stop…my head from hurting."

Noah's face lost its scowl. "What?"

"My…my head started hurting. Like little needles were stabbing at my brain. I don't know, it was weird, and it started when Odette got mad, so I just wanted to get away for a bit and clear my head."

"Is it still hurting?"

"No." Juliette rested a hand at the base of her neck. "No. I'm sorry, Noah. I didn't mean to drag you out here after me."

"It's fine. I'm just glad you're okay." Noah didn't say anything else as they turned up the dirt pathway that led back to the palace.

Juliette chewed the inside of her cheek, pressing a hand to her heart and realizing Noah wasn't in his uniform. He must have been in his room or in the hangar, off duty, which meant he left the palace in a hurry to come after her.

How did she always manage to drag him along?

"I'm sorry," she said again.

"Stop apologizing."

Juliette felt her chest deflate. "Sorry. I mean—seas, I don't—I don't know what to say." She nervously laughed.

Noah slowed. His touch was noticeably softer as he turned her to face him. "What happened?"

Juliette drew a steadying breath, irritated when her eyes watered.

Noah's face immediately changed. "What's going on?"

"It's…it's nothing." Juliette swallowed hard, willing her voice not to shake. Tears spilled onto her cheeks. "I don't know, I didn't—I was fine, taking notes, and then I felt that pain in my head—"

"Who were you taking notes for?" Noah's frown deepened, confused.

Juliette licked her lips, trying to stop the tears. "Odette had a cabinet meeting and wanted me there to take notes so I could retranslate everything back to the House Leaders. I don't know what happened, but she got mad at one of the military guys and started yelling, and then she yelled at *me* and told me to go to my room. Then my head started to hurt."

"You were in Odette's cabinet meeting?"

"Yes. I'm sorry I made you think something was wrong, but I know you don't like it when she's upset and—"

Noah waved a hand in the air. "It's fine; don't worry about it."

Juliette wiped her palm on her face, wanting to keep crying, crying until things were better, until Odette loved her. But that wouldn't happen. "I'm sorry I worried you."

Noah's mouth twitched in a smirk. "Please, butterfly, stop telling me you're sorry. You don't have anything to be sorry about."

Butterfly. Despite the worry turning her mind into a jumbled mess of chaos, Juliette's chest filled with warmth. Chills shot down her arms, and she smiled, the smallest bit of relief washing through her. She swiped at the moisture on her face. "Okay."

"Luckily I walk fast. Are you okay? She didn't hurt you, did she?"

Juliette shook her head. "No."

Noah almost smiled, his hand sliding from her forearm to her hand. She reflexively moved against him, wrapping her shaking arms around his waist.

"I'm sorry I talked to you so sharply," he murmured against her. "I saw you moving quickly outside the palace and thought…well, I don't know what I thought, but I worried something serious was wrong."

Juliette almost laughed, taking a deep breath in, trying to focus on the emotions she could feel. She felt warm at Noah's touch, she felt safe, even if it was just for a moment. Relief that Odette wasn't going to come after her, at least right now, gave her a sense of peace. She felt his arms around her, and she could feel the muscles in his back, and smell the faint traces of the soap he used. Some of his hair tickled her cheek. She crushed her eyes shut. He had always been her safe place, and she hoped he always would be.

Noah pulled back, slowly, deliberately.

Juliette moved to let him go, but his hand loosened around her wrist, dropping almost to her hand. His fingers brushed the top of her palm, sending a spark of electricity up her arm.

She definitely felt *that*.

"Noah," she whispered. She loved him. She'd always loved him, but at some point, that love had turned into something deeper. She wasn't sure when, only that, whether he knew it or not, he held her heart.

Noah's eyes dropped, just for a second, to her lips.

The air in her lungs hitched. He started to move closer, and she thought for one glorious second he was finally going to kiss her, but then he pulled back and rubbed his nose with the back of his hand.

"We uh, we should get back," he whispered.

"Yeah. Yeah, we should." Juliette cleared her throat. She smoothed her hands down the front of her dress, turning and walking with him back toward the palace. She wanted to apologize again for worrying him. He was good and kind and brave and strong, and he deserved far more than being trapped in the palace with her.

No, *because* of her.

"Have you had dinner?" Noah asked, walking around toward the side entrance.

Her stomach immediately growled. "No."

"Come down with me, we'll hang out there for a bit."

Juliette hesitated. "It's late; you weren't asleep?"

"No, I was working on the ship. If you want to come work on it as well, you're more than welcome to. I knew you were busy, so I thought I'd tackle what I could by myself."

As they approached the palace gates, he stooped down again and she slid to the ground with a grunt. The palace loomed in front of her like a forbidding monster that was waiting to devour them. Her feet grew heavy, and she slowed her pace.

"Jules?"

With a shaky sigh, Juliette blinked her eyes clear. Having been outside the palace for the first time in what felt like forever, going back made her feel like a criminal returning to the scene of a crime. Like she was sentencing herself to prison again.

"Just…taking one last breath of fresh air." She took a quick inhale and continued forward. Back into her prison of ice and stone and shadows.

Chapter Forty-One

Something shook her room with such force it woke her. Juliette reflexively tightened into a ball, drawing the blankets around her. Books and glass trinkets fell from their shelves and crashed to the ground. A low cry escaped her mouth as the room continued to shake, the intensity growing with each second.

"Princess!"

Juliette peered out from beneath her blankets. The guard standing outside her room—Luis—burst in, crossing the floor and scooping her up, blankets and all. He moved to a corner of the room and set her on the ground, crouching over her to shield her from any furniture that might fall. One of the screens mounted on the wall crashed to the ground, followed by a lamp on her nightstand.

Juliette instinctively held on to Luis's lapels, having nothing else to hold on to. He pressed in closer, shifting so she wasn't cramped but still protected. She squeezed her eyes shut and said a silent prayer that Noah was okay. There wasn't much in his room that could have fallen and hurt him, and she doubted he was sleeping through all this.

Juliette crushed her eyes shut. *God, please keep him safe.*

Finally, after an eternity, the shaking died down. It seemed like it had been hours, but it couldn't have been longer than twenty seconds.

"Are you hurt, Your Highness?"

Juliette shook her head, letting out a shaky exhale. "No, I'm okay."

"Are you sure?"

"Yes, I'm fine."

Luis waited a solid minute, probably waiting to see if there would be any immediate aftershocks, before standing up and helping her to her feet.

"Can I get anything or do anything for you?"

Juliette started to shake her head but stopped. "Would you just make sure Noah is okay?"

"Of course." Luis inclined his head before moving back outside and closing the door.

Juliette stood up and sank onto her bed, still shaking from adrenaline. She wasn't even sure if, on the off chance Noah *wasn't* okay, anyone would tell her. Why would they bother to report to the princess that one of the guards was hurt?

Juliette drew a deep breath, starting to pick up the things that had fallen. She'd have to ask Daisy to vacuum up the broken glass tomorrow at some point.

Someone softly knocked on her door, and Noah poked his head in a moment later.

Relief washed over her, and she didn't even realize how tense she was until her shoulders dropped. She stood up, darting forward and throwing her arms around him, realizing too late there was glass on the floor and she didn't have shoes on.

He hugged her back. "I'm fine, I'm fine," he said. "Are you?"

"Yeah. More startled than anything."

Noah glanced around at the mess. "Did you step on

anything?"

"No, I don't think so. They're getting bigger each time, it seems."

"Yeah, I know. Magnitude was 6.1."

"Really?"

"According to the news report." Noah brushed his hands together and casting a look around. He held a hand out to her, helping her jump over the mess of glass to the carpet by her bed. She looked at their intertwined fingers. Despite the darkness, she realized he had nice hands. It was an odd thing to notice, but they weren't too big or too small, his fingernails were short but smooth, and there was a small collection of freckles on the back.

"I'll see you tomorrow," he said, stepping toward the door.

"Sleep well," she replied.

Juliette sighed, sinking onto her bed. A part of her—well, okay, *all* of her—wished he'd stay. Or at least kiss her forehead or something. She slid back beneath the blankets, arranging them over her and then watching Noah close the door after him.

Oh well. It was wishful thinking.

With a sigh, she reached for her tablet and checked the status of the quake across the country. It seemed to have been centered in Anadia, so the rest of the Houses weren't as severely impacted.

She was about to snap her tablet back off and try and get some sleep, when she spotted a pile of blankets on the small table beside the door.

Knowing she wouldn't get much more sleep, at least not here in her room, Juliette slid on a pair of thick sweats, grabbed her hoodie and the pile of blankets, and started down toward the garage.

It was almost spooky, being there alone, but it felt good to have the time to herself.

She cleaned out the single cabin, dusting it from the top down, replacing the old sheets and blankets, and sweeping the ground. The bathroom sink still needed to be replaced, but that would have been a bigger job. She checked the sink in the galley, and it worked, so they could always use that.

Once the bedroom was as clean as possible, she moved out into the living area. The sofa was built in, so she beat out as much dirt and dust as she could, then wet a rag and scrubbed at the dirtier spots.

It felt good, cleaning. There was something therapeutic about it. She imagined she was cleaning the crevices of her mind, ridding herself of all the unwanted clutter that consumed so much of her thoughts.

Finally satisfied she'd gotten the interior of the ship in at least livable condition, Juliette collapsed onto the bed. The blankets smelled like hers, and it brought the smallest sense of comfort. Like maybe she could belong here.

She fell asleep and dreamed of unleashing a terror of technological warfare on Odette.

Chapter Forty-Two

Odette told herself, repeatedly, that queens don't run. They walk, quickly, if need be, but never run. The heels of her shoes clicked on the slick, marble floor.

It was almost midnight, but the quake had roused her, and she couldn't go back to sleep until she checked that everything was fine.

With a nervous sigh, Odette rounded the corner and took a series of stairs down into the palace sub-levels where a smaller, hidden infirmary was located. She paused at the door, locked, and punched in the security code.

_Sapphire

Odette shoved the door open and stepped inside. She knew the way without a guard, but it was still strange to be up at this hour, wandering the dark halls, completely alone.

"Your Majesty, I expected you'd be down shortly," the woman behind the counter said as Odette walked in. She stood up, dipping into a quick curtsey and then gesturing to the side. "She's fine."

Odette brushed past her, jogging down the narrow hallway toward one of the three rooms. The largest. There were two nurses inside, one of them picking up things that had fallen on the floor, the other checking on a small figure nestled on the bed.

"She's fine?" Odette asked, shoving the door open.

"Yes, Your Majesty."

Odette didn't take her eyes from the girl lying on the hospital bed, watching her perfect face. Her chest was rising and falling, slowly, steadily, peacefully. A mess of pale blonde hair spilled over the side of her pillow. Her eyelids, lavender beneath the blue lights, remained closed. The machine tracking her heart rate was beeping steadily. She was safe. She was alive.

She was perfect.

Odette pressed a hand to her chest. She didn't know why she thought something might have happened; there had been far worse quakes than that, but seeing Sapphire alive and safe made her weak with relief.

The quakes. They were getting worse. What happened when they were strong enough to shake the palace foundation?

"Would you like to sit with her, Your Majesty?"

Yes. Odette wanted nothing more than to sit with her little girl, her precious Sapphire, forever and never leave. Well, actually, the one thing she wanted more than that was for Sapphire to wake up. To look around, to see the world around her, to run and come to the ball. To live the way she deserved to live, not hidden behind glass walls.

Dr. Violet had better come through with that serum.

"No. No, I can't." Odette straightened. "I have to go, but I want three nurses in here with her at all times, and if anything happens to her, it'll be your head."

The nurse paled but nodded.

Odette turned and walked away, heading back to her room. She didn't know when she'd started crying, only that her face was drenched in tears by the time she sagged against her closed bedroom door. She hated being so powerless. She hated that her soldier program still had so far to go before she could even hope to test the other things it could do.

Taking another series of deep breaths, Odette straightened. She forced herself to go back to bed, knowing she'd need a decent night's sleep before tomorrow.

Because tomorrow she was going to talk to Dr. Violet. It was time to speed the process up, no matter the cost. If it meant more testing, fine. Her country needed defenses, and Sapphire had lived her entire sixteen years of life asleep.

Odette ended up waking by the eight o'clock trumpets. She thought for certain she'd be up before then, but she was grateful for the extra rest. She got herself dressed, not even bothering to call for a maid to come dress her, and then ran a comb through her silky curls. She sent Natasha a ping, asking her to meet her in the dining room.

Natasha made it there before Odette.

"I want to meet with Dr. Violet this morning. I want that trigger implemented by the end of the week," Odette said, crossing the room and taking a plate and the buffet. "Speaking of, I came up with a name for it."

Natasha didn't reply. She waited until Odette had finished filling her plate before approaching the buffet for some breakfast of her own.

"Sagitta. It's Latin, for weapon." Odette took a seat at the head of the black, wooden table.

"I see."

"I want to meet with Dr. Violet this morning, can

you have Juliette ready for me?"

Natasha nodded, reaching for her tablet beside her. "Yes. Is ten o'clock okay?"

"Fine." Odette waved a hand in the air.

"In the meantime, I have some final details for the garden party I'd like to go over with you, if that's suitable."

Odette groaned. As hard as she worked to keep the palace and herself in the news, sometimes she wished she wasn't quite so adamant about it. She wasn't in the mood to be talking about party plans, not when there were more pressing matters, but given that she'd already planned the event, she couldn't back out now.

"What details?" Odette asked.

Natasha gave her a list—the final menu, her new dress was finished being altered and needed to be tried on one more time, and additional horses needed to be brought in for the inspection of the guard ceremony.

Right after breakfast, Odette marched straight to the infirmary. Dr. Violet was there, ready and waiting.

"Your Majesty."

"Progress report," Odette snapped, not at all in the mood for flattery.

Dr. Violet turned her tablet on.

"Have you been able to implement the trigger?" Odette asked, tapping her foot.

"It's in the works. The last time Her Highness was here, I was able to simulate a dream sequence to harness the adrenaline we need to release," Dr. Violet murmured, tugging at her shirt's collar. "I'm working on advancing the affirmations into the serum itself, I'll just need to run a few more tests on it, then on her."

"Fine. I've already told Natasha to have her ready

to come this morning, will that be sufficient?"

"Yes, that will be perfect."

When ten o'clock rolled around, Odette took her place behind the glass window so she could watch without having to sit in that horrible room.

When Juliette was brought in, fighting against the guards holding her as she usually did, Odette almost halted the process so she could beat some sense into Juliette herself.

Dr. Violet didn't seem fazed, so Odette let it slide. She watched with borderline fascination as Juliette was strapped down onto the table, such a contrast from Sapphire, who was content to lie peacefully.

Dr. Violet didn't say a word. She loaded a syringe and very calmly inserted the needle into the underside of Juliette's arm. She had to do it three times because Juliette wasn't relaxing. As soon as the solution drained into her arm, the fight instantly left Juliette. She tried, in vain, to weakly break free, only for her head to drop onto the padded table and her eyes to fall closed.

Odette fought the smile from creeping onto her face. Juliette's suffering was an added bonus to this whole ordeal, and she didn't pretend to regret it.

Odette took a step forward, closer to the glass. She watched as another syringe was loaded, Dr. Violet explaining that this solution would momentarily weaken Juliette's mind, stripping her subconscious of reason and leaving her susceptible to instructions.

Dr. Violet then placed a set of microbes on Juliette's temple that had a series of subliminal thoughts of Noah being threatened. Juliette's need to protect him would, theoretically, surface when that feeling was released into her brain, giving Dr. Violet the chance to see how strong the serum's response was.

"I'd like to leave her here for at least an hour, to let her body go through the rejection process while we monitor it," Dr. Violet said, her voice projecting through the speaker.

"Rejection process?" Odette repeated.

"Her body has been reacting negatively to the serum itself, so I'd like to do it in gradual doses, that way if and when she begins to reject it, we can tone down the strength of it to essentially trick her brain into accepting it."

Odette turned her attention to the screen, though she didn't fully understand. She watched Juliette's brain activity. It was stable. Odette's heart skittered, daring to imagine Sapphire being given the same set of injections, but with the purpose of stirring her brain to wake up.

"I'd like to reintroduce the idea again in two days, and then we can test it," Dr. Violet added.

Odette resisted the urge to pick at her nails. Two days. They'd know in two days if this whole experiment would come of anything.

Chapter Forty-Three

"Are you sure? One hundred percent positive?" Noah asked for the ten-millionth time.

Juliette didn't stop knotting her hair on the top of her head. "I told you; Odette doesn't get up until eight, at the earliest. She's got her stupid garden party today, so it will take her a blessed hour or two to get ready, and the ceremony is at eleven. That gives us at *least* two hours, and at most three. Plenty of time to get to town, scout around a bit, and come back with no one the wiser. There are plenty of guards and maids around her and the gardens, which will take the focus away from us."

"What about the security at the gates? How are you going to sneak past those?"

"Through the one in the back, where the guard towers have a blind spot that we can duck behind while I override the gate code."

Noah heaved another sigh, but he stooped for his hoodie, tugging it over his head. He tucked his gun in the waist of his pants, confident the bulkiness of the hoodie would hide it.

Juliette was dressed more casually than she usually was, wearing a simple pair of pants, one of Noah's old T-shirts that fit him when he was twelve, and her blue sweatshirt. Her shoulder bag was slung over her shoulder, and her hair hung free.

She wanted to go down to the city, and she wanted him to come with her. There were some computer parts she needed and hadn't been able to acquire on her own.

Everything in him told him that was a bad idea. Odette would be furious if she found out, Noah could be fired—or worse, and he really didn't want to think about the "worse"—any number of things could go wrong. After expressing his concerns aloud and Juliette still wasn't deterred, he gave in.

It was just now six, and he thought for a moment to at least tell Mason or Luis that he was going, on the off chance Aaryn noticed his absence, but thought better of it. He wouldn't want them to get in trouble by not saying something when he shouldn't have been leaving the palace grounds without authorization.

"You have your list?" he asked as they started through one of the back entrances to the palace, up into fresh air.

Juliette held up her tablet. "Yes."

Noah shivered, the cold air shocking his system. If he hadn't been fully awake before, he certainly was now. As they walked, leaving the relative safety of the palace, the instinct to pull her back and keep her behind him was strong, but he fought against it. If they wanted to blend in, they needed to act like two normal people.

Not a princess and a guard.

After Juliette disabled the passcode at the gate, they slipped through and were able to make it down to the main city in only twenty minutes.

There was a secondhand salvage shop toward the edge of the city. Noah kept an eye out for a public trolley they could grab, and when he did, they hopped on. Juliette had way more fun than he did. She held on to the side, grinning into the wind, her hair billowing out behind her.

Noah tried to relax, wanting to enjoy the small field trip and getting to spend time with her outside the confines of the palace.

"Is that it?" Juliette asked, jerking her chin toward a small building at the end of the street.

"Looks like it."

"Does this thing stop, or do we just jump?"

"I think we jump." Noah took her hand. "Ready?"

The trolley was moving slowly, so it was easy to stick the landing. As they jogged to the side of the street, Noah didn't let go of her hand. Not because he felt like he had to, but because he wanted to. Her skin was soft, and her hand fit perfectly in his.

Noah held the door for her, and they both slipped through.

The shop was brightly lit, with glass display cases along one wall, and floor-to-ceiling shelves filling the rest of the space. A small check-out desk was at the far end of the store, and one of the light bulbs was burnt out.

"Seas," Juliette breathed.

Noah tried not to laugh. "Focus."

"Right."

Juliette started walking, slowly, through each and every shelf. She never stopped moving, though she sometimes slowed to a crawl. Noah watched her, fascinated with the way she would examine two things that to him looked identical, but to her were worlds apart.

"I don't suppose we have time to stop for coffee, do we?" she asked, pausing before approaching the check-out counter.

Noah glanced at his watch. It was almost seven forty-five. They'd need at least another half hour to get back to the palace. "If we're fast, I think we can make it."

Juliette grinned, carefully setting her basket of items on the counter. She kept her head down, her hair obscuring her face just in case the clerk happened to be paying super close attention. Thankfully her lack of media coverage helped conceal her identity.

Noah handed her his card, loading their purchases into a large paper bag. He'd stash it in the ship, and then she would come down later and sort through everything.

"Thanks," she murmured, handing him his card back.

Noah stuffed it into his pocket, taking her hand with his free one. "Are we good?"

"I believe so."

They started back outside. In the short time they'd been in the store, the city had woken up. People were walking around, shops had sidewalk carts set up, the same trolley was rolling lazily down the street.

"So why the urge for coffee?" Noah asked, glancing around for a coffee shop or café.

Juliette shrugged. "I've never tried it before, but it's always sounded good." She stopped, looking at a small establishment on the other side of the street.

They crossed at the next light, and thankfully there weren't a lot of people in line ahead of them.

"We can get it to go," Juliette said, glancing at her own watch.

Noah cast a glance around. His gaze clashed with

the barista behind the counter, who was smiling almost sheepishly at him. Noah's eyebrows twitched. He glanced down at the front of his sweatshirt, thinking maybe he spilled something on it.

Rather abruptly Juliette took a step back, shock on her face.

"What's wrong?"

"I don't need coffee. Seas, I'm so sorry, I wasn't even thinking." She shook her head, heat flushing her cheeks.

Noah frowned, confused. "What? Why not?"

"Because I don't have…you know, money. It's bad enough you have to front the bill for parts to the ship. I wasn't paying attention."

Noah waved a hand in the air, taking her arm when she turned to get out of the line. "It's fine. I'll buy you a coffee." He was trying not to smile, her sincerity endearing.

"You don't have to."

"I know." He shrugged. "I want to. Besides, I want one now that we're here, and it would be rude not to get you one as well." He took a step toward the counter when the person in front of them stepped to the side.

Juliette's smile wavered, but excitement brimmed behind her eyes.

Noah glanced up at the menu above them. "What do you want?"

She shifted her lips, thinking.

Noah ordered for himself a plain coffee while she deliberated. As soon as both orders were placed, they moved off to the side to wait. Noah's eyes wandered to the window, his stomach clenching at seeing a pair of royal guards meandering down the sidewalk. They didn't appear to be in any hurry or looking for anything specific, but Noah didn't relax until they were out of sight.

Their orders were called, so Noah collected both cups, handed Juliette hers, and then they started back out onto the street.

"So what's the consensus?" he asked, dropping his gaze to her cup.

"It's very strong. I think it needs more sugar, but I like it. I can understand why it makes breakfast better."

Noah laughed. "What are your thoughts on the garden party later today?"

Juliette shrugged. "I'm indifferent about it. I didn't realize there was such a thing as a 'greeting of the guard' ceremony, have you heard of it before?"

Noah shrugged, sipping at his drink. "Nope."

"Odette was saying how Demetria needs more money for the shield, and the only country interested in helping, she doesn't want, yet she's going to shell out money for a party and pointless ceremony."

Noah scoffed. "Figures." He glanced at her from the corner of his eye. "You aren't even a little excited about it?"

"For the garden party?" Something akin to a smile crept onto her face. "Maybe. A little nervous though."

"Yeah? Why?"

Juliette shrugged. "Because we're supposed to each ride a horse through the line of guards, and I haven't ridden a horse in a while."

"You'll be fine, and I'll be riding beside you just in case something happens."

Juliette's eyes snapped over to his. "Seriously? I assumed you'd have to be with everyone else."

He shook his head. “You and Odette will each get a personal guard. I checked the rotation already and traded shifts with Mason, so I’ll be next to you the whole time. Camron Rajaram will escort Odette.”

Juliette visibly relaxed. “Oh good. I’ll breathe so much easier then.”

Chapter Forty-Four

Juliette darted into her room, quickly changing out of her street clothes and back into her nightgown. Her stomach rumbled, and she glanced at the clock. It was only a quarter to eight. She had fifteen minutes until a maid would be up with her dress and do her hair. Her heart was in her throat, but she had made it back safely.

She couldn't wait until they were out of the palace.

While waiting for Daisy to come, she moved to the window and sank down onto the ledge, unable to keep the smile from her face. She couldn't see the gardens from her room, but she had a nice view of the forest.

"Your Highness?"

Juliette glanced to the side as Daisy walked in with a floor-length riding dress in her arms. A brown riding jacket that hung past her knees was draped around the hanger. Juliette's smile warmed. It was beautiful. Easily the nicest dress she'd ever owned.

She stood up, moving to her vanity and sinking down.

Daisy started brushing her hair, working the tangles free. While she was busy, Juliette picked up her tablet and easily accessed Odette's personal program so she could look at the guest list. She even went so far as to check her guards' rotation to see when Noah would be with her and for how long.

She wasn't nervous about the party, knowing Noah

would be there.

Excitement beginning to build, Juliette tried to hold as still as she could. Her mane of hair was dressed with various oils, then laced back in a loose half fishtail braid. Once her hair was finished, she was helped into the dress. A pair of smart leather riding boots completed the outfit.

Giving herself a quick once-over in the mirror, Juliette smiled to herself. She'd never actually dressed up and been primped to this extent. Hopefully Noah would notice. Well, obviously he'd notice since she always wore the same round of dresses, but hopefully he'd *like* it. Hopefully when they parted ways at the end of the night, he'd go to sleep thinking about how much he wanted to kiss her.

Stepping into the corridor, she made her way outside to the stables. A pair of horses were being brushed and saddled.

Odette was already there, dressed in an elegant red and gold satin gown with a slit going all the way up her right leg. She kept arranging the folds of the fabric to show off her long limb.

Juliette fiddled with the ends of her hair, a flicker of envy rising in her chest. Odette was a good seven inches taller, and most of her was legs. She took every opportunity she could to show them off.

"Ah, little sister." Odette smiled brightly, spreading her arms out as if to hug her.

Juliette snapped her eyes up. She stood frozen as Odette embraced her in a way that couldn't have been more awkward if it was staged. Only after catching a glimpse of the press gathered beyond the stables did it click.

The event was being televised. Of course it was. And Odette could be nothing less than the perfect queen and loving sister.

"I see the swelling in your eye has gone down," Odette muttered, a smile still plastered on her face.

Barely managing not to roll her eyes, despite the flutter of nerves that planted itself in the pit of her stomach, Juliette moved back toward the horse designated to be hers and started running her fingers along his shiny coat. Out of the corner of her eye, she watched Odette gracefully mount.

"Your Highness?"

Juliette turned, accepting the hand of a stable attendant. She tried to mimic the way Odette gracefully mounted, but wasn't sure she succeeded.

Once Juliette was seated, another attendant held the hem of her dress so she could swing one of her legs back over without flashing anyone.

She liked riding side-saddle. It made her feel graceful and elegant. She almost fell but managed to catch herself.

"I'm fine." Juliette chuckled. Thankfully the attendant walked the horse out of the stable, so she only had to focus on keeping her balance.

"What's the holdup?" Odette snapped as Juliette rode up beside her.

Juliette stifled an eye roll. *How in the seven seas should I know?*

A guard, dressed in the more formal royal guard uniform, approached Odette. Juliette breathed a sigh of relief, glad to not have to be alone with Odette for very long. As Odette started forward, the guard steered his mount into place just off to the side. Her eyes roved his face, a leer crossing her lips.

Juliette turned her gaze away just in time to see Noah approaching. A smile stretched across her lips, her face warming as he came within arm's reach.

Noah dipped his head, the faintest smile tugging the corner of his mouth as his eyes quickly skirted her dress, then back up to her face. "Your Highness."

Juliette chewed her lip, fighting back a smile. She waited until he turned his gaze elsewhere before casting him a more thorough glance. His pale green eyes were almost white, offset by the dark colors of his uniform and his wavy blond hair that hung just past his jaw. Her eyes darted to the royal seal embroidered on his left shoulder, visible only in certain lighting. A symbol of his rank. She didn't realize he had been promoted, and the realization sent a pulse of pride through her mind.

He kept his gaze fixated ahead as they started along the dirt path toward the courtyard where the rest of the royal guards were lined up. It was a sea of black-uniformed guards. The House leaders and their families had come all the way to the city of Anadia, and the queen's court as well as a few of the higher-ranking aristocrats. They all stood just outside the guard formation, watching with admiration.

Juliette tried to find Lord Atworth. Or more specifically, Atticus. She'd seen him a few times in security videos but had never paid him much attention. She was curious about him now, after Noah said how nice he was. Most of the House Families weren't nice to those beneath them.

Which was odd, because it wasn't like they did anything to earn their positions. Most of them were handpicked by Odette.

Odette paused as the guards moved unanimously aside and formed a pathway.

Juliette centered her attention on the road in front of her.

The Demetrian anthem blared from unseen trumpets, filling the spring air with a beautiful melody that didn't seem to fit with Odette. Polite applause rose from the sidelines. For the first few minutes, everyone's attention was focused on Odette and all her glory. As she and Juliette continued slowly forward, Juliette realized more and more gazes were gradually turning toward her.

Her face growing warm, Juliette looked down at her saddle. Her hands started trembling, and she clenched them tighter around the reins, fighting the urge to scratch at her wrist. Seas, everyone was looking at her—if she in any way messed something up, she'd be in a world of hurt. Odette would be mad, and she'd probably be sent to Dr. Violet right away.

Her horse jerked, and Juliette immediately slackened her hold, her heart leaping to her throat and hammering against the sides of her neck.

Noah's hand gripped her horse's reins, steadying her. "Deep breaths; you're okay."

Juliette breathed a silent sigh of relief. "Thank you," she whispered.

When Odette reached the end of the walkway, she turned her horse around to face both the guard and the spectators. Juliette did the same, stopping just behind and to the side of her sister. When Odette swung out of her saddle, her dress billowing out around her, every single one of the guards brought their fists to their chests in perfect synchronization.

Juliette couldn't help smiling at the meticulousness of their movements, watching as they held their positions.

Odette, however, was already walking away without so much as a backward glance, turning to mingle with the aristocrats who had made their way toward her.

Juliette glanced at Odette, then again at the guards. She scowled at her sister's back. Didn't she realize they were waiting for her to salute back and dismiss them? Though the sun was blocked by the snow, the brightness was still filtering through, and it was quite bright out. Juliette suspected they would stand there forever without being formally dismissed.

Juliette saluted, and they relaxed their stance.

Odette snapped her head around, her attention caught by the movement. She glanced at Juliette, frowning.

Juliette smiled sweetly.

"Your Highness?"

Shaking, Juliette took someone's hand—Noah's—and dropped to the ground, her face growing warmer by the moment. Her legs trembled, and she almost tripped. Her heart was suddenly hammering inside her chest. She felt Noah's hand on her back, but her feet were rooted to the ground.

"Did she see that? Did she see me?" Juliette asked, her voice barely above a whisper, her hands shaking.

"No, she didn't see you do anything."

Juliette sucked in a lungful of air, but her feet refused to move. Seas, what was wrong with her?

"Jules, hey—breathe. You're okay, she didn't see anything." Noah ducked so he could look at her.

"You're okay. Take a deep breath."

Juliette swallowed, nodded, then let the air in her lungs out. Noah nudged her toward a canopy of tables laden with food just inside the gardens.

"I'll be close. Try and have fun," he whispered.

"No promises." Much to her dismay, Noah melted into the background as soon as they entered the gardens. He'd stay with her. He wouldn't be far away.

Juliette looked around for a friendly face, wishing she could have stood wherever he was stationed and just watched. Even if he didn't want to, or couldn't, talk. She recognized all of the members of the court and their families as well as a few of the newly appointed House Leaders.

If she could find Atticus, she bet he would be safe to talk to. As she looked around, searching, she started to grow nervous that at any point someone would look at her and recognize her. Not as their princess, but as the girl who had made it possible for Odette to control them.

Juliette squared her shoulders.

Chapter Forty-Five

Juliette glanced around, involuntarily trying to find where Noah was. Unfortunately for her, he knew how to blend into a crowd.

In fact, she realized as she looked around, she didn't see any guards anywhere, but there had to be more than Noah and whoever escorted Odette. There were easily two hundred people here.

Clenching her hands into fists, Juliette watched Odette flutter around with a grin on her face as though she didn't have a care in the world.

"Your Highness!" a voice said.

Juliette jumped, turning as a middle-aged man walked up toward her. His hair was iron grey and combed back, and he wore an expensive looking suit that couldn't have been very comfortable. Juliette tried to place who he was as he bowed.

"You're looking well, if I may say. It's so good to see you."

"Thank you. I'm happy to be here," she replied, smiling and hoping he couldn't tell she had no idea who he was.

"May I introduce you to someone?" he asked, cocking his head to the side.

Juliette nodded politely, still smiling. She followed him as he started toward one of the tables where people were seated. She sifted through her mind the different pictures of the various members of the court and House Leaders. She was pretty sure he was one of the representatives from House Atworth.

The man rested his hand on another person's shoulder, and the young man seated at the table stood up, dressed in the typical fashion for a member of the aristocracy. His smile deepened when he saw Juliette, taking her in.

Juliette immediately bristled.

"This is my son, Ransom West."

"West, please," the young man said. He smiled, his teeth perfectly straight. He politely reached for Juliette's hand. Unlike his father, West's tie was loosened, his sleeves were rolled up to his forearms, and his jacket was slung casually over his shoulder. "A *genuine* pleasure, Your Highness."

Juliette smiled. "Likewise."

"Why does the queen keep a gem like you hidden away?"

Juliette blinked. Laughing, she hedged. "Um…what?"

"*West.* Perhaps Her Highness would like something to eat?" the man suggested, his eyes hardening.

"Well, it seems to me that if *Her Highness* did, she could ask herself." West winked at Juliette, patting his father on the arm. "Besides, there's an endless string of servants around. That's what their job is, and I would hate to rob them of that pleasure. Your Highness." West dipped his head in half a bow before disappearing into the crowd.

"My apologies, Your Highness," the man said, the muscles in his face taut. "My son is a bit flighty."

Juliette pressed her lips together, not sure what to

say. She politely excused herself and crossed to a table with appetizers. Daring to glance behind her, she saw West mingling with a few young girls who seemed much more interested in touching him than talking to him.

Odette appeared beside her, like a snake slithering through the sand. She looked perturbed as she loaded her plate with several mini cakes.

"Are you enjoying yourself?" she asked, her voice quiet but sharp.

Juliette hesitated. "Yes."

"You seem to be quite the topic of conversation," Odette continued, delicately licking the frosting from one of her fingers. Her lipstick didn't budge.

Juliette paused with a crystal glass in her hand, her eyes twitching. "Me?"

"Yes, you. What I can't figure out is why. I know you almost blew the entire…" Odette waved her hand behind her. "*Thing* back on the horse, so why is everyone singing your praises?!" she hissed, keeping her voice low. Her voice was tense, her onyx eyes glittering with hatred, yet she managed to keep the sweetest smile on her face as if they were in casual sisterly conversation.

Juliette blinked slowly. "I almost blew what thing?"

"The walking down the pathway on the horse! I saw you, getting flustered on the saddle and almost causing a stampede."

"A stampede? With two horses?"

Odette scoffed, stabbing a piece of pastry in a way that made Juliette jump. "Just try not to freak out about nothing again, okay?" She set her plate down and stalked off into the crowd.

"Wouldn't dream of it. That's your job," Juliette muttered to herself.

"Older sisters. Can't live with them, shove them back where they came from, am I right?" West made a show of shaking his head stepping up beside her and filling his glass with more punch. He pulled out a small flask out of his pocket and poured a dark liquid inside.

Juliette's eyebrows twitched. "You have an older sister?"

"No." West scoffed. "But I've gone out with a couple girls with older sisters and…" He trailed off, shuddering. "They're never fun."

Juliette felt her eyebrows twitch. The urge to badmouth Odette was strong, but she didn't want to risk word getting back around.

West jerked his chin. "I take it you don't ride all that much."

With a grimace, Juliette shook her head. "No, not really. I think I've only ever ridden one time before, but it was so long ago I don't even remember."

"Eh, well. You're beautiful, so I doubt anyone was paying attention to how you were riding," West added casually, taking another drink and looking at her over the edge of the glass.

Juliette froze. Did he just call her *beautiful*? She'd never been called that before in her life. He must have been teasing her. "Oh, well, hopefully. I mean hopefully that no one was paying attention to how I was riding. This was more of Odette's thing. I couldn't care less about ceremonies."

"Oh come on, don't tell me I'm the first guy to ever tell you you're beautiful," West said, completely ignoring the second part of what she said.

Juliette's lips parted, but no words came out. No, actually. Noah had called her beautiful before. Or, at least he'd called her pretty. Or that she looked nice. But it was basically the same thing.

West seemed amused, but then he sobered. "Hm. Well, you're beautiful, so don't let anyone tell you otherwise." He winked at her again before downing the rest of his drink and disappearing back into the crowd.

Juliette glanced around, relieved to discover Odette was in deep conversation with a group at the other end of the gardens. Her eyes settled on a tier of cupcakes, and she quickly snatched a plate.

Making sure no one was watching her, she grabbed two of them. Ducking through the bushes, she secured them in a little crevice in the wall and covered them with a napkin.

Chapter Forty-Six

Noah kept a discreet eye on Juliette, watching as she mingled with the various members of the court. She used to always talk about how she couldn't wait until she was old enough to participate in royal social events, but over the past few years, she hadn't shown that level of excitement for public events that she used to.

He could tell she was nervous, but she seemed to be growing more comfortable with the passing minutes. Noah felt the smallest bit of relief. She was slowly coming out of her shell and acting like herself again.

Seas, he hoped getting away from the palace would begin to eradicate all the harm Odette had been inflicting.

Noah's blood started to grow hot when that Ransom character started talking to her, an overly flirtatious grin on his face. When she glanced over her shoulder, making sure Odette was out of sight, his eyes skirted over her dress.

Move along, good sir, Noah thought to himself with barely a concealed scowl. *She's not a party favor you can use and abuse for your own fun.*

Only when he finally walked away did Noah start to simmer down. He watched, invisible, the people walking around. Some were talking, others were sitting at tables eating. Odette was standing in the midst of a small group, all smiles and laughter.

Noah dragged his gaze away from her, trying to find Juliette in the crowd. Through the sea of black suits and boldly colored dresses, it took him a few minutes to find her. The brown brocade dress she was wearing hugged her in all the right places, making her look taller than she was. Her dark hair was hanging down her back, and Noah found himself daydreaming about running his hands through it.

Juliette crossed to one of the other tables laden with desserts and picked up two cupcakes.

A shriek caught Noah's attention, but it was just one of the girls with Ransom. She ducked away from him, and he caught her, shoving a handful of frosting into her face.

"Oh, *gross!*"

Noah looked back across the crowd, but he didn't see Juliette. He was just about to move to a different place when Natasha approached him.

"Her Majesty would like you to take Her Highness away from the party now."

Noah almost frowned. "Where?"

Natasha shifted uncomfortably. "Anywhere but here."

Noah dipped his head. He started toward Juliette, who had reappeared and looked excited about something. Her eyes sifted through the crowd, looking for something. Looking for him. Again.

Their eyes met, and her face lit up at seeing him approach.

"Let's go for a walk, Princess," he whispered.

Juliette's face brightened a little more, and she relaxed into a smile, not even questioning it. Noah guided her in front of him the way she was supposed to be. He tried not to pay attention to the way her dress hugged her narrow waist.

Rounding a massive wall of shrubbery, she crouched to the ground and pulled two cupcakes out from a little nook. They were covered with a silky white napkin.

"I saved you one," she said with a grin, walking back to him and holding one of them out.

Noah continued walking, not pausing to take it from her. "I'm on duty, Princess."

Juliette scowled. "You're not allowed to eat anything when you're on duty?"

"Not with you."

"Fine, I'll eat them both. Will you at least *hold* the second one? Or does that go against your 'on-duty' rules?"

Noah slowed, waiting for her to catch up. He reluctantly took the extra cake, relieved when they entered the woods and left the sounds of the garden party behind.

The air started to grow cooler, and a light breeze rustled the fallen leaves across the moist dirt. Juliette took a deep breath and let it out, tilting her face to the sky and smiling.

Her free hand bumped into his, and he stole a quick glance at her. She was so *stunning*.

He looked down at her hand, tempted for a split second to wrap his fingers around hers, but afraid that even out in the woods wasn't enough privacy.

"So where are we going?" she asked.

Noah shrugged. "Wherever you want."

Juliette frowned. She glanced over her shoulder back toward the palace, then shook her head. "She asked you to take me away, didn't she?"

Noah didn't answer.

"She's never happy, is she?" she asked, forcing a laugh. "I'm silly and embarrassing, she hates me. People *kind of* like me, she still hates me. She's just determined to hate me, isn't she?"

Noah was silent, wishing there was something he could do. But there wasn't anything he could do. There was never anything he could do but sit back and watch Odette rip her apart and then help her pick up the pieces.

Lightly shaking her head, she smiled at him. "I started working on a dress. Back before our *plan*, but I thought I would bring it and finish it anyway."

"Oh yeah?"

"Mm-hm. I had to redo a few spots on the top, but I finally got it. I'll show it to you, if you want."

"Of course."

Juliette's smile deepened, and she leaned into him.

Noah tensed. "Watch the cupcake. Come on." He cocked his head, pulling her toward a patch of clean grass deeper in the woods where they had some added privacy. She pulled her hair over one shoulder, sinking to the ground.

Noah sank down in the space beside her, taking the bottom half of her cupcake when she broke it off. She had mentioned one time that cake was just a holder for the frosting and would oftentimes discard the parts that didn't have any on it.

"I'd eat just a bowl of frosting if it wasn't frowned upon," she'd said, laughing.

Noah, however, was the opposite and preferred there be little to no frosting. They made good cupcake partners.

"What does it look like? The dress," Noah asked.

Juliette brightened, delicately licking the frosting from her thumb. She turned so she could face him, resting her elbow on the log. "It's pale pink, almost white, and has a full skirt with a cinched waist, and ties around my neck. Almost like a halter top, but not quite. I wasn't sure I was going to like it, but I think I do. And it's a really good dress to spin in."

Noah smiled lopsidedly.

"Have you seen Odette's dress? For the ball?"

Noah shook his head, swallowing his disdain for the queen and eating another bite of cake. It had lost some of its sweetness.

"It's so gorgeous, and it's really big and poofy and strapless. And the entire front is covered in diamonds. She looked so beautiful in it." She trailed off, the admiration evident in her voice.

Despite all the things Odette did to her and how much she hurt her, Juliette still wanted her sister's approval. Her sister's *love.*

"I wished she liked me," Juliette murmured with a distracted sigh. "Is that silly, after everything she's done and is still doing?"

Noah's throat was dry. "No, not at all."

"I mean, she doesn't have to *like* me, you know? I get it. We don't have to be super close, and not everyone gets along well with everyone, but…underneath all that she doesn't even *love* me. Just…as a sister."

Noah stopped eating, his heart ripping at her pain. He wished he could say something that would take everything away and make it all better. He wished he had the magic answer as to why Odette hated her so much. But he didn't. There was nothing he could do to fix it.

Juliette exhaled slowly.

Noah turned toward her. "There's nothing wrong with you. There's no reason other than her own wickedness for keeping you locked away, and feeding you lie after lie."

The corner of Juliette's mouth twitched in the start of a smile, but it never quite made it.

"Hey." Noah cradled her face so she'd look back at him. He brushed a tear that spilled with his thumb. "You *matter*. Anyone with half a brain in their head can see that, *please* believe me."

Juliette almost smiled. She automatically leaned into him, resting her head on his shoulder. "I believe you."

"Good." Noah raked his fingers through her hair.

"Maybe once we're gone and she realizes what a great sister I was, she'll miss me," she added with a headshake.

"It would serve her right."

Juliette lifted her head so she could look at him. The inside of her lips were tinged red from the frosting in a way that was majorly distracting. "Thank you. I don't say it nearly enough, I know, but…thank you for being here. For always lifting me up when I feel down," she finished, her voice barely audible. "For running away with me."

Noah gently pinched her chin. A hint of a smile cracked his lips. "I like taking care of you. It makes me feel useful." He shook his head, tucking a strand of hair away from her face. "You are *everything* I have."

Juliette pressed her lips together in a smile. “You’re everything I have, too.”

“Well then we’re a good fit,” he replied, leaning back against the tree.

She leaned back beside him, playing with the hem of her sleeve. “I’m glad you’re here,” she whispered.

Noah sighed dramatically, nudging her with his boot. “Yeah, I know. I’m glad I’m here too.”

Chapter Forty-Seven

Noah checked his alert feed several times as he and Juliette walked inside, making sure the queen hadn't issued an order for Juliette to be brought back to the party. So far no demands had been sent, thank the skies, and he couldn't imagine Odette missing her, so Juliette seemed to be in the clear.

"I thought you were working the party?" Mason asked as Noah walked into the kitchen. His eyes immediately darted to Juliette, and understanding dawned on his face.

Noah didn't bother answering. He reached into the cooler for a few pre-made meals and started heating them up.

"Your Highness," Mason murmured. "I'll, uh, talk to you tomorrow?" he asked, glancing back at Noah.

"Sounds good."

Mason took the rest of his dinner and vanished out of the kitchen.

"He doesn't have to leave," Juliette said when he'd gone.

"He might be going to bed. He's got a weird sleep schedule."

"Oh."

Noah glanced at her from the corner of his eye. She looked tired. He nodded to one of the empty chairs at the table. "Come on, sit down, I'll make us something to eat."

Juliette took one of the empty chairs, drawing a leg up. She was still wearing her dress from the party.

Noah pressed his lips together. "So what'd you think of the ceremony?"

Juliette shrugged. "I thought it was cool, but Odette seemed so disinterested; I don't know why she bothered with it."

Noah laughed. He handed a plate to her, then cocked his head to the side. "Want to eat while we work?"

"Yes please," she replied.

They made their way down to the garage, food in hand. Noah had made decent progress with the engine, and he wanted to start it and see how it paired with the computer system once Juliette had it finished and installed.

"Did you clean in here?" he asked as he stepped into the living area.

"I did." Juliette grinned. "It smelled musty, and I couldn't take all the dirt."

"Looks good." Noah stooped for one of the toolboxes he had spread around, digging through it. He flipped a switch on the control panel, relieved that lights flickered on.

Juliette pulled herself up into the cockpit, sitting in the doorway. Her legs dangled over the side.

She finished her midday snack, then scrambled inside the ship and did some more tweaking on the computer. She said it worked beautifully on her tablet, but the first time she plugged it in, the ship didn't respond.

"How's it going up there?" Noah asked after they

had been working in silence for almost an hour. He moved to the door of the cockpit, resting his arms on the threshold.

"Good. I think I've got it, now I just need to plug everything in and see." Juliette sank back on her heels, reaching behind her for a wire and twisting it into place. The status bar on her tablet was green, so she unplugged her tablet and connected the computer to the ship.

Noah leaned forward.

"So far so good."

Noah grinned. He jerked his thumb toward the control panel. "Should I turn the engine on?"

Juliette dusted her hands together. "Give me one second," she said, checking something on the screen. "Okay, go ahead."

Noah pulled himself into the cockpit, taking a seat at the pilot's chair. He flipped a series of switches, starting the ship's engine, half expecting it to putter and die. It revved to life and held a steady rumble.

Juliette was grinning so broadly it looked painful. "Okay, okay, okay, let me run a diagnostics check," she said, tapping around on the screen. "Looks good. The oil level is low, and the engine pressure is high," she added, looking up at him.

Noah nodded, standing up and reaching for a lever above his head. "I can fix the engine pressure, but we'll have to take care of the oil another time." He jumped to the ground and made a few adjustments on the outside of the ship.

Juliette gave him a thumbs-up. "Better! The solar panels are activated, and I can read them on the computer. Obviously we have no solar charge, but at least they're working," she added, leaning out of the doorway.

"Great. What else?"

"Besides the oil, nothing. The fuel levels are registering as full, which is good. I was afraid the gauge was broken, but it's not." She looked up, grinning. "We're good."

Noah sagged against the ship, relief making him weak. He almost laughed. They did it. Freedom was just around the corner.

Juliette jumped to the ground, grinning from ear to ear. She threw her arms around him, and Noah easily caught her, lifting her off the ground and holding her in the tightest embrace he could. He felt her hands in his hair, her breath on his neck. He set her down, pulling away just enough for him to look at her.

He dipped his head toward her, but instead of kissing her, he rested his forehead against hers, setting her back to the ground.

She swallowed, and he could feel her heartbeat in her neck. "Noah—"

"I can't, butterfly," he whispered, shaking his head. His throat tightened, and he swallowed, every fiber of his body alive with electricity.

She moved one of her hands to rest on the back of his wrist, her blue eyes sparkling. She barely nodded. "It's okay."

Noah drank her in. Her beautiful face, the radiance of her eyes, the flush of her lips, the faintest dusting of freckles across her nose. He shook his head. "No, it's not. If I kiss you…I don't think I'll be able to stop."

Juliette pulled away just enough so she could touch her fingers to his lips. Her eyes flickered up to his.

"Then don't stop."

He studied her face for two and a half seconds before his resolve crumbled. He slid his hands to cradle her jaw, closing the space between them and sealing his lips against hers.

Juliette groaned, gripping his waist.

A galaxy of stars and suns exploded around them. Her lips were soft and sweet, her hair a waterfall of velvet. He reminded himself to pay attention to her body language, coaxing her to keep going, but ever mindful not to take it too far. His hands ran through her hair, cradling her head. Their noses brushed against one another. A tear trickled down her face, turning their kiss salty.

He took a step forward, pinning her against the side of the ship. He held her tighter, kissed her longer. One of her hands moved back into his hair, making a gentle fist. Her other arm wrapped around his shoulders.

"Juliette," he whispered against her lips. He kissed her again, then her jaw, her cheek, her nose, her closed eyelid. He buried his face in the crook of her neck.

She choked on a laugh, drawing in a shaky inhale, unable to keep a smile from her face. His thumb grazed the side of her cheek, trailing over her flushed and slightly swollen lips as he turned his head and kissed the soft spot behind her ear.

Noah captured her lips again, feeling the smoothness of her cheeks, the warmth of her skin against his. She arched into him. One of her hands gripped his waist. The hem of his shirt must have shifted, because he could feel her hand on his bare back.

"Butterfly, let's fly away," he whispered. Noah

wrapped his arms around her again, holding her. His entire body was shaking. He didn't know how long they stood there, together, in the cold garage. It could have been minutes, or it could have been hours.

"I should probably go back to my room and get some rest before tomorrow," she murmured against him.

Noah let her go, glancing at his watch. It was almost one. "Yeah. That's…that's a good idea." He slid his hand down to hers, lacing their fingers together. He kissed her again, quickly, before walking with her back up the stairs, into the main area of the palace.

Chapter Forty-Eight

Odette couldn't turn her mind off. She had hardly slept last night, and this morning she felt no better. She had sent Natasha to collect Juliette and bring her to the infirmary for her next round of injections, but even the prospect of making some genuine advancements to Sagitta was doing little to lighten her mood. She couldn't take her thoughts from her little girl down in the sublevels of the palace. Her little Sapphire—who should have been just as awake and alive as Juliette, except she wasn't.

Juliette, who had taken more of Odette's attention than she should have. Who had taken more of her *parents'* attention than she should have.

Odette worked her jaw until it ached. She'd never forget the morning her mother was alerted that an abandoned baby had been discovered at the palace kitchens.

With it being less than a month since her own granddaughter had been born and then immediately hospitalized, Odette would have thought her parents would understand. They didn't *need* another baby. The royal family was fine as it was.

"It's not about us being 'fine,' Odette," her mother, always so flighty and self-centered, said softly after one of the maids had brought the abandoned baby into her mother's bed chamber.

Odette couldn't believe it when she'd been told, so she had to drag herself out of her own bed to see for herself.

"No, it's about you still not being happy with just *me* as your daughter," Odette spat, shooting a glare at the squirming baby her mother was bathing in a basin of warm water. Which was ridiculous given that she looked clean and healthy. It was evident she had been fed and taken care of.

Pain had flickered across her mother's face, an image Odette had seared into her brain to this day, but she didn't care. Her mother was cold and heartless to even think of letting a street orphan into the palace and parading her around as a princess.

"My Sapphire is lying downstairs with tubes stuck in her! She's struggling to stay alive, and you're wanting to adopt another baby?! This one is not a newborn, she's at least six months old. They'll be the same age! You think I can't see what you're doing? You're trying to make me forget *my* baby!"

"No one is trying to make you forget Sapphire," her mother murmured softly, picking the baby up and wrapping her in a blanket. She bundled her so perfectly and then set her gently down in a cradle. She walked around toward Odette. "We can have two new babies. They don't have to compete with each other."

Odette yanked away from her mother. "And they won't! Sapphire is a royal born princess, while that thing is *nothing* and a no one!"

"Odette, she's someone's daughter. Maybe a young girl who was in your position, only because she wasn't born into the privilege of having a palace, couldn't keep her baby and had to give her away."

"People who can't afford to make mistakes should be more careful." Odette raked her fingers through her hair, her anger growing. She wished her mother would leave, just for a minute, so she could hurl the baby out the window. End her life so there wasn't an issue to be had. It would be quick and painless—seas, she wasn't completely heartless—so then her mother's attention would be given solely to Sapphire.

"Perhaps."

Odette scoffed.

"Why don't we go down and sit with Sapphire for a while? Just the two of us? I have a new blanket and a headband I bought for her." Her mother opened one of the dresser drawers and pulled out a few neatly folded baby garments.

Odette grabbed them and hurled them into the fire. "Oh you'd part with your street spawn long enough to visit your granddaughter?"

Her mother's face changed, turning from sympathetic to disappointed. *Disappointed*! As if Odette was in the wrong, not the other way around.

"You're just as bad as *he* is," Odette hissed.

"Odette—"

"It's not enough that I have to endure being abandoned—" She caught herself. She never told her mother of her secret love or how quickly things had escalated. How quickly he'd cast her aside the moment she told him she was carrying his child.

The look of sympathy on her mother's face only angered Odette further.

She banned both her parents from setting foot in Sapphire's room, ordering any palace staff to refuse entry to them. Which, she realized now looking back on it, she didn't really have the authority to do. But they listened. Her parents never saw Sapphire.

Never got to hold her or play with her or see her run.

Now, just sixteen years later, Juliette was still here. Still taking attention away from where it should have been, still mocking Odette with her very existence.

It was a pain no one should have to bear, yet Odette bore it. And she bore it well. She would take her suffering and turn it around for the good of the kingdom. She would make use of Juliette.

"Your Majesty?"

Odette jumped, turning as Natasha walked in. She looked uncomfortable.

"Her Highness is being prepped and is almost ready for the first trial."

Odette straightened. Stood up from her vanity. "Good. I want to watch."

Natasha bowed, waiting until Odette had walked through the door before following after herself.

"How is she doing?" Odette asked. She hoped Juliette was just as miserable as she always was.

"She's doing fine."

Odette scoffed. "No thanks to that guard, I'm sure."

Natasha smiled sympathetically, but she said nothing.

The entire walk to the infirmary, Odette thought of Sapphire, hoping she was close to opening her eyes for the first time in her life.

Chapter Forty-Nine

Odette was standing on the other side of the glass, her hands clasped in front of her. Anyone who was watching would have thought she was completely indifferent, but Juliette knew she was simmering beneath the façade. She only ever came to the infirmary with her when she wanted to talk to Dr. Violet. But now she refused to step inside the room, instead opting to stay and watch through the glass window as if Juliette was an animal in a cage.

Juliette crossed her ankles, swinging her legs and chewing her lip. Her eye was back to normal, thankfully.

Dr. Violet walked in a moment later, pushing a cart of vials in front of her.

Juliette glanced back at Odette, holding her gaze when Odette rolled her eyes. It probably went unnoticed by Odette, but Juliette wanted her sister to know she wasn't afraid. Even though she was starting to tremble.

"Did you do those tests I gave you last week?" Dr. Violet asked, tapping on her data tablet. She looked irritated. Well, more so than usual.

Juliette licked her lips. "Yes."

"Every day?"

"I said yes," Juliette drawled.

"Good. I know you don't like needles, but we have

to do at least three today. I'll try and do them quickly, but if you hold still and relax, it will go by faster."

Juliette swallowed, blinking the moisture from her eyes and swallowing. She forced a nod, imagining her and Noah outside his ship again. The way his hands felt on her face, on her waist. The press of his lips against hers.

Dr. Violet grew silent as she loaded a syringe with one of the liquids and turned toward Juliette.

Juliette's vision started to blur, and she dug her fingernails into her palms, forcing air into her lungs. Already her vision started to speckle, the back of her head feeling like it was falling asleep. *Breathe, breathe, breathe*, she told herself, over and over again.

Dr. Violet grabbed her arm and inserted the needle into the soft side of her forearm.

Juliette barely stifled a groan, the edges of her vision turning white.

"You do this every day, Princess, just calm yourself, and we'll be done soon," Dr. Violet said as she tossed the needle into a hazard waste basket and reached for another one.

"I'm perfectly calm," Juliette retorted, jerking her arm back when Dr. Violet withdrew the needle.

Two guards stepped forward, and each one grabbed one of Juliette's arms, forcing her back.

Juliette stifled a groan as an additional needle was inserted into her other arm. She winced, a dull ache spreading up her shoulder and down her spine. With one last final attempt to twist free, Juliette let out a cry, but the guard's hold remained strong.

Dr. Violet withdrew the needle. "That wasn't so bad, now was it?"

Juliette swallowed, forcing air into her lungs. She couldn't find the will to respond. The edges of her vision were speckled with stars, and pins tickled her fingertips. A dull ache started to creep up from the base of her neck.

"I'm going to say something, and I want you to tell me the first thing that comes into your mind, understand?"

"I…I do." Juliette's body started tingling, and she forced her eyes open. She shivered against a wave of fear, rubbing her palms against her eyes.

"Keep your hands down."

Juliette jumped at the sharpness of her tone, but she silently obeyed.

"*Bezopasny.*"

"Safe," Juliette immediately replied, the strange word filling her mind with the picture of safety. She and Noah, sitting together. Noah holding her. Protecting her, laughing with her. She wished Noah was here with her right now. Dr. Violet wouldn't do anything she didn't want her to if Noah was there. He'd protect her.

"*Yazyk.*"

"Language."

"*Pet.*"

Juliette almost smiled. "Sing." Noah told her once that she sang beautifully. She didn't remember consciously trying to get his attention or make him take notice, but he did.

Dr. Violet looked pleased.

"*Ocjraniath.*"

Juliette was silent, a slow breath leaving her lungs. Her mind went blank, an ache pulsing behind her eyes. "Um…"

"*Ocjraniath.*"

Something pricked Juliette's brain, and she cringed, pressing her hand against her forehead. *Ocjraniath.* She knew that word, though from where she wasn't sure. "Guard?"

"Good."

A headache had started at the base of her head, and Juliette closed her eyes against the harshness of the lights. The tissue paper crinkled beneath her as she bunched it in her fingers.

Dr. Violet started loading another syringe.

Juliette recoiled, trying to back away. "Wait, wait, wait, you said—"

The two guards appeared again, holding her still as Dr. Violet grabbed her arm and thrust the needle into the crook of her elbow.

Juliette clenched her teeth together as tears trickled down the side of her face. She had to close her eyes when Dr. Violet attached several microbes onto her arms and temples. The computer tracking her brain functions and heart rate started beeping faster, and she swallowed against the panic she felt rising.

"Your Majesty?" Dr. Violet turned to the window.

Odette nodded once, and the glass turned into a one-way mirror. Juliette was staring at herself, sitting awkwardly on the exam table wearing nothing but a thin gown. Her skin looked deathly pale under the light, and she cringed.

The computer mounted on the wall in front of her flashed a set of foreign text.

Ной в опасности

Juliette sucked in a breath, the headache spreading across the back of her head up to her eyes. *Noah is in danger.* She could hear the machine tracking her heart going berserk, and she recoiled against a flash of pain.

"Juliette, what are you thinking? What's going on in your mind?"

Juliette was silent. Her chest rose on its own accord as her lungs drew in a deep breath. Another sharp pain pricked the back of her head, and her eyes watered, her neck arching to make it stop. A shrill ringing made her want to slam her hands against her ears, but the tubes prevented her from doing so. Tears welled up in her eyes, and when she blinked, they spilled over.

"It's…he's…"

"Juliette?"

Additional tears trailed down her face, and she shivered. Her eyes settled on the back half of the room, which had been stripped of furniture and now had five guards standing at attention. Had they always been there?

Goose bumps rose on her arms.

"W-what's happening?" Juliette asked, her voice beginning to tremble. Tingles of fear crept up her throat, and she wanted to crawl into a hole and hide. "Where is he?" She blinked, and she shivered, wrapping her arms around herself. The urge to run and escape crawled up her throat, and she fought against the urge to scream. "Did I pass the tests? Did Odette hurt him?" Her voice broke on the last word.

If Odette was upset, she'd hurt him.

"No. But I need you to listen to me very carefully," Dr. Violet said slowly. She lowered herself onto the stool, rolling closer so she could look right into Juliette's eyes. There was a cruelness in her gaze. "See those guards?"

Juliette turned, glancing at the five men again, confused. “Yes.”

Dr. Violet smirked. “*Noy vie opasnosti.*”

Juliette shrieked, arching her back as the pain from her head exploded down her spine.

Noah was in danger.

Shaking her head, her hands formed fistfuls of her hair, and she stumbled from the table, all coherent thoughts vanishing from her mind. She had to get to him, she had to save him.

Her eyes snapped up, filled with a hatred she had only felt once. She screamed, a bone-chilling, blood-curdling cry, before launching herself at the guards the way a tiger would attack her prey.

She could tell that the guards were more surprised than anything, but by the time she reached them, it was too late. Juliette yanked a gun out of someone’s holster and shot two, point blank, before a third managed to kick the weapon out of her hand. She grabbed his wrist, twisting his arm until he roared in pain before kicking his arm the wrong way.

With another shriek, Juliette thrust her fist into another’s face and wrapped her arm around his neck. She thrust her heel into the fourth’s stomach, using the momentum to propel herself into the air and gripping the fifth around his neck. With a powerful jerk, she snapped his neck, and he fell to the ground.

Dr. Violet took a step toward the glass. “Your Majesty, we should—”

“No.” Odette’s voice snapped back as Juliette efficiently took down the last two guards. As she landed back to the ground in a crouch, ready to spring toward her next nonexistent victim, Odette’s voice came out again over the PA system.

"*On vie bezopasnosti*."

Juliette's eyes rolled back, and she collapsed to the ground.

Except she didn't fall to the slick, tiled ground of the infirmary. She fell to the soft, carpeted floor of her room. She didn't remember making any sound, but she must have.

Her door flung open, and the guard standing outside her door burst in, weapon drawn.

Noah. He was in danger. He was dying. Odette was going to torture him.

"Don't hurt him!" Juliette shrieked.

The guard rushed forward, pointing his gun around the room, but he was looking for a threat in the wrong place. They were after *Noah*!

"What happened, Princess?"

Juliette tried to tell him to go make sure Noah was safe, but nothing came out. She was crying too hard, and she couldn't figure out how to form the words.

The guard paid her mindless babbling no mind as he felt her arms for a wound that wasn't there and then searched the room. Another guard hurried in at her continued screaming.

"Call Noah, get him up here," the first guard said.

"*NO!*" Juliette shrieked. "No, no, no—leave him alone!" she called. "Don't hurt him!"

"It's okay, Your Highness, no one's going to hurt you or anyone else. Are you in pain? Did something happen?"

Juliette shook her head. She wanted both of them to leave so she could run to Noah's room and make sure he was okay, but she was afraid that she would find his room empty and abandoned and covered in blood.

"Are you in pain?" the guard asked again, sinking beside her and taking her shoulders.

"No—he's—in—danger," she hiccupped. "I have to get to him before Odette—"

"Who's in danger?"

A third guard darted inside.

It was Noah!

"Jules? What happened? What's wrong?" He was in front of her, deftly feeling her arms and looking her over for any signs of injury.

Juliette tried to respond, but sobs wracked her body at seeing him alive and unharmed. She fumbled to grip his hands, but they were still moving over her. He thought she was the one hurt.

"Talk to me, butterfly; what's happening?"

Juliette found it hard to take a breath. "They…were going to kill you—I tried to stop them—there were too many. And Odette knew, and she just *stood* there, and he…he *touched* me!" She tightened her arms around him, trying to ward off the unseen danger simply by being closer to him. The room was shaking so hard she thought the ceiling might collapse. But wait, no, *she* was shaking.

"Who touched you?"

"I don't know, I couldn't see him, but I…" She cried harder, almost coughing. "I could feel his hands. You have to run!" She buried her face in his shoulder while simultaneously thinking to push him away. She sobbed against the pain in her sternum, trying to fold into an even tighter ball.

"Juliette!" Noah shook her—hard.

Juliette let out a cry of pain, his thumb digging into

a tender spot on her arm.

Noah either didn't notice or ignored her. "Wake up; you're dreaming. I'm fine, there's no danger. It was just a nightmare—"

Desperation made Juliette cry harder. Her limbs turned to jelly, and her head fell back, her neck a wet noodle of uselessness. She had to warn him. He needed to run. "I'm not dreaming—they were going to hurt you! There were…so many…and you were *there*, you said it was beautiful when I sang…and we were safe…" She squeezed her arms tighter around him, tears streaming down her cheeks and her face growing hotter.

"We *are* safe." Noah's fingers gently moved the neck of her shirt aside, looking at the bruise on her shoulder. He pulled back ever so slightly, frowning. "Is this from Odette?"

Juliette's head twitched. "No, it's from…" She trailed off, tears still streaming down her face. "It's from one of the guards. The guards who were going to hurt you. He…he hit me."

Noah's face relaxed ever so slightly, though why, Juliette didn't understand. He let her go only to cradle her face. His voice softened as he continued, "It was a nightmare. A very realistic one, but just a nightmare. There's no danger, no one's trying to kill me."

Juliette shook her head, pulling him back, frustrated he didn't believe her. It wasn't a nightmare. It couldn't have been. It was so *real*. The fear of knowing he was going to die, the desperation of wanting to save him. How could her mind trick her into something that intense and terrifying?

"Look at me, butterfly." Noah turned her face back

up to meet his gaze. “It was just a nightmare.”

“No, it wasn’t!” She glanced to the side, her eyes darting around her room. *Her* room. The computer sitting on her desk, her Bible resting on her nightstand, her bed, her window…the black sky pressed up against the glass with no stars to keep it up where it was supposed to be.

“See? No danger.” Noah tucked a strand of hair behind her ear, following her gaze around.

“It wasn’t a nightmare,” she said again, wiping her nose with the back of her hand. She glanced back down at the bruise forming on her shoulder, and she shuddered, remembering the weight of the impact. Remembering icy fingers touching her leg, her chest, her waist. Even as she thought it, the memory started receding into the back of her mind.

“You probably hit it when you fell,” Noah murmured.

Confusion muddled her thoughts. “I’m…I’m not crazy, Noah, it just…it was so *real*,” she whispered, shivering as additional tears trickled down her face. He didn’t believe her. She knew it. He never believed he was in danger; he was always concerned for *her*.

“I know. I don’t think you’re crazy. Take a deep breath. You’re okay.”

Juliette shook her head, forcing air into her lungs. She bunched her fists into her hair until her scalp ached.

Noah gently worked her hands free and pulled her against him again, raking his fingers through her hair in a gentle contract. She snaked her arms around his waist, forcing air in and out of her lungs and wishing she could fall asleep wrapped in his arms. He held her for several minutes, letting her calm down, before he gently pushed her away so he could look at her.

"I need you to try and remember one thing."

Juliette looked up at him.

"Did someone touch you?"

Juliette blinked. Yes. No. Maybe. Her eyebrows sank in concentration, and the effort gave her a headache. Another tear trailed down her face, and she licked her lips. "I…I don't know," she murmured, squeezing her eyes shut. She looked at him, despair clouding her face. "I don't know. I think…" She hesitated, her shoulders sagging. "No, I guess not."

Noah didn't seem overly appeased, but he managed a slight nod. "Okay, just keep breathing." He pulled her back against him, shifting one of his legs around her so she was wrapped in safety.

Juliette crushed her eyes shut, sucking in another breath. Her heart kept thudding against her ribs, seeming to grow faster and faster even as the details of the nightmare slipped away, leaving only a cold fear in its place that she tried to ignore. She kept her eyes closed, moving her hand to Noah's wrist.

"You went to the doctor's yesterday, that's probably what brought on the nightmares," Noah murmured.

Right. Yesterday. The infirmary. The endless number of shots and strange liquids, even more so than normal. Odette was there, that she remembered.

Juliette tightened her arms around Noah, even as her body began to convulse all over again. Her heart was beating too fast. She could feel it in her throat, in her brain, in her eyes. Her arms twitched. Noah's arms tightened around her.

"Jules, you're okay. Hey, breathe. Juliette, look at me."

Juliette's vision turned hazy, a mixture of darkness and light blurring in front of her face. Black specks filled her vision, and she couldn't breathe. A hand reached inside her, crushing her heart, shattering her spine.

"Juliette!" a voice, deep and frantic, echoed in her ears. She could feel something warm on her arms, on her face, around her legs.

Then, there was nothing.

Chapter Fifty

Noah paced the length of the hallway outside his room. He hadn't slept for the rest of the night, not after what happened. He wasn't sure if it was a seizure or an extreme panic attack. Whatever it was, it had caused Juliette to shake so hard he was afraid she would hurt herself. He managed to keep her relatively contained, but she ended up passing out, which, at the time, he had almost been grateful for.

She'd been under observation at the infirmary, thankfully by Gr. Greene, not Dr. Violet, for almost four hours. Noah wasn't sure what was going on, and he doubted he'd be told.

Reaching the end of the hallway, he started back down the other way. He wished Mason was awake, if nothing else for someone to talk to and think out loud with.

Noah strung a hand through his hair, sinking back against the wall and dropping his head into his hands. She had to be okay. She had to be. It wouldn't be fair, after everything that happened, for her to die or be bedridden for the rest of her life.

Noah finally stood up, starting toward the gym and needing to let out some of his pent-up rage. He headed straight for the punching bags, not even bothering to wrap his hands.

"Hey, Noah."

Noah didn't even turn around. It was Meyer, and he was not in the mood. "Not today, Meyer," he snapped.

Meyer didn't take the hint. He came up to Noah, smacking his shoulder. "Come on, man, it's—"

Noah wheeled, slamming Meyer against the wall, wrapping his fists around his shirt. "I said not today," he seethed.

Meyer didn't push back. "I wasn't going to start anything."

Noah huffed.

"Your girl's in the hospital. You're upset. It's okay. I'm sorry."

Noah waited for the punch line, waited for him to jab at him, but he didn't. There was no mocking in his face. Noah took a step back, letting Meyer go. Meyer tugged his shirt down.

"If you, you know, need anything." Meyer shoved his hands into his pocket, jerking his shoulders in a shrug.

Noah worked his jaw. "Thanks."

Footsteps caught their attention, and they both turned as Mason jogged into the room. "I just heard. What happened?"

Noah shook his head. "I don't know. She…she had a nightmare. Luis was on duty, thank the skies. She was panicking because she thought I was in danger—I mean really panicking—and then…I don't know, she just kept getting more and more worked up, and then…she passed out. Or had a seizure. I don't know. She stopped breathing, but her heart was racing." Noah turned his face to the ceiling, blinking his eyes clear.

"Is she stable?" Mason asked.

“I think so. But, I mean, no one will tell *me* anything, so I have no idea.” Noah filled his lungs to the bursting point, then let the air out in a sigh.

“I bet I could get Daisy to find out,” Mason said, backtracking out of the room.

Noah took off after him. They didn’t get very far before Noah’s wristlet vibrated. He stopped, frowning.

“What’s wrong?”

“It’s Natasha. She’s calling me to the infirmary.”

“Maybe Juliette’s asking for you.”

Noah darted back to his room, quickly changing into a uniform and then tearing up into the palace, toward the infirmary. He slowed, pausing to catch his breath and steel his face into stone, before continuing forward.

Natasha was pacing outside the doors, worry plastered on her face. Odette was nowhere to be seen.

“Is she—?”

“She’s fine. She hasn’t woken up yet, but she’s breathing on her own, and they were able to get her heart rate back to normal.”

Noah dragged a hand down his face. “Skies above.”

“I already made a report to Odette, but she won’t see it until she gets up, so you have a few hours if you want to go in and sit with her.”

Noah wasn’t sure why Natasha was being so nice, and in all likelihood, it was some kind of trap, but now all he was concerned about was making sure Juliette was okay. He took a step forward, relieved when Natasha didn’t follow him.

Juliette’s door was open, and she was asleep. A white blanket was tucked around her. She was still wearing her nightgown.

Noah hesitantly took a step closer, not wanting to startle her. He rested a hand on her wrist, lightly grazing her skin. "Hey, butterfly. I'm glad you're all right. Don't push yourself, okay? Get as much rest as you can."

Juliette barely stirred. She almost groaned, her eyes blinking open.

Noah pulled the wheeling chair over, sinking down beside her and keeping his hand on her wrist.

Juliette's eyes fluttered open. Her head immediately lolled to the side, looking at Noah. She almost frowned, pulling her hand back. "What are you doing?"

Noah blinked. Cleared his throat and then nervously smiled. "I just wanted to make sure you were okay."

Juliette scrambled to get up, almost falling off the bed. "Get away from me! I didn't do anything!"

"I know, it's okay. Odette's still asleep. It's only five—"

"Who are you—what are you doing?! *Get away from me!*" Juliette shrieked, backing against the wall, disrupting the curtains at the window.

"Jules—"

Natasha appeared in the doorway, her eyes wide with alarm. "Juliette, what's wrong?"

Juliette's eyes darted between Natasha and Noah. "Who—who are you?" Tears welled in her eyes, spilling onto her cheeks when she blinked. "What's happening?"

Noah's heart stilled. He could only stand frozen, though he locked eyes with Natasha, who looked equally concerned. She opened her mouth to say something, but Juliette let out another half-hearted cry, sinking to the ground.

Noah wanted nothing more than to go to her, to comfort her and remind her she was safe, but she was still looking at him like she was afraid of him. Like she had no idea who he was.

The door opened again, and this time it was Dr. Greene who walked in.

"Princess, are you doing okay?" she asked, carefully. "I heard you yell."

Juliette shook her head, still crying.

"What's going on?" Dr. Greene crossed the room, crouching down beside Juliette. She spoke gently, as if worried she would frighten Juliette by speaking too seriously.

"I don't know—I don't know what they want." Juliette shifted, pressing the back of her hand to her mouth. "I didn't…I didn't do anything."

"I know." Dr. Greene looked over at Noah and Natasha. "Could we maybe give her some space?"

Noah could only blink, dumbfounded. He swallowed, turning from the room and walking back out. Natasha was right behind him.

"It'll go away. Whatever's confusing her, it'll go away, and everything will come back to her," she said.

"What is Dr. Violet doing to her?"

Natasha opened her mouth to reply, but Odette appeared around the corridor. She at least had the decency to look mildly concerned.

"Your Majesty." Natasha dipped into a bow.

"What in the skies is happening?" she demanded. "I got your alert, and it woke me. What's wrong with her now?"

"She had another seizure, it would seem," Natasha replied.

Odette sighed.

"And, as of right now, she can't remember…anything, from the looks of it."

At that, Odette's expression shifted. "What?" Her eyes shifted to Noah, recognition crossing her features. "She can't remember you?"

"It doesn't appear so, Your Majesty," Noah replied.

Odette was silent for several seconds. For once, she was at a loss for words. "Well, it…it's probably just temporary. All the other effects have been," she added, glancing at Natasha. She waved a hand in Noah's direction. "You can go."

Noah bowed, then turned and started down the hallway.

Chapter Fifty-One

Juliette's head hurt so badly. She couldn't stop crying, even as Odette walked in and demanded that she get it together and stop acting like a baby.

"My…head…I can't…think…" Juliette sobbed, tears trickling down her face, her nose running.

"Then stop thinking!" Odette cried.

"Your Majesty, I might suggest we give her some space to…to let her brain rest," another woman said. Another doctor, though Juliette had no idea who she was either. She barely remembered Natasha, only after Odette reminded her.

Juliette's brain felt like it was being squeezed. It was making her nauseous.

Odette, for some reason, listened to the new doctor. She crossed her arms over her chest. "Then what do we do? How do we fix this? If she can't remember anything, she can't be triggered!"

"That's not necessarily true. The trigger is just meant to create an emotional reaction so that Sagitta will be activated. If I've implemented everything correctly, which I believe I have, it won't matter."

Odette still didn't look happy.

"Trust me, Your Majesty, this isn't a setback. I mean, it is for *her*, but—"

"I don't care about her. I need this serum to work. If it works and memory loss is a side effect, then that's a hit we'll have to take. Can we test it again and see if it still works?"

The other doctor—Dr. Violet, Juliette thought Odette called her—hesitated. "I would prefer to run some tests and see what's going on first."

Odette shook her head. "Fine. Do whatever you have to do, but I want to try it again."

"We will. Your Highness, why don't you come on back up on the bed, and let's see if we can make you more comfortable?"

Juliette would have laughed if it didn't hurt. They were all talking as if she wasn't there and were now going to treat her like an idiot? She didn't have the strength to resist and let herself be pulled back onto the bed. She was barely aware of Dr. Violet checking her heart rate, then sticking something on the side of her head that connected to one of the computers. A light shone in her eyes, causing her head to pound even harder.

She barely managed to lean over the bed before throwing up.

Finally, after what felt like hours of being poked and prodded, she was left alone. Natasha walked with her back to her room, and Juliette collapsed onto the bed. She tried to take in her surroundings, tried to find something that struck a chord with her, but everything was new.

New and different and terrifyingly unimpressionable.

Trembling, Juliette raked the hair away from her face. She stood up again, moving to the window and peering out into the trees below.

She thought something fluttered in her

peripherals—a butterfly?—but it disappeared so quickly she thought she must have imagined it.

Butterfly, let's fly away.

The voice sprang unbidden into her thoughts, a needle to her brain. Juliette cringed, backing away from the window and closing the drapes.

Chapter Fifty-Two

"You're…what?"

Noah, his hands shoved into his pockets, leaned back against the kitchen counter, bumping a box of pastries by accident. "Yeah."

Mason blinked at him. Opened his mouth. Closed it again. "You're serious? You're actually…?"

"Leaving the palace."

Mason dragged a hand down his face. "You're crazy. You both are."

"It was her idea. But now it's not a strong want, it's a need. I have to get her out of here. I can't sit back and do nothing anymore; I've been doing nothing for six years."

"You haven't *known* for six years," Mason said softly.

"I did. She told me when she was ten, six years ago."

Mason froze.

Noah swallowed. "She told me, six years ago, that Odette was hurting her," he repeated, his voice barely above a whisper. "I didn't know the extent of it, but I knew she wasn't safe."

Mason's lips parted. "If you get caught, you'll be killed, and she'll be tortured even more."

Noah shrugged. "Then we can't get caught."

Mason choked on a laugh. "Sounds simple

enough."

Noah waited for him to say something else, afraid to press that matter and push him away altogether.

Finally, Mason sighed. "I suppose I could agree with all of the above," he murmured with a faint smile, cupping the back of his neck. He blew air out from between his lips, his cheeks puffing. "What do you need from me?"

Noah's shoulders dropped with relief. "Seas, thank you."

"Don't thank me yet, I haven't done anything."

"You're helping. That's enough to warrant a *thank you.*" Noah cleared his throat, straightening. "The biggest obstacle right now is getting the tracker in the ship disabled. Juliette was going to take care of that, but in light of what's going on, I don't want to wait for her to *maybe* get better and remember how to do it. I did some research, and evidently there were some issues with the tracking box on that particular model, but I haven't been able to figure out anything past that."

Mason shifted his lips to the side. "I'll do some digging and see if I can get it disabled without sending an alert, but if not, we might have to wait until the moment you're ready to leave."

"And alert someone I'm gone?" Noah's eyebrows shot up.

"No, I can tell Aaryn I need to do some repairs on your ship, and maybe a few others to keep suspicion down, and have it disabled."

"Won't he realize it's still down after a few hours?"

"Probably. But, by that time, you'll be gone. Once you're out of the palace, it won't matter."

Noah barely shook his head. That wasn't ideal at all. He had done some rough calculations and estimated he'd need at least six hours to get to the gate in Fatir.

"It will be our last resort," Mason added. "But, like I said, I can see what I can do to override it manually and discreetly."

"I might have something that will help with that," Noah continued, pulling out his tablet. He'd written everything down on the recall for his ship's make and year so Mason could read over it. "I don't know if that will help *us*, but, given that that specific ship had issues with tracking equipment, I thought it was at least worth noting."

Mason studied Noah's notes. "Yeah. It might be, at that. Can I look at it again? Your ship?"

Noah nodded, shoving away from the wall. "Yeah, of course."

Mason jogged with Noah back through the maze of corridors, toward the garage, down to the second level, and then into Noah's ship. Noah hung back, watching with rapt interest as Mason poked around the underside of the control panel again.

"I hesitate to *count* on the recall, because not literally every single ship had an issue with tracking equipment." Mason scooted out from beneath the ledge, tapping around on his tablet. "Only the majority of them. We can't know where this one sits."

"No." Noah picked at a piece of paint chipping from the wall, drawing a knee up.

"How long have you guys been planning this?" Mason asked after several seconds of silence.

"Running away? She first mentioned it…maybe three months ago? Two? In all honesty, I had been very loosely toying with the idea for a few years, but didn't give it any serious thought until she said she was leaving."

Mason inclined his head in understanding. He pulled himself out from beneath the ship, shoving his hands into his pockets. "I'm glad. I've noticed her changing."

"Who?"

"The princess. Whenever she was in the queen's presence, or being yelled at, she's started to…I don't know, pull into herself. I can remember when she was younger being so full of fire, spunky, almost. But recently, I feel like she just doesn't care anymore. About anything. She just…"

"Disassociates."

"Yeah. Disassociates from life."

"I've noticed that too." Noah shifted his lips. What was worse, *Juliette* noticed that about herself. She was worried she was going insane, that her brain was killing itself and she'd forget who she was entirely.

"Okay, I think I might have a few options," Mason finally said.

Noah perked up. "Yeah?"

"Maybe." He glanced at his wristlet. "My shift starts in ten minutes, so I won't be able to get started on it now, but let me think on it, and I'll check it out as soon as I can."

"Thanks." Noah stood up, feeling like he should say or do more as a show of gratitude, but not sure what.

Mason, however, didn't seem to be waiting for anything. He nodded once, the faintest hint of a smile tugging at the corner of his mouth, before disappearing down the corridor.

Noah breathed a sigh of relief.

Mason was going to help them get away.

Chapter Fifty-Three

Noah's wristlet vibrated, startling him awake. It was only five, but he intentionally wanted to wake up earlier so he could see about going to visit Juliette. He had made himself stay away from her for an entire day, giving her time and space to get her bearings, and it was killing him.

Maybe, after she had some time, he could talk to her and talk her through what happened.

As he neared her room, not entirely sure what to do or how to approach the situation, Noah slowed. She was sitting on the window ledge at the end of the hallway, staring out the window. She barely turned, seeing his reflection in the glass.

"I'm sorry, I didn't mean to startle you," he said. "Your Highness."

She shook her head. "You didn't."

Noah cleared his throat, moving into position at the side of her door. He didn't think he'd ever felt more awkward than he did right now. He had to keep reminding himself everything would be okay. They'd been set back, but as soon as she was away from the palace, her memory would come back. She just needed some time.

"We used to play hide-and-seek." Juliette's voice was a whisper, but it wasn't a question.

Noah forced a nod. "We did. I always won."

Her expression didn't change, save for the subtle frown on her eyebrows. "Why?"

"You sing when you're concentrating. Playing games was no exception, so it was easy for me to find you."

The smallest smile tugged at the corner of her mouth. Her eyes flickered toward him. She started to say something when her head snapped to the side.

Noah's heart crumbled impossibly more, focusing his eyes on the wall opposite him as Odette and her entourage came down the hallway.

Juliette stood up, a little slowly.

"I want to try and jog your memory," Odette said by way of greeting. "Dr. Violet thinks it would help if we pretended nothing has changed and go on about our normal routines. You were good with computers; do you remember that at all?"

Juliette hedged. "A little. I think."

"Good. Here's a list of past assignments you've completed. I want you to duplicate them, and I want them done by the end of the day."

Juliette hesitated. "What…what happens if they aren't done in time?"

Odette almost smiled. "I'll break your wrist and see if that will bring some memories up." She turned and swept down the corridor.

"At least I remember I hate her," Juliette muttered.

Noah would have laughed if he hadn't been so worried.

"I'm going to go in my room and work on this," she added, talking to Noah. "Do you…do you usually come into my room with me?"

"I have before, but not all the time."

She pressed her lips together, as if thinking about it.

"I'll stay out here unless you need something," he said quietly, not wanting her to feel trapped.

"Or we could go to my study," she countered.

Noah almost smiled. "Whatever you want."

Once Juliette was settled in her study, with a spreading of tablets around her, Noah took up his post just inside. He would have liked to have been able to keep working on the ship, but he didn't want to be too far from her on the off chance she needed something.

Or remembered him. Either one.

From where he was standing, Noah could just make out her screen—the blue text scrolling up and down the tablet, the endless string of letters and numbers that somehow made sense to her.

Or, at least, they used too.

Her fingers never stopped flying over the screens. Every few minutes, she'd pick up a stylus and make some kind of note or swipe something across the screen.

At some point she started humming, her brows knotted in concentration. The hiccups interrupted her song—she always got the hiccups at the most random times.

Noah tried to find comfort in that. She was singing; her core habits were still there. She wasn't gone. She would remember. She would be fine.

"I can't do any more," she whispered. "I don't…I can't remember what to do now."

Noah froze. He certainly had no idea how it worked. "How much have you done?"

She rapidly blinked, turning her eyes to the ceiling.

"Half the list."

"That's a start, why don't you take a break and give your mind the chance to rest?" he suggested, glancing at his watch.

Juliette swallowed. Reluctantly nodded.

Noah breathed a sigh of relief. He glanced at the clock, surprised it was almost noon. "It's lunchtime, are you hungry?"

"A little."

"Then why don't you eat something, and then we can come back here?"

"Yeah, yeah, that…that'll be fine." Juliette replied, but there was an emptiness behind her eyes.

Noah held the door for her, walking closer to her than he should have. She got lost a few times, and, much to Noah's disappointment, Odette was in the dining room when they arrived.

"You look tired," Odette said, barely looking up.

Juliette hesitated. "I am, a little."

Odette waved a hand in the air as Juliette crossed the room and started filling her plate at the buffet. "How's it going?"

"Fine. I'm making progress."

"Good." Odette smiled. "There's hope after all."

Juliette started around the table.

A frown settled over Odette's face. She reached a hand out, and Noah twitched, but she only gripped Juliette's shoulder. "You have to eat more than you do; you're *way* too thin."

Juliette yanked her arm back. She sat down at the space beside Odette.

Noah worked his jaw.

Odette slapped Juliette, hard, on her cheek. "Do not

yank your arm from me." She spoke so calmly, so easily.

Noah worked to keep his face neutral. Days, he only had to get her through a handful of days, and they'd be, hopefully, leaving. He was going to do it—he was going to get her away if it was the last thing he did. His heart started beating faster at the thought.

Besides her red cheek, Juliette looked unbothered. She sipped at the water in front of her.

Odette went back to eating. As soon as she finished, she stood up without a word to Juliette and disappeared.

"I wish she'd go away and *stay* away," Juliette murmured, standing at the dining room window. The bruise on her eye from a few days was finally starting to get better, but her cheek was red.

Noah didn't say anything, though he wholeheartedly agreed.

"I want to try and finish this," she added waving her tablet.

Noah nodded.

As they walked back toward Juliette's study, Noah's mind spun. Odette's ball was in a week, which should give him and Mason plenty of time to get the tracking equipment disabled. The challenge would be to keep Aaryn in the dark or come up with a valid excuse as to why they were messing around.

Noah realized he needed to come up with a way to re-broach the subject of running away to Juliette.

Chapter Fifty-Four

Juliette returned to her room, not her study, and spent the rest of the afternoon by herself. Noah wanted to be able to go and work on the ship, but he was hesitant to leave her on the off chance she needed something.

Or remembered him. Either one.

She didn't want dinner when Daisy brought her up a tray. By the time Luis came up to relieve him for the night, Noah was eager to *do* something.

"How is she?" Luis whispered.

"I don't know. She hasn't really talked much." Noah licked his lips. "You'll let me know if she…needs something or something happens?"

"Of course." Luis started to say something else, but a sniff, followed by a delicate sob, came from Juliette's room. "Or, you know, you could just go in there now since you're already here."

"She doesn't know who I am," Noah snapped under his breath.

"So? You were friends before, so there was obviously something about you she liked, and it's not like you've changed."

Noah hesitated.

"Maybe put on some normal clothes though so it's more casual and not so intimidating?"

Noah shifted his lips to the side. "Yeah, okay." He

jogged downstairs, quickly changed into some dark jeans and a sweatshirt, then came back up to her room. He shot Luis a grateful look before knocking on her door.

A muffled "come in" was the only thing he heard, so he cracked the door open. Juliette was sitting at the foot of her bed, her arms wrapped around her legs. Tears stained her face.

"My head hurts," she mumbled. "I did most of Odette's list, and it's starting to come back to me, at least a little, but…I can't do any more. Everything hurts *so bad.*"

"Okay, then take a break," Noah replied quietly, stepping inside. He left the door open an inch or so, then crossed the room and sank down opposite her. "Try and sleep, maybe you'll feel better in the morning."

"It's only seven."

"So?" Noah shrugged. He started to collect her tablets. Being careful not to disrupt anything on the screens, he set them on her desk.

Juliette reluctantly handed him the one in her hands.

"You've been working hard," Noah commented.

"I set up a router, wrote a new firewall for Odette's personal tablet, and reconfigured the palace's security network." Juliette's words trembled, and she spoke as if she had done something wrong and was afraid of getting caught.

"Then you've earned a rest."

Juliette was silent, so Noah crossed the room and picked up a handful of blankets from her bed, as well as her pillows and her favorite blue hoodie. She stayed frozen to the spot, her eyes unfocused, even as Noah set the hoodie next to her and arranged the pillows behind her so she could lean against the bed without hurting her back.

"Jules?"

A tear dropped onto her face. "Everything hurts."

Noah's heart couldn't have hurt more if someone stabbed a knife into his chest and twisted it. He sat down beside her, reminding himself he was a stranger to her. She didn't feel the same way about him as she did two days ago.

"I don't remember you," she whispered, looking up at him.

"I know. It's okay."

"No, it's not. I remember…certain things, but I know there's more."

"What things do you remember?"

Juliette licked her chapped lips. "Butterflies. I don't know what that means, but…it was important, wasn't it?"

Noah almost smiled. "You like butterflies, and when we were…" His head twitched in a shake. "I started calling you butterfly because it seemed cute, at the time." He jerked his shoulders in a shrug, aware of how ridiculous it sounded.

"I like it." Juliette sank her head into her hands, barely stifling a groan.

Noah's eyes roved to the bruise on her eye. He lightly grazed her skin, thinking too late that he probably shouldn't touch her like that anymore.

But then she turned to look at him, leaning into his touch.

Noah wrapped his arms around her, relief surging

in his entire body when she moved closer to him, resting her head on his chest.

"It's okay to give yourself time to heal."

"What if I can't ever remember?"

"Then you'll make new memories. Better memories."

Juliette sniffed, then groaned.

"Your head?"

"Yeah."

Noah moved his hand to the other side of her head, moving his fingers in small, slow circles. "You sure you don't feel like eating something?" he asked, noticing the full plate on her coffee table.

"Not really."

Noah didn't press it. He shifted, moving his other hand to the other side of her face, while keeping her supported. At least she seemed to be warming back up to him.

"You kissed me."

Noah almost laughed, but he managed to steel his face. "And you kissed me back."

"I would have been an idiot not to."

This time Noah actually laughed.

"Was I good?"

The question caught him by surprise, but he swallowed back another laugh, worried she would think he was mocking her. "You were fantastic. Not that I have anything to compare it to, but it certainly set the bar high."

She laughed, then immediately cringed.

"Sorry. Okay, *butterfly,* no laughing until your headache's gone."

A comfortable silence settled over them for several

minutes. Noah had no idea if whatever he was doing to her head was in fact helping, but she didn't ask him to stop, so he didn't.

Around eight, Noah asked her to eat again. She cleared half her plate and finished two glasses of water, before curling up next to him on the floor again. He reached around her for one of the blankets, draping it across her shoulders and then scooting down and lacing his hands behind his head. He really wanted to get down to the garage at some point, but the ship might have to wait.

"Do you want to go back to your room?" she asked, turning to look over at him.

"I'm fine. Unless you want to go to bed?"

She hesitated. Shook her head. "I'd rather talk to you some more, if that's okay."

"Of course." Noah nodded once.

While Juliette got up to use the facilities, he stuffed a few more pillows behind him, getting as comfortable as he could.

Juliette returned, wearing his hoodie, and settled on the ground beside him. *Right* beside him.

Noah hesitated, then started running his fingers through her hair, scooping his other arm beneath her shoulders. Her eyes blinked, slowly, before she turned onto her side, one of her arms resting on his stomach.

He started telling her about his trip again, knowing how much she enjoyed hearing it the first time, and hoping that if she was quiet for a long enough stretch of time, she'd fall asleep. He told her about the ship, and how long of a flight it was, how peaceful the days were, alone in the cockpit.

He didn't stop moving his hand through her hair.

"Once we landed, you could just feel the temperature shift. It was *so* much warmer and drier there than it is here. I didn't realize how moist the air here is," he added, looking down at her.

She was asleep.

Noah breathed the smallest sigh of relief. He should have moved her to her bed and gone and worked on the ship, but at the moment, he was in no hurry to move. He kept talking, telling her about their plan—her plan—to run away. About how, as much as he hoped she would wake up and remember everything, he didn't want her to work too hard at it. She needed to give her poor brain the chance to heal.

Around nine, he pulled his tablet out of his pocket and scrolled around on the news for a little while.

A cross between pride and worry flashed through his mind when he realized just how many people were talking about her. Her appearance at the greeting of the guard ceremony had taken off, and several sites analyzed her outfit and hairstyle.

She had been seen in public before, but never for so long and never so blatantly. What was even more surprising was finding several budding *fan* sites under her name. The gifts she had been sending to the various houses had become a hot commodity, and young girls were eager to get their hands on them.

He worried how the queen would react.

"You've got fans, Jules," he murmured.

Juliette slept for a while, during which time Noah pored over the instruction manual for his ship and even managed to find an in-depth article on restoring a ship like his that included ways of disconnecting the tracking beacons and identifying chips, before he decided Juliette was sleeping soundly enough to move her to her bed.

He started to untangle her arms from around him but slowed. Seas, he hoped she was going to be okay. He wanted her to remember him, and all their history, but more than that he wanted her to be *okay*.

Carefully sliding his arms beneath her, Noah lifted her up. Her head drooped against his shoulder as he moved around her bed.

Noah frowned to himself. She was small. Too small. She had always been petite, and he'd noticed she seemed to have lost some weight, he just didn't realize how much.

Juliette took a deep breath in as he set her down on her bed, her eyes fluttering open.

"Try and sleep some more," he whispered, bringing the heavy quilt up and over her.

"But it's still early," she protested, trying to push herself up and still half asleep. "You were going to take me to the gym."

Noah's heart skittered. "We've got plenty of time." He could tell she was trying not to fall back asleep.

"No, we don't. We're running out of time." She started to say something else, tears gathering in her eyes.

"I'll stay with you. I'll stay here," Noah said quickly.

She froze, one hand gripping the blanket.

Noah gently worked it free, guiding her back down onto her pillow and drawing the blanket back up and around her. "I'll stay here, I promise."

"You need to sleep, too," she murmured, her eyes closing.

Noah faintly smiled. “I will.” He waited until her eyes had closed again and her breathing turned steady before standing back up and closing the curtains in front of the windows.

Chapter Fifty-Five

Juliette took a deep breath and let it out, arching her arms above her head in a stretch, her hands bumping into the headboard. Her eyes fluttered open, and she had a brief moment of confusion at seeing the curtains drawn at her windows. She lifted her head, glancing at the clock on her nightstand. It was only two thirty, but based on the pitch blackness filtering through the closed curtains, she guessed it was two thirty in the morning.

Stifling a groan, she turned onto her back. Her headache seemed to be getting better, but she didn't want to move too quickly and risk agitating it.

She turned over onto her other side, her eyes settling on Noah, sprawled out on the ground just beneath the window.

Juliette smiled to herself, pain pricking her head. She wanted to remember more about him. She kept getting flashes. Moments that felt like pieces to a massive puzzle she couldn't even begin to understand.

She slid out from beneath her blanket and pulled it free, carefully draping it over Noah and then curling up opposite him.

"What are you doing?" he mumbled, his eyes still closed.

Juliette froze, one arm curled beneath her head. "Nothing," she whispered back.

"You have a bed."

"Oh is that what that big thing is?"

"Jules…" Noah sighed.

"Go back to sleep, it's the middle of the night—" Juliette sucked in a gasp as the floor started trembling.

Noah's eyes snapped open. "Under the bed."

Juliette scrambled to crawl under her bed, glad her bed was on the taller side and the space wasn't overly cramped. The shaking intensified as Noah slid in behind her, though his fit was a little tighter.

"C'mere, c'mere." He awkwardly pulled her back toward the wall, wrapping her in a cocoon of safety as the ground shook harder and harder. She could hear things falling and glass shattering around them.

"Great seven seas," Noah said, loud enough to be heard over the noise. His arms tightened around her shoulders, and one of his hands held the back of her head.

Juliette shouldn't have felt as safe as she did. She knew they had a history, knew there was established trust and mutual affection, but she couldn't wrap her mind around it. Not entirely. Yet with his arms so tightly around her, she'd never felt safer in her entire life.

He said he kissed her. She wished she could remember that, if nothing else.

He held her until finally, *finally*, the shaking stopped.

Even after the ground was still, she held on to him. Adrenaline was pumping through her veins, and it was several seconds before her heart started to slow.

"We used to run through the hallways during these quakes and see who would fall first," Noah said, his arms staying around her.

Juliette almost laughed.

"What are your thoughts on stargazing?" he asked.

"Stargazing? I don't…I don't know. Why?"

"Just curious. You and I have a list going of things we want to do when we get out of here, I thought I would add stargazing to it."

Juliette thought about it, frustrated when her mind stayed empty.

"We'll go camping and stargazing and horseback riding and swimming and go to the beach and have picnics every day."

Juliette smiled, trying to picture it. "Okay." She adjusted her head, feeling his heart thumping against her ear. "Do you want me to move so we can get out?"

Noah was quiet for a beat. "No."

Juliette breathed a sigh of relief, the tension she didn't even realize she was carrying melting from her shoulders. She was glad when he didn't loosen his grip around her, though she couldn't imagine it was very comfortable for him. She wanted to ask if he wanted to move a little.

Noah's hand started running through her hair, and her eyelashes fluttered. The back of her throat tightened, and she swallowed against it.

When she did finally drift off to sleep, her mind was filled with dreams. *Good* dreams, though she couldn't quite understand what they were. Her thoughts were entirely centered around Noah.

She was actually sad when she was startled awake during the eight o'clock trumpets.

"Time to go back," Noah whispered.

Juliette filled her lungs. Back to reality. No more

daydreams, no more hiding beneath her bed and dreaming of a faraway land and a faraway dream and a faraway reality. She waited until Noah had released her before inching out from beneath the bed.

Her room was in disarray from the quake last night, and she was glad she had thought to put the flower crown in a protective case as it had tumbled to the ground and lay pinned beneath her vanity chair.

Fortunately, there wasn't much that was glass, but even still Noah told her to wait by the bed while he cleaned the floor of the smaller things.

"I'll ask Daisy to come up," Noah said.

"Thank you."

Noah stooped for his sweatshirt.

Juliette took a step toward him. "Noah?"

Noah paused, his eyes searching hers.

"Thank you. I…I wish—"

Noah closed the distance between them, and Juliette's heart ricocheted. "Don't. You don't have to be sorry or try to make me feel better. I want you to be safe. I want you to be healthy and happy. Don't wear yourself into the ground trying to remember me. It will either come back to you, or it won't."

"I want it to."

Noah pressed his lips together. "I want it to, too. But I also want you to not be in so much pain."

Juliette's eyes darted to his mouth, set just so.

"Do you still want to go to the gym today at some point? You may have mentioned that in your sleep last night."

Juliette blinked. "I did?"

Noah nodded.

"Yeah. That…I'd like that."

Noah shot her a smile before turning and slipping from the room.

Juliette stared after him for several seconds, her mind replaying yesterday morning and last night.

Noah's smile, the way he looked at her, the way he held her and ran his fingers through her hair. The way he did all of those things despite everything. She played those moments over and over again until she was sure they were engraved in her memories forever. She wanted to remember, but if that wasn't possible, she wanted to start off a new set of memories with a bang.

Chapter Fifty-Six

Juliette arched her back. Noah said she had come to the gym with him before, and she tried to hold on to that so she didn't feel quite so awkward.

"Are you okay?" he asked when he neared her room.

"Ish."

"How's your headache?"

"Better."

Noah smiled. "We'll take it easy today, just in case."

Juliette filled her lungs, walking with him down the corridor toward a small door built into the wall that led to another series of small hallways that eventually spit them out into a large room filled with exercise equipment.

There were a few others in the room, so Noah guided her to an empty corner. While he did pull-ups, she sank to the ground and did some push-ups. The back of her head pulsed when she went down, so she didn't do too many of them.

Sinking back on her heels, she watched Noah finish his set. The edges of her vision blurred, and she crushed her eyes shut. The base of her neck tingled, and she could remember, vividly, sleeping in his bed. She didn't remember what brought her to his room, only that she was afraid, and he let her take the bed while he slept on the floor.

Her eyes welled up, and she tried to remember more. Why was she afraid? Why was he so willing to give up his bed for her?

"Jules? Hey, what's wrong? Does your head hurt again?"

Juliette shook her head. Noah appeared in front of her, his eyebrows drawn in concern. He lightly rubbed her arm, and she fumbled for his hand. "You're…so thoughtful."

Noah looked like he might laugh. "What?"

Juliette blinked, slowly. The inside of eyelids felt like they were made of sandpaper. She opened her mouth to say that something was coming to her, but she couldn't hold on to it long enough to figure it out.

"Take a breath."

Juliette pressed the heel of her hand to her forehead. There was a bruise somewhere on her face—her cheekbone, right below her eye. It was from Odette. Odette had hurt her. She had tried to hurt Noah.

Noah took her face in his hands. "Look at me."

She did.

"You're okay. If something's coming to you, let it. Don't try so hard; let your mind remember on its own."

Juliette blinked her eyes clear, though she wished he wouldn't take his hands from her face. She filled her lungs, then pushed herself up.

She worked out for a little while longer before going back up to her room to shower and dress for the morning.

A small tinge of dread settled in her stomach. She knew she'd be going back to the infirmary today, as per Odette's instructions before she left. She'd been trying to tell herself over and over that it would be okay. The doctors were trying to help her, they were trying to fix whatever caused her to lose her memory.

She would survive. She would remember Noah.

Sitting with her back to the heating vent so her hair would hopefully dry faster, Juliette played around on her tablet while waiting for either Noah or another guard to come up and get her for breakfast.

Chapter Fifty-Seven

Odette tucked one of her legs beneath her as she settled back against her settee. She stifled a yawn, tired from the day’s events and ready for a good night's sleep. She’d just stood up when there was a gentle knock at her door.

Odette straightened the tie on her silky robe.

Natasha walked in a moment later, her face oddly bright.

“What is it?”

“I just received word from King Philippe.”

Odette’s heart stopped. A wary grin crept onto her face. “And?”

“He would like to move forward with the proposed marriage alliance.”

Odette drew back, surprised. She thought for certain he would have decided against it, which, in all honesty, she wouldn’t have been overly disappointed about. “It took him long enough.”

“I thought you would be pleased.” Natasha smiled.

Odette strung a hand through her silky hair, sinking back down onto the settee. Oh, to not only be finally rid of Juliette, but to have a way into France, a way into the rest of the world, all rolled into one beautiful package.

“I’m sorry to interrupt your evening, Majesty, and I thought to wait to tell you until tomorrow morning but thought you’d want to know right away,” Natasha added.

Odette waved a hand in the air. “Not to worry.”

In the meantime, Odette now had a slew of things she needed to start organizing and getting done. Since Dr. Violet was finally making real progress, Odette was confident the serum would be perfect before the end of next year, which meant Juliette’s usefulness would be at an end.

“I wonder now if you *should* have waited until tomorrow to tell me because now I won’t sleep,” Odette added with a laugh.

“My apologies. Can I have one of the maids bring you some tea?”

“Yes, actually, that would be wonderful,” Odette added with a hiccup. Skies, she hated the hiccups. She wished she knew what brought them on.

Natasha bobbed a quick curtsey and disappeared. The tea arrived in only a few minutes, complete with a few pecan cookies.

While she sipped at her tea and nibbled on the cookies, Odette contacted King Philippe. One of the things she’d explicitly told him was she wanted to keep the whole thing under wraps for the time being.

Around midnight Odette finally shut her computer off and started toward her bed. She paused at the window, peering up toward the sky. It was black, no stars visible through the ever present snow, but she could imagine what it would look like to finally look out the window and see stars glittering in the night sky.

Oh, to see the sky! The sun and the moon and the stars and clouds, even *rain*. To feel the warmth of the day from nature, not artificial life supports placed throughout the palace to keep the temperature.

Odette laced her hands together behind her head and stared up at the ceiling, the grin plastered to her face.

Chapter Fifty-Eight

Juliette's eyebrows sank together lower on her forehead in concentration. Noah watched her in his peripherals, hiding a smile. She was supposed to be handing him things when he asked her to, but when he went to get something for them to eat, she had taken one of his books and started reading. He left her alone, while he slid beneath the control panel and neatened up some of the wiring.

He had reminded her of their intended plan of escape earlier yesterday, and though she had no memory of it, and it didn't ring even the slightest bell, she was eager to come to the garage with him.

"Do you have a pencil?" she asked. She blinked several times, as if clearing some dust from her eyes. Her eyes, Noah noticed, were bloodshot.

"Check in that little cubby," Noah said without getting up.

Juliette stood and crossed the room, crouching down to dig around a small box. Noah's eyes narrowed, watching her. Was she moving slower, or was he being paranoid? Her spirits seemed to be up, at least a little bit, but her movements were slow. Lethargic.

Noah made a note to see if he could covertly get her to take a nap at some point.

Clearing his throat, focusing his attention on the ship in front of him, Noah took a deep breath, starting to grow nervous. Skies above he was really stripping his ship of all palace connections. He and Mason had spent hours poring over the black box, learning everything they could. It was time to actually do it.

If anyone found out, they'd all be in serious trouble.

"I bet the first person to test fly one of these things was *terrified*," Juliette murmured with half a frown, looking up at the ship.

"Oh yeah?" Noah asked, trying not to let her see how nervous he was.

"Yeah."

Noah drew a steadying breath. He didn't even let himself look over at her, afraid she'd be looking at him and start talking again. Sweat trickled down his temple. He removed a small chip, tucking it in his other hand to destroy, and replacing it with a blank one.

He did it again and again, one at a time, until all the trackable components of his ship had been replaced. He checked his tablet, expecting Mason's name to flash up at him any second with a warning to stop. Mason had offered to take over for Aaryn while he was out working with some new recruits, giving Noah a slim window of opportunity to get the ship stripped.

Noah breathed a sigh of relief when five minutes passed and there was no word from Mason. He dropped his head down and closed his eyes, sweat making his hair damp.

"Are you okay?" Juliette asked.

"Yeah. It's just really hot under here," Noah replied with a grunt as he slid out and wiped his forehead with the back of his hand. He sent a quick nex't to Mason, double-checking that nothing had come up.

Mason responded right away, saying he was in the clear.

Noah dragged a hand down his face, finding it wet. His hands were shaking, his heart was fluttering madly in his chest, and the back of his shirt was drenched.

Juliette picked up a few crackers from the plate of snacks beside her, her eyes wandering around.

"Hey would you do me a favor?" he asked, willing his voice not to shake.

Juliette looked over at him.

"Grab me some water from the kitchen? Sorry, my hands are a mess," he added, holding up his greasy hands.

"Yeah, sure." Juliette set the book down and disappeared.

"Okay, Lord, please let this have worked. Please, please, please," Noah whispered, running a quick diagnostics check on the ship to make sure everything was running smoothly and he hadn't damaged the mechanics.

Mason appeared, jogging down the stairs, smiling. "We did it."

Noah held his hand up in a high-five.

"Where's the princess?"

"She went up to the kitchen."

"She knows though? About the escape plan?"

"She does." Noah wiped his hands off on a rag and then tossed it in the trash. It was beyond salvaging. "I want her to show me how she does a check on the ship's computer, just to make sure they're still talking to each other."

"Smart."

"House Atworth and House Apatite should change names since all the food comes from Atworth," Juliette said as she came back down into the garage, a glass of water in her hand. Her eyes landed on Mason, and she stopped, awkwardly smiling.

"Yeah, that would make more sense." Noah chuckled. He downed the water in a single gulp, not seeing the need to mention that "Apatite" and "appetite" were spelled differently.

A light frown settled over her face. "Odette was going to take me to Canyons once. I think. But she didn't. She gave me some new tablets instead…for some reason."

"What? Odette? Do something *nice*?" Mason muttered on his way back up the stairs.

Juliette must have heard it because she almost laughed.

"Here, let me take those," Noah said, taking the books from her.

"That was Mason, right?" she asked, lowering her voice to a whisper and walking closer to Noah.

Noah nodded. "Yes. Me, Mason, and Luis are all *your* guards. Luis mostly works night shifts outside your room."

Juliette rubbed her wrist, letting out a shaky sigh. "Do you have any schoolbooks left from when you were in school?"

Noah paused. "I think so. Why?"

"Can I read some?"

"Sure. Any one in particular?"

Juliette shifted her lips to the side, stepping in front of him when he grabbed the door. "Any on Demetria's history? I thought I'd scan over some of that and see if…well, if any of it comes back."

Noah grinned. "Yeah, that's a good idea."

He and Juliette started upstairs toward his room, where he dug around for some old school textbooks. "History," he repeated, flipping the book around and handing it to her. "Flip through the first chapter and see if that's what you're wanting."

Juliette took it, flipping the cover open and scanning the pages.

Noah balled his hands into fists, then shook them out. Maybe he should go for a run or do something to get all this pent-up nervousness out.

Chapter Fifty-Nine

Juliette's eyes fluttered open, and she sighed. Exhaustion tugged at her eyelids, and she turned onto her side, frowning as an ache spread through the muscles in her shoulders. Despite the stiffness, she felt better than she did yesterday. Her head didn't hurt nearly as bad as it had been.

The clock on the table said it was only four in the morning.

Juliette flipped over onto her stomach, fixing the pillow beneath her. There was a heaviness in her mind that didn't seem to be lightening as she woke up. Odette hadn't come near here, and Dr. Violet had been seeing her every day since she woke up with no memory.

She didn't like how jittery she felt, even now, in bed, this early in the morning. The first thing she thought of was how much she wished Noah were here. She didn't doubt she had been in love with him, and even with her limited memory, she understood why. She wanted to love him again.

Tonight was Odette's ball. Tonight was the night, according to Noah, they had planned on running away. It didn't seem as climactic as she thought it should have. She didn't even know what still needed to be done, or what her role had been. Noah said it had been her idea, and that for the past two and a half months they had been working together on it.

She still didn't know what was wrong with her, or what Dr. Violet was doing to fix it, but given everything that had been happening the past few days, she was starting to feel…lost. There were so many things she knew she *should* have been feeling but wasn't.

She wanted to feel something more for Noah. She wanted to be excited to leave. She wanted to resent Odette the way she should have. She wanted to feel stronger in herself.

Seas, she wanted to feel *like* herself.

All she felt was empty. It had only been five days since she had lost all memories of her life. She had hoped things would come back to her more and more. Every once in a while, she'd see something, or hear something, that would give her a sense of déjà vu, but that was it.

With a sigh, Juliette pushed herself up and wandered into her closet. The racks were lined with dresses of all different colors and fabrics. She didn't think she was going to the ball tonight…not if she and Noah were running away.

But she couldn't remember. It was Odette's ball, why would she miss it?

Juliette blinked at her closet, trying to find a dress appropriate enough for a dance. Did she even know how to dance?

After staring dumbly at her options for far too long, Juliette changed into a light pink, gauzy dress that was a little too long without any shoes and then stepped out into the corridor.

Preparations for the ball had been underway since yesterday morning, and Juliette wanted to look at the ballroom and see what it looked like.

Odette would no doubt be imprisoning herself in her room until the ball began, having every known beauty treatment imaginable done. At least that gave Juliette the freedom to walk around the palace and enjoy everything before the hundreds of people arrived.

The foyer had been decorated with beautiful flowers and garlands, the courtyard scrubbed and cleaned and polished, the hallway cleaned of dust, and the wood floor polished until it shone like a mirror—only to then have a red carpet rolled out over it.

She wanted to spend the hours leading up to the ball with Noah, but she hadn't seen him all morning. It might have been his day off.

After breakfast, where she ate two bites of her casserole, Juliette took a walk through the gardens with a guard who wasn't Noah, paced up and down the corridor outside her bedroom until her heart was racing, and then took a quick shower followed by a long bath.

She sat in the hot water—the temperature being maintained by the jets—and watched the bubbles shimmer and pop around her. Leaning her head back, she closed her eyes and played with a pendant around her neck. There was a rose etched onto the surface. It struck her as familiar, but it must have been because she just walked through the gardens.

Juliette studied the bathroom, looking for something that would catch her attention. There was a bowl of grapes on the counter beside the tub. She must have brought them up. Or maybe a maid left them?

She nibbled on the fruit. The skin crunched between her teeth, a burst of sweetness exploding in her mouth. She drew her knees to her chest, trying to peer out the window. It was too high for her to see from the tub, but she could imagine the dozens of cars driving up through the palace courtyard and the beautifully dressed men and women stepping from them.

With another sigh, Juliette dunked beneath the water and blinked the droplets from her lashes. She craned her neck to look at the clock. It was only four, and she remembered someone saying the ball started at seven.

Reaching over and picking up her tablet, Juliette puttered around a few of the programs she'd set up, the lines she'd tapped into, the computers she'd hacked. She hated that *that* was what she remembered the most of.

With a sigh, she finally got up and wrapped the robe around herself before stepping out into her room and looking at her array of dresses again.

It was the longest three hours of her life, but she managed to stay busy wandering around her room, rearranging her shelves, digging through her slim array of clothes, making a few more necklaces and bracelets for the maids, and playing games on her tablet.

Finally, around five o'clock when she was sure Odette was in her room getting ready, she slipped the gown she had picked out over her head. The white-pink dress fit her perfectly, the layers of chiffon swirling around her feet and the waist easily conforming to her own. The long skirt made her look taller than she was, and the flowing skirt accentuated the few curves she had. Her hair had dried curly, so all she did was pin the top half of it back with a ribbon before securing a butterfly tiara on the top of her head.

Managing to smile in her reflection, Juliette left the

safety of her room and started toward Odette's wing.

Odette was in her room. Juliette wasn't sure if she had ever been here before, but it felt strange.

"What…do you think you're doing?" Odette, seated at her vanity, looked at Juliette through the reflection in the mirror.

Juliette froze. Her eyebrows came together. What *was* she doing? "I was…I'm ready for the ball," she murmured. "It's…it's tonight, right?"

Odette scoffed, standing up and starting toward Juliette like a tiger salivating over her prey. "You call that a *gown*? Little girl, I'm afraid this is barely passable for a *dress*," she added, gathering up a handful of the beautiful material in her fingers.

Juliette clenched her jaw. "I know. I tried to find the nicest one in my closet, but there wasn't a lot to choose from."

Odette chuckled. Her eyes flickered up to Juliette's hair. "And did you just wake up, or is that intentional?" She yanked the tiara off her head, taking a few hairs with it and tossing it to the side. It clinked and rang as it bounced on the tile in the bathroom.

Juliette gave a low cry of pain, involuntarily taking a step back. She slapped Odette's hand away, putting space between them, her heart racing in her chest.

"I thought I told you once already, you stupid, *stupid* girl; you're not going to the ball! I don't care what you're wearing. I wasn't going to let you go when you had some semblance of a brain in your head, there's no way I'd let you go now that you can barely remember your own name!"

Juliette wanted so very badly to leap up, to snap that she didn't have any idea what Odette was talking about and tell her to leave her alone.

"Did you hear me?" Odette hissed, leaning down and getting in Juliette's face.

Juliette glanced at the maids standing off the side, wishing one of them would step in and help her. "Yes, Your Majesty. I'm sorry. I thought…I thought I was supposed to go."

Odette almost smiled. "You thought wrong. I keep telling you, if you don't know something, don't just guess."

Juliette blinked. "Right. Of course."

Odette rolled her eyes. "Go back to your room and stay there. I don't want to see you again for the rest of the night, understand?"

Juliette was shaking, but she didn't know why. Tears sprang to her eyes, but she didn't know why. Swallowing, she pushed herself up and took off down the corridor. She didn't know where she was going; she didn't even know her way around the palace anymore. She wanted to go up, as high as she could, and look out at the world. She wanted to feel something, just for a moment, even if it was fear.

She ran, faster than she should have, given that her dress was too long. She wasn't sure when she started crying, only that when she slowed down, the front of her dress was dotted with moisture. She pressed the back of her hand against her mouth, wanting to scream but afraid of Odette finding her. Hurting her. Killing her.

Another corridor branched off to the side. Juliette took it, having no idea where it led. She must have been closer to the front of the palace than she realized, because when she paused at the end, she could see the foyer down below. People were arriving, trickling into the palace like waterdrops.

Juliette wanted to go up higher. There was a narrow stairwell, tucked in the corner of the upper balcony. She started toward it, slowing down and keeping her eyes trained on her surroundings in case someone jumped out at her. She tripped, the heel of her hand slamming into one of the stone steps.

The stairs went up forever, twisting in a spiral. Juliette kept going. Her heart thudded harder, the tears on her face having dried up.

When she neared the top of the stairs, she paused, surprised to see a small landing, at least two stories above the ballroom. She must have been closer to the roof of the palace. Even this high up she could hear the music, see the faint glow of the lights.

She dared to inch closer to the balcony, to look down over the sea of people. Many of them were still pouring in through the opened doors, speaking and mingling with one another. The women's gowns were *stunning,* made of all different colors and styles, their glittering diamonds visible even from way up there. She wondered how many of them she made. No one was dancing yet; dinner hadn't started, and neither had Odette been announced.

Arctic skies, everything was so *beautiful.*

Juliette groaned, her eyes widening as she tried to take everything in. It was stunning. Much more so than she ever could have imagined it.

Juliette tried to lean over the banister to see what was beneath them, but she was afraid of falling.

After a solid thirty minutes of letting the guests continue to arrive, all the while Juliette grew more and more excited at seeing the different dresses, the Demetrian anthem blared from invisible trumpets.

Juliette tried to inhale but choked. She moved back, afraid of being seen, until her back hit the wall.

She sank to the ground, wrapping her arms around her legs and burying her face in her knees.

Chapter Sixty

Noah planted his feet, pushing the back of the ship as hard as he could. Mason, on the other side of him, was doing the same. There was a small landing pad on the outside of the door, but getting the ship up the incline without turning it on was taking more effort than he realized.

"Almost…there," Mason grunted.

They crested the top of the hill, and then pushing became easier. Mason darted around to the front, hopping into the cockpit and pulling the brake, bringing the ship to a stop.

Noah was panting.

"Man, you gotta work harder in the gym if you're breathing that hard." Mason laughed, jumping down to the ground.

"Shut up," Noah replied, annoyed when the simple words exhausted him. He climbed into the ship, checking and double-checking the engine. Mason knew how to run a diagnostic on the ships computer, so while he did that, Noah checked the list on his tablet and made sure, once again, there was nothing he'd forgotten.

Nerves planted themselves in the base of his stomach. Within the hour, he and Juliette would be leaving.

"You okay?" Mason asked.

Noah nodded, standing up and dropping the seat of the sofa back down. "Yeah. It's just…sinking in."

"Don't tell me you're having second thoughts." Mason's words, though accusatory, were laced with emotion.

Noah shook his head. "No. It's…surreal, I suppose."

"It won't be, as soon as you're out of here and see the sky and feel the sun."

Noah pressed his lips together. "You sure you don't want to come?" He'd asked the question so many times already, but he couldn't not ask it again.

"I'm sure." Mason clapped his hands, rubbing them together. "Alright, engines are good, computer's good. You've got food and water; the heating and cooling units are functioning. I'm guessing Juliette's the one who cleaned, because it looks great in here and I've seen your room."

Noah laughed.

"The water tank is filled, you're all fueled up, and I checked the oil levels. What else?"

Noah wracked his brain, but nothing more came to mind. He once again consulted the list on his tablet.

"Where's Juliette?"

"In her room. Daisy went up to get her."

As if on cue, Daisy appeared coming through the back door. "She's not in her room. I can't find her."

"What do you mean?"

"Exactly what I said. I don't know where she went. I tried to scan the ballroom but couldn't get close enough with everyone still arriving."

"Odette wouldn't let her go to the ball," Noah mused. "Not without a dress, and I know for a fact she doesn't have one."

"Maybe she's in the library?"

"I looked in all the usual places," Daisy added. "But feel free to double-check."

Noah, trying not to grow worried, called up a smile. "She probably went for a walk, I'll look around."

"Don't you have her location on your tablet?"

"She's not wearing her watch. She must have taken it off. It's fine, I'm sure everything's fine."

Mason and Daisy exchanged a glance.

"Daisy, do me a favor and check the gardens?" Noah asked, taking the stairs two at a time. He thought about changing into his uniform but didn't want to risk running out of time. Instead, he took the servants' passages back toward Juliette's wing. He looked in her bedroom and any other place she might be in her wing of the palace, but they were all deserted.

He even went to the infirmary, but it was closed for the night. The next place he thought of was the room Odette had turned into a prison cell. The door was open, and the room was empty.

Starting to grow increasingly concerned by the minute, Noah came up short. He tried to think of where else she would have gone, voluntarily or involuntarily. He kept moving, thinking he may as well start looking in the places he otherwise wouldn't have, since he was out of ideas.

As he neared the front of the palace, the sound of music and voices filled the air. He was about to turn away, when his eyes settled on a narrow stairwell, tucked in the far corner of the second-level balcony.

She wanted to watch the ball, in that one moment when she'd forgotten they were planning to run away.

Noah crept up the stairs, his heart still thumping against his ribs. Cresting the top, he scanned the area and was about to turn away when his eyes landed on her.

She was sitting with her back to the wall opposite the balcony. Her eyes were open, but she didn't look at him as he neared her.

"Hey, butterfly. What are you doing?" he asked, carefully sinking down beside her.

She drew a steady inhale. "Nothing. I was going to go, but Odette said I couldn't."

"I know. I'm sorry." Noah cleared his throat. "We were planning on leaving tonight, do you still want to? Or have you changed your mind?"

"Leaving?"

"The palace. You helped me work on the ship yesterday."

She hesitated. Dropped her gaze. "Right."

"Do you not remember that?"

"I do. Kind of. I keep thinking things are real that aren't. And vice versa." She tried to laugh. "It's very confusing."

"It's only been a week. Less than a week, actually. You need to be patient with yourself."

"I don't want to be patient!" she cried. Thankfully the noise from the ballroom drowned it out. "I want to remember! I want to know why Odette doesn't love me, I want to know why you do, I want to remember why I stayed here for so long and what pushed me over the edge to decide to leave. I want to remember deciding to leave! I want to…I want to feel *something*, and all I feel is empty."

Noah weighed his words carefully, reminding

himself the night was young and they had plenty of time. "Then let yourself feel empty. Take it in. Process the emptiness. Don't try and force yourself to fill in the blanks."

"I'm not."

"Good. You remember some things. Like hacking! And that's not easy, trust me, you've shown me some of the things you've done, and it's way over my head."

She almost smiled. "I suppose."

"Do you remember how to walk? What country you're in? You're name? *My* name? You remember things. Not everything, but you aren't starting from scratch."

Juliette shook her head. "I'm sorry I've been such a mess the past week."

"Don't be sorry." Noah followed her gaze out toward the balcony. "Do you want to dance?" he asked, trying to think of something he could *do* to pull her out of herself, or even distract her.

Juliette was silent for several seconds. She lifted her chin from her knees, barely nodding. "Yes."

Noah stood up, offering her his hand. She seemed to hesitate, but she took it, and he carefully pulled her up, leading her out toward the center of the balcony. He rested a hand on her waist, taking her other hand. She moved against him, her arm wrapping around his waist, her head resting on his shoulder.

They moved with the rhythm of the music, not exactly dancing, but moving together. Noah leaned his cheek on the top of her head, realizing that tonight wasn't going to work. They'd have to leave another time; they'd have to wait until she had a stronger grasp on what was going on.

Whatever had caused her memory to glitch had messed with her in more than one way. She was a shell of the girl she had been, and Noah knew it would take time for her to climb back out. He held her tighter and felt her arms tighten around him. He was suddenly acutely aware of how many of his thoughts centered around her, how much of his attention had her at the core. She had always been special to him, and he had been a fool to take it for granted and not recognize the direness of her situation.

Now it was too late. He'd missed his chance to really and truly protect her, and now she was the one to suffer for it.

Noah blinked his eyes clear.

Chapter Sixty-One

Juliette's heart hadn't stopped racing since Noah put his arms around her. The music danced through the air, like golden ribbons weaving their way through her. When she rested her head on his shoulder, the smallest sense of calm descended. Peace. Safety.

She was safe.

She remembered him at the hospital, how he'd been the first person in the room. Odette hadn't come until later, and she'd been so upset over something else, she didn't even care. She yelled at Juliette, telling her to remember, giving her tasks to help boost her memory, demanding that the doctor *do something*.

Noah had told her it was okay, that she didn't need to remember everything right away, that she needed to give herself time and be patient.

"Noah?"

"Hm?"

Juliette swallowed. "You planned on running away tonight, right?"

"It was your idea," he clarified. "I just kind of...kept things moving in your absence."

She remembered the ship. She remembered Odette yelling at her, that she had to see Dr. Violet from now on instead of Dr. Greene. She remembered as a child, never sure what would bring on the next whipping, or how to avoid them. Odette had learned to be sneaky, to keep her treatment of Juliette from her parents and threatening Juliette with more abuse if she said anything.

Her back twitched. Odette had whipped her on the day of her birthday party. Then again a few days later.

"Are we still going to run away?" she asked. He hadn't said anything about it, so maybe things changed.

"That was the plan, but if you changed your mind, it's okay. We can go another day, or if you want to stay, we can stay."

"You'd stay?"

"Of course." The corner of his mouth twitched in a smile. "My place is right next to you. Whether that be here at the palace, as your guard, or running away, as your…well, I don't know what I'd be to you then."

Juliette lifted her head, looking up at him. "You love me."

Noah drew a long inhale, then let it out slowly. "There has never been a day that I haven't loved you," he whispered. "That I haven't been *in* love with you. You have been the center of my world for as long as I can remember, even as a kid. All I ever wanted was to marry you and make you mine, to see you smile and make sure you were safe and protected and cared for, and to sit by every day and watch that woman tear you apart is more than I can stand."

Juliette tried to take in the rest of what he was saying, but her mind was having trouble moving past the first sentence.

One thing she knew, despite the gaps in her memory or the confusion of her surroundings, was how fiercely she loved him back. She opened her mouth to tell him, but nothing came out. Her eyes dropped to his lips. She didn't give herself the chance to think; she cupped his face and stretched up to kiss him.

He kissed her back, gently at first, but Juliette didn't want him to be gentle. She wanted him to *kiss* her. She wrapped her fingers around the front of his shirt, pulling herself against him, snaking an arm around his neck. She felt him groan, a slight rumble deep in his chest.

Abruptly, his kiss turned harder. Desperate. One hand cradled her jaw, and the other gripped her waist. He forced her mouth open, backed her against the wall. His fingers dug into her side, and she gasped, wanting him to hold her tighter and kiss her harder.

Their kiss from the garage came flooding back, with such an intensity she would have lost her balance if Noah hadn't been holding her. She remembered how, at the time, it had exceeded every expectation she ever built in her mind—every daydream, every fantasy, every hope.

Somehow, this kiss knocked that one out of the first place. Her wildest dreams paled in comparison. She wanted him to kiss her forever. She wanted to bury herself in him and in the safety and love he gave her. She was caught in an avalanche of passion, strong, powerful, and unable to stop it if she tried.

Finally, instead of trying to keep up, she surrendered to him as he continued to kiss her with a bruising intensity, knowing he wouldn't really hurt her.

Then, as if watching them through a video, her memories started to resurface. Odette threatening to sleep with him to get a rise out of her, her taking her frustration out on Noah, angry she was so powerless. Odette hitting her at dinner, and Juliette hitting her back, defending herself. She felt

She gasped for breath, drenched in the softness of Noah's lips against hers, trailing across her cheek, down her neck. The tingling in her sternum grew, shooting all the way down to her toes. He shifted, burying his face in her hair, kissing her neck. She willed him to pull her tighter and hold her closer.

His grip tightened around her for a brief moment before his hands slid to her hips, and he captured her mouth again.

Adrenaline raced through her veins. Her hands found his waist, slipping beneath the hem of his shirt and feeling the smooth panes of his muscles. She heard his breath hitch.

His pale green eyes pierced into her soul, and she couldn't have looked away if she wanted to.

Juliette didn't know when they had stopped moving, both rooted to the ground, their gazes locked onto one another's.

"I'm sorry," he whispered against her, brushing away the remnants of her tears. "I didn't mean to—"

Juliette shook her head, surprised to see moisture in his eyes as well. "I love you, Noah. I want to leave this ice-forsaken prison," she breathed against him. He kissed her. One of his hands touched her neck. "I want to leave Odette."

Noah swallowed.

"I want to leave the palace, tonight; I don't want to wait another minute."

Noah didn't reply. He kissed her again, until they both had to stop for breath.

Juliette blinked, her brain fuzzy. She touched his cheek, wanting to sear him into her brain so she would never, ever forget this feeling no matter what happened. "I remember. At least…at least the big things. I remember *you*. I love you, Noah. I love you so much."

Noah cradled her wrist, kissing the palm of her hand. "Then, if you're sure, we should go, before the ball ends."

Juliette swallowed, but the tiniest bit of light crept into her eyes. "Butterfly, let's fly away?"

Sunshine broke through Noah's face in a smile.

She took a step back, then glanced down at her dress. She hadn't realized what she was wearing until now, but it was the pink one she had started making a while ago. The one she planned on wearing tonight to celebrate their escape.

Noah's hands slid from her neck to her shoulders. "Can you disable the security feeds outside your room and outside the garage?"

Juliette blinked. "Yes." The answer came easy. She'd done that kind of thing a thousand times before.

"How long will it take?"

"Just a few minutes once I'm in the system," Juliette replied. He gave her a reassuring squeeze, pulling her into a tight hug. She licked her lips, trying to remember where she had left her data tablet. It must have been somewhere in her room.

"I'll walk with you back and then go down to my room to get my things. Once you've got them disabled, send me a nex't and I'll come back for you."

Juliette nodded, and he slid his hand down to hers, leading her toward the stairwell.

As they walked through the corridors, empty and abandoned, Juliette's resolve strengthened. She was already trying to figure out how she could change the security feeds so their absence wasn't noticed until it was much too late.

Odette wouldn't even realize she was gone, and when she did, she'd be looking for a phantom. Creating entirely new identities for each of them would be a bit more of a challenge, but she was confident she'd figure it out. She *would* figure it out. She and Noah were going to leave and never come back.

And she would never see Odette again.

A word about the author...

Abigail lives in sunny California, though she's always dreamed of moving to a rainy climate (the gloomier and cloudier, the better!). She is an avid reader of all things sci-fi, fantasy, and romance. When she isn't reading, writing fanfic, drafting a new manuscript, reorganizing her desk for the millionth time, reading her Bible, watching Star Wars, studying, scrolling Instagram and TikTok, playing the piano, or spending time with her family...she's probably dead and local authorities should be called. The Princess and the Guard is her debut novel. Abigail can be found on Instagram and TikTok @abigailjgrace

www.ingramcontent.com/pod-product-compliance
Lightning Source LLC
Chambersburg PA
CBHW072307020726
47501CB00002B/417
9781509262779